ALASSIAN BORN

Alassian Born

LYNN OAKWOOD

Red Ink Books

ALASSIAN BORN
Copyright © 2024 Lynn Oakwood

All rights reserved. No part of this publication may be reproduced or transmitted by any means without the prior permission of the author.

To request permission, contact Lynn Oakwood at www.lynnoakwood.com.

All characters in this book are fictitious and any resemblance to actual person, living or dead, is purely coincidental.

ISBN 978 90 833539 0 6
ISBN (Hardcover) 978 90 833539 1 3

First Edition, July 2024

Red Ink Books
www.lynnoakwood.com

*This book is dedicated to the memory
of my grandmother
Rosa.*

She made the most delicious cordon bleu.

"He could dimly see the grey forms of two elves sitting motionless with their arms about their knees, speaking in whispers."

        J.R.R. TOLKIEN, The Lord of the Rings

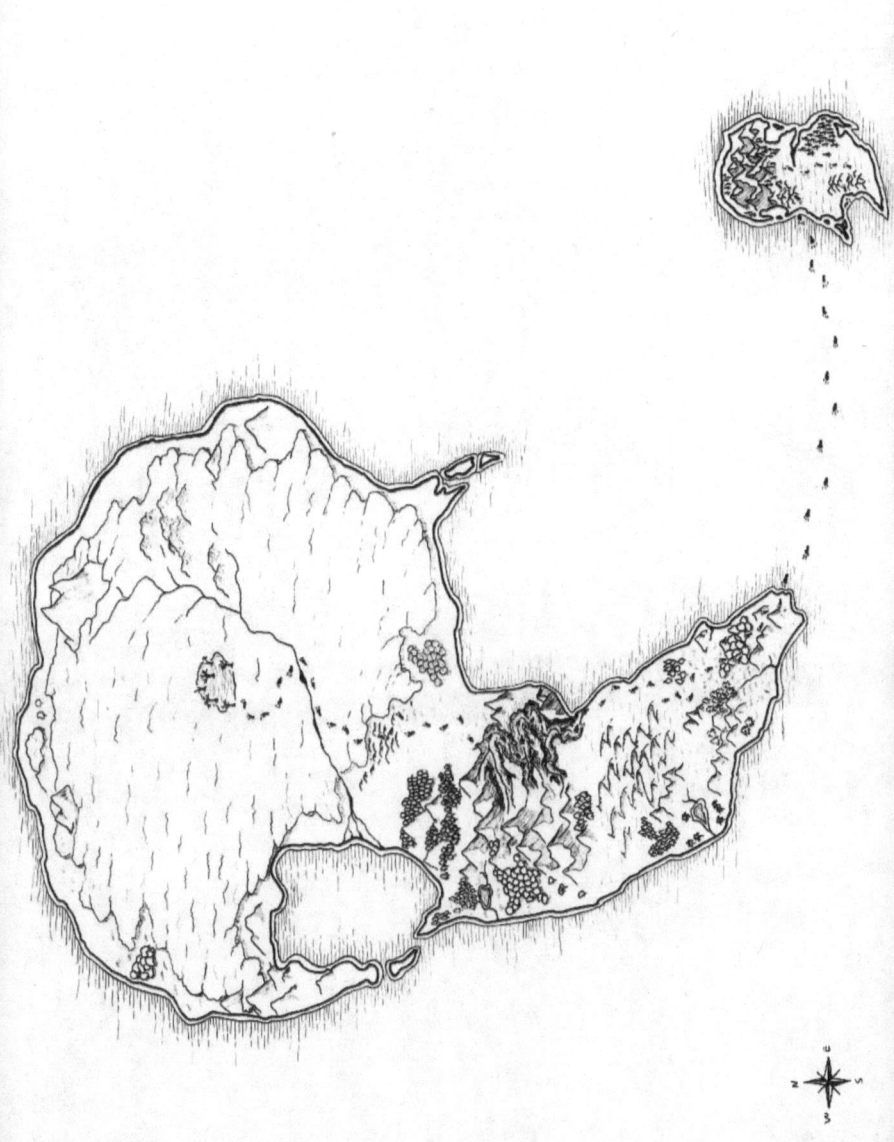

PROLOGUE

It was a wooden gate in the closed fence surrounding the garden. It was very big and dark, with thick mahogany doors that shone in the sunlight. It wasn't magical or special. Father had said there were things in the world that were special, but this wasn't one of them, this was just a wooden gate.

And yet to the child, sometimes it didn't seem like a gate at all. Sometimes it shimmered, filling with minuscule lights that quivered and fidgeted bumping into one another, pushing and pulling. He could see shapes beyond it, shapes made of colorful bright lights that didn't stand still, but moved like living things, walking this way and that, beating wings in the sky, shaking branches in the wind. They did all the things that living things do.

There was a world beyond the gate, a world he could glimpse through the fabric of the gate itself.

Father called it the *outside*.

Outside there were voices, not voices that the child could *hear* but voices that just *were*. Only, they hadn't always *been*. They'd begun *being* the first time the gate had not seemed like a gate, and they had not stopped *being* since.

1
THE CHILD

HE WOKE TO THE chirping of a bird perched on the sill of his open window, his eyes heavy from a tiring, troubled night. He sat up and rubbed the dribble from his mouth with the heel of his fist. The sun was low, hidden beneath the branches of the trees, but the day had begun to warm. It was already time. He gasped.

He bolted out of bed, crashing clumsily into the door trim before stumbling through, missing the first step down the staircase. He caught the wooden handrail and hugged it tightly, proceeding to descend each step carefully till his feet found the safety of the short grass. He ran, calling out as he crossed the shaded garden, "Father! Father, can I go with you?"

Miriethal paused with a hand against the gate. The many long braids of his chalky hair brushed the grass, swaying gently, before catching up to the new state of things, becoming still. When he turned, the rays of morning lit a frown on his face. He gazed down, his ivory eyes each inked with only the tiniest black pupil. He said, "Not today, child."

"Then when can I go?"

"When you are older."

"How much older?" He had not been old enough the last time this had happened, and he was, now, nearly four years old.

"When you have grown to match my height," his father said. "Now stay with Tashira. I shall be back soon."

Tashira roared sleepily from somewhere among the garden trees; then she was silent.

He sat in the grass watching the gate doors close and hide his father from sight. The morning dew wet his naked legs and small braies, but that particular problem did not concern him. A much bigger problem did.

It had taken him well over three years to become as tall as he was now, and unless he found a better way to do it, it would likely take him another three or even four years to match his father's height. That would simply not do. He was done with staying at home, done with being left behind, and done with being a child. He wanted to see the wonders beyond the gate, to meet the strangers that lived outside, and to go with his father into the forests he'd glimpsed all about.

Home was not always a bad place to be, and actually, it was usually just fine. It was a great house of living trees, of wooden walls, a roof made of reeds, and far above, a green canopy of leaves. Great roots stretched out from the ground like folds of cloth, so tall that he had to bend his head back and look up to the sky to see where they merged into trunks. The hot sun shone over a garden of grasses and weeds, and berry-laden shrubs, and the air smelled of flowers: the yellow lionprides with their manes of round petals, the tiny white whispers huddled densely in clusters, and the red tulips, their cups raised to the skies.

He knew the trees that made his home were very old—his father had told him so. He also knew that trees required plenty of water and sun to grow. So when the sun rose above the highest branches, he walked to the green pond at the garden's heart and stepped in the middle of it. He stood there like a tree, his arms outstretched to the blue sky. The water nuzzled his hips.

He didn't feel himself getting any taller. Only tired, and slightly cold.

When Tashira woke from her long nap, she demanded he came out of the pond and play with her. He chased her as she bounded about the garden, and she let him climb on her back and hustled him around in a frenzy. But when their games bored her, she went to lick her black fur dazzling clean and dozed off in the sun, leaving him alone with his worries.

In the late afternoon on the following day, his father returned, looking disheveled, with a bright red dot painted on his forehead and a line on his lips.

Father kneeled to kiss him on the cheek, then without a word headed up the spiral staircase to the warm wooden rooms overlooking the garden.

He followed upstairs. "Why can't I go with you?"

Father leaned his ivory sword against the wall and bent to untie the laces of his leather boots. His hands moved wearily, yet with urgent impatience. "I am tired, child," Father said.

These words were of no use to him, because already his own eyes, which had been light and lively before Father's return, had since become heavy and slowed with a terrible drowsiness. He pouted and watched Father undress, toss his white robe at a chair, miss, pick it up, and hang it over the back. Father lay on the wide puffy cotton mattress, pulled the sheets over himself, and closed his eyes. At last, peeking toward him, Father said yawning, "It isn't . . . saaafe for a child."

He, too, yawned. He rubbed his sleepy eyes with his fists, then yawned again. His steps were light and silent over the wooden floor. He climbed onto the wide mattress, slipped under the sheets, huddled close to his father's warmth, and soon fell fast asleep.

"TAKE ME WITH YOU!" he said one day when he was five. He was in his room above the garden, sitting on his small bed still warm from the night's sleep. The first light of morning came through the open window.

"You know I cannot do that."

"But I can hunt with you, I can!" Hunt, he had learned, was what his father did when he was gone for days, sometimes one day, sometimes two or three. Once, it had been more days than he could even count, although back then he had been too small to add past the number of his fingers, and in truth he could not be sure it had been as many days as that, because once or twice he'd forgotten how many fingers he'd already counted. He had done a great deal of crying when his father had come home at last, ill and weak.

"I do not need you to hunt with me, child. What I need is that you stay hidden, that you stay safe. You stay here." Father's gaze was earnest, and his word final. "I must go, now."

Burning tears filled his eyes as Father turned his back to him. His lips began to tremble. He did not watch him go, but curled into a ball under the bedclothes and breathed in damp air, sweltering in his own breath. When he could no longer bear the heat, he slipped the linen from his head and used it to dry his eyes and nose.

Later that day, he perched on the balls of his feet in the warm grass, his lips pursed tight and a frown pushing his brows down. The closed gate stood mockingly in front of him. From each of the two doors, a thick twisted handle hung some distance above the ground. He reckoned that if he stretched himself on his toes, he could reach the handles with only the tips of his fingers. But he would definitely reach them.

"I'm going out," he said.

Tashira made not the slightest move. Her huge black feline form lay seemingly asleep in front of the doors. Her pretense did not fool him. He had pondered the matter long that morning, back in his room. There would be no stopping him.

He rose upright. "I know you hear me."

Tashira opened a round yellow eye, as big as a full-grown apricot, and looked at him. She did not move.

"Let me pass!" he ordered.

The *kaara* opened her other eye and stood up on her hefty, furry legs. She was much, much taller than he was. She bent her head down so that her snout almost touched his nose. Then she growled. Between her black lips flashed walls of pointy yellow teeth. Her thick fangs split apart, her pink tongue flattened against the floor of her mouth, and a roar boomed out of her.

But his mind was made up, and he was not afraid. He brought forth focus to his eyes and made them shine with ruby light. He watched Tashira's shape brighten with the inner flow of her energies. He no longer saw black fur. Instead, he saw the life's movements within her body: the beating of her heart, the seeing of her eyes, the thinking of her mind. Her shape was dense and smooth as marble, yet it shimmered from within with strength and motion. He raised a hand, and ushered her aside—gently, because Father had taught him he must be kind to the weak. Against her will, the forest cat plodded away from the gate; then she stood immobile in the grass and watched him.

He let his focus wane, and his sight stilled.

Stretching on his toes, he reached for one of the metal handles. He could only just touch it. Leaning against one door, he slipped his fingers behind the handle of the other, and pulled.

THE CITY OF IRIETH dwelled at the heart of a lush jungle of ages past. Houses fashioned from wood and living trees hid beneath the green line of the high canopy, as a coral reef lying unseen in the depths of the sea. Its people were wise and long-lived, with pale skin, white hair, and ivory eyes. They called themselves "Alassians" and counted the years of their lives in centuries. The children born in the city were few—only one every decade or two—so that all children were known by all and loved by all. For life was precious to the Alassians, and especially that of a rare child of their kind.

So when a boy three feet tall, dressed in loose garments

of rosewood red, made his appearance outside the keeper's home in bright daylight—a slight figure in the thin gap between hefty doors—the Alassians came to stare and wonder. The child stood still and watched them in return. Until then, he had only known one other who was the same as he, Alassian and not a creature of the wild: his father, Miriethal. Now he saw others, many others—tall people gathering round, talking to one another, looking at him. Fear came into his heart and held him speechless.

One of the people stepped forward—the robe, brown like the earth, whispered in the grass step after step until it stopped.

The boy looked up at the face smiling down at him, but he did not see it smile, he saw it grin.

The stranger spoke, but the boy did not hear the words, for his heart beat too loudly. He turned, and ran. Through the garden, past the pond, up the stairs, and into his room. He shut the door with a slam and sank his weight against it, hugging his knees with his arms. There he shook with sobs. And he dried his cheeks, and he cried, and sobbed.

When Keeper Miriethal returned to Irieth bearing the red marks of a hunt, he found the gate to his home open and a crowd gathered outside. He walked through the people quickly and stiffly. They asked him questions: about a boy—A boy? A little one—who was in that room—Where? Up there—hiding—He'd been hiding in that room for the better part of the day.

"I shall go see this boy," the keeper said. He pushed the heavy gate closed, slowly and silently.

Outside, the crowd lingered until sunset. Then calm fell.

Miriethal stood by the garden pond, his gaze trapped in its shallow depths where a maze of weeds lay blackened by the night. Tashira, darker than darkness, circled around him and around the hole in the ground. She looked at her sire's face. Her sire stared unmoving into the pond, deep in thought.

It had been five long years. Only now was Irieth beginning to resemble a shadow of itself, the memory of the loss fading away. And now. Would they ask the question now? Would they ask about their guardian? Their strength? Their heart? All they had seen was a child, and a child was no guardian. The guardian was will of steel and heart of fire, the mightiest and most adept of Alassians. The power did not belong with the young and untrained. The ruby light had faded, reunited with the flow of the world—lost, it must be sought anew. Miriethal had named this the truth five years ago, and he alone knew otherwise. Except that, now, they had seen the boy.

The following day there was a knock on the gate. Miriethal emerged from within with the look of one who had kept vigil through the night. Outside his home, in the feeble morning light, stood a falyn—a male Alassian—with an old and stern face. The falyn's long hair fell to his feet in thin braids that lay on the ground behind him, fine as a blanket of frost. His voice was taut and bitter. The two spoke for long, the visitor now and then peering behind the keeper's shoulders, through the doors left ajar, and the keeper seemingly untroubled by the intrusion.

That day, Miriethal spoke to anyone who sought him

out, neither denying nor confirming the truth, agreeing only to what had been seen. A boy came out of this home, a boy ran into that room. Had there been a boy? So he had been told. Did the boy live in this home? A boy *had* lived in this home. Who was this boy? A young child, it seemed. Who were his parents? That, he had not been told. He spoke humbly and patiently, and one by one all the visitors were turned away.

The afternoon was beginning to darken, when a furious banging shook the gate. Outside, stood a tall young falyn, his face marked with a thick line of red paint over the eyes. Miriethal met the silent glare with unease, then stood aside to let this falyn in.

Alone in his room, the boy had not eaten or slept since the day before. His father had not tried to come in, but had asked for the door to be open. The door remained closed. He was still afraid, terrified, though not of the people, not since yesterday. At first, between one shameful sob and another, he had realized with horror that in his hasty escape he had left the gate open. He had listened hard for anyone who might come in, but no one had, and returning home, Father had closed the gate. Through the long hours of the night, nothing more had happened. In the morning there had been a coming and going of people, none, however, had gone past his father and entered their home. So he no longer feared the people outside; yet an unexplained dread filled him, and the slightest noise made him gasp with a pounding heart.

When presently, this falyn was let in, the boy at last got out of bed and ran to the door. There he stopped like a fly caught in a web, hands against the wood, heart beating fast. He listened intently—though not with his ears, for he was too far to hear the words spoken. This falyn's heart was angry and fierce. His rage roared like the squall before a storm. Suddenly, he yelled, and his voice lashed against the closed door and was muffled.

Curiosity won over the fear. The boy reached for the knob, pulled the door open, and crept to the stairs. He saw below him, in the garden, his father and a stranger deep in argument. Tashira, like a shadow, circled them both with a predator's pace, slow and deliberate, her big yellow eyes on the stranger.

He was a slim figure with wide shoulders and strong arms, taller than Father by a few inches. The color brown was all about him. Baggy brown trousers that stopped tight at the knees, a dark brown leather jerkin, and a wide brown sash at the waist. Into the sash he carried two black-sheathed swords with polished bronze handles. His hair was pure white, brighter than Father's chalky tone, and shorter; it was plain instead of braided, and tied in a narrow stream that hung behind his back, brushing his thighs when he moved.

"I will hear none of your riddles," the stranger was saying. His voice, although irate, was silvery clear. "No more, Keeper. Have you lied to me?"

Father did not reply.

"Is he? Or is he not? Answer me!" His command snapped like the cracking of a whip.

Father averted his gaze a moment, then quietly said, "Forget what you think you have learned, please. None of it must leave these walls. No one can hear of it."

"I have learned nothing!" barked the stranger. "You have told me nothing. If you want my silence, then give me the answers I seek. Talk!"

"You must quiet your anger," Miriethal said. "You must learn to be patient."

"Why are you doing this to me!" cried the stranger, and the strain in his voice betrayed despair. "I was left with nothing. Now I . . . Why?! Why won't you answer me? You are cruel. You are hurting me. And I have done you no wrong."

"I am sorry, young one."

There was a pause. Silent, unspoken words. Stares.

"If you say nothing, I shall have to ask *him*. Where is he? Where is the boy?"

Miriethal stood silent.

"Then keep your secrets! I will look for him myself."

The stranger turned, and quick as a shadow, Tashira bounced in his way, growling and hissing, big and brawny and black as pitch darkness, almost as tall as he.

Nimbly the falyn drew a sword and held it between himself and the kaara. Glaring at her with hard rage, he said, slowly so that his words were clear and full of silence, "Do not try to stop me, or I will fight you both. I seek answers, not blood. Yet blood will spill if you demand it."

But after he had spoken, his hand began to tremble. His grip wavered. His sword fell on the grass with a dull thump. His gaze searched the garden then flicked to the stairs. There, he saw the boy.

He was small and thin, fair-skinned, and with snow-white hair less than an inch long—as is true of all Alassian children his age. But his eyes shone bright red, as none of the children's do. He was crying silently, his lips pressed together, his brows furrowed, and heavy tears dripping from his chin.

Without speaking or moving, the falyn watched the boy cry and sob a little, the glow of his eyes slowly fading until they turned white and dull, the power stowed away.

Then the keeper spoke. "He is. But no one must know. I beg of you."

The stranger collected his sword from a bush of white whispers that had flattened beneath its weight, and sheathed it. Again he looked up at the boy. "No one will know," he said. His gaze lingered a moment in scrutiny. Then he turned, and left.

IN THE OPEN KITCHEN, thickly roofed with tangled leafy vines, a small fire crackled in a high circle of gray rocks, casting long shadows on the earthen floor.

"Father? Who was that falyn?"

He was sitting at the oaken table by the fire, looking into a bowl of steaming soup. Before his answer came, he stirred the food four times slowly with a slim white spoon.

"Someone you may one day know as your kin," said his father, "but not today. Today you are my son, and he is no son of mine. Eat your supper. It's getting cold."

He ate obediently, though the dense, orange soup tasted bland to his palate. When the bowl was empty, he said, "I'm sorry, Father." The words came out in an indistinct mumble, so that he was not sure they had been heard.

"Come. It's time to sleep."

Father took him by the hand and led him upstairs to the bigger of the two bedrooms and to the wide cotton bed in which he had not been allowed to sleep for over a year. Tonight he was allowed again. He cried, and Father held him in his arms until the sobs passed. Sometime after that, he fell asleep.

That night the keeper watched the darkness grow and then brighten again. When at last the morning light flooded the room, he slept, but only until the little one awoke. They got up late and went about their day with a silence and stillness that stayed with them for many days to come.

Then one morning, his father told him, "Tomorrow, we go into the forest."

His mouth fell open in a wide "O", and he did not think to close it for quite some time.

"We leave before dawn, so you will go to sleep early tonight."

He did not sleep that night.

Before the sun rose, he and Father rode on Tashira's back into the deep, unending jungle. Tall tree trunks rushed by them in a blur of brown and green, and the smell of earth, trees, flowers, and wood, filled their senses. The ground and the air were moist and did not dry even as the day went on, for daylight was timid beneath the high jungle canopy.

Everything he saw that day was a marvel. He grinned and giggled until his cheeks hurt and his breath was all out of him, then he grinned some more; and to his delight, Father laughed along with him till his white eyes were bright with tears.

He pointed at things, asked about them, and listened to his father tell him about the tree with smooth white bark, the stream that flowed fast and babbly, the huge red flower with the white dots that looked as if it might suddenly spring up and begin to walk, and many, many other wonders.

As the light of day began to dim, he kept his eyes from closing for as long as he could, but when twilight came, he slipped into quiet dreams.

In the small room above the garden, Miriethal laid the child in bed and kissed his forehead. Then with a tender smile on his lips, he murmured, "Sweet dreams, Guardian."

The next morning, and for many mornings to come, the boy awoke thrilled with excitement, dreaming of the day when his father would surely say: Tomorrow, we go into the forest. This time, he would make sure to sleep the night before, so that he could be awake when they returned home in the darkness of midnight. He did not ask his father when next the day would come, for that would certainly scare the time further away. Instead he waited, and once and again, his patience was rewarded.

THIS DAY WAS SILENT and hot, he was eight years old. His father was asleep on a blanket of vivid grass by the great riverside, cloaked in a robe of silver chiffon and wrapped in the heat of a sunbeam that shone intrepidly through the green canopy. Father had returned from a long hunt only the day before and was tired. Tashira was with them as she always was when they ventured into the jungle. She, too, was asleep—not because she was tired but because she was a cat and often did just that: she slept.

He was not far, and wide awake. He had climbed a blooming nut tree, and was ten feet above the ground, standing on a cluster of coconut-sized pods and holding tightly the thick twigs that grew all around the trunk, rough and old near the bark and green and smooth at the tips. The tips were covered in green buds, some of which had opened into big flowers with six red petals and a heart filled with pink and yellow stamens. Between two of these flowers hid the little creature he was chasing after: a red squirrel with black almond eyes, a cream belly, and a tail like a tongue of flame.

"I got you," he whispered, beaming at it. He stretched out to touch it. The critter hopped past his hand and ran up his arm to his shoulder, then leaped, spread its wing-like arms, glided softly, and dived into the tall grass below.

"Not fair!" he laughed.

He hurried down after it and snooped about in the sea of green. The squirrel re-emerged, standing up on an old tree root. It looked his way with a fat nut in its tiny fingers. He carefully went to crouch near it, and offered his open hands. The squirrel gave him the nut.

"I'm not hungry," he giggled.

The furry creature sniffed his fingers, then leaned forward. He felt the light pressure of the creature's gentle touch, its hard nails thin and sharp. He waited very still.

Finally, the squirrel climbed to retrieve the nut and began to nibble it right there on his hands. He held his breath, his cheeks stinging with glee.

The creature paused, listening. It glanced around, its head twitching left and right and back; its tail flickered once. Quick as a heartbeat, it scrabbled up his arm and slipped inside his clothes—*Hide!*

He jolted upright. Then he froze. Warm against his belly, the critter shuddered. His own body shivered, but he held himself still, for the fear he felt was not his own.

His belly squeaked.

"Hush, little one," he said inside his clothes. "What scares you?"

The creature kneaded his skin, scratching him with little nails, quivering and sniveling.

He inhaled deeply to ease his own tremors. He looked up and cast the fear out through his breath, clenching his fists. Bracing himself, he brought forth focus to his eyes.

About him the jungle shone and twinkled with life, full of currents and light. The leaves of trees shimmered green around him and above him. High in the sky, the wind blew white and bright, and the sun wove the world red. Down below, the earth sparkled densely with stars, myriads of tiny lives. He looked upon the one essence of all things, and in it, he saw a darkness, a wrongness, a slithering mass of steaming emptiness that swam in the multicolored currents of the river, thirty yards away. He blinked. The darkness leaped from the water, headed for the white brightness of his father's form.

He waved a hand at it, and slapped it back into the river. Then he sprang forward.

The squirrel's nails tickled him as the critter scuttled out his clothes to flee the opposite direction.

He kept his eyes on the darkness. He'd wished to cast it all the way beyond the river, but instead he had only managed to shove it back in the water. And now it leaped again, shooting out from the river's depths as an up-diving falcon. He threw himself at it, arms outstretched, uncaring of the rock that tricked his foot. His mind locked around a frigid emptiness as his chin smacked the ground.

He lay there sniffling soil. The fall had lashed at the nape of his neck, and he'd whacked his teeth together. His hands were open on the ground, palms up. In the air above, his mind held the icy emptiness.

He got to his knees.

Father lay sleeping beside him, unaware of the danger aloft. It was a snake, a pit viper, twenty inches long, flimsy, its round bulging eyes crowned with a crest of scales, its mouth gaping, the fangs drawn out. He could discern the creature's features through the steaming darkness that seeped from its marble-like body. But where he should see the light of living flesh, of a heartbeat, of flowing blood, he saw veins and masses of pulsing blackness. The creature's life was spent, eaten away. It did not think. It neither sensed nor felt the world around it.

He held the snake suspended between parted hands. What was inside it tried to move; he pressed his mind stoutly around it and held it still.

With the fingers of his right hand, he clasped the creature's feeble living essence, with the left, he tugged at the darkness. He wrenched it all out in one vigorous pull, and his hands snapped apart. The snake fell limp on the ground, lying there unmoving, its life force faintly guttering.

The darkness, like a black vapor, tried to dissipate. He closed his hands around it, his fingertips nearly touching. He squeezed it into a dense globe of icy nothingness and watched it. He watched it pulse with the beat of a heart. And he began to feel . . . wrong.

Cold. He felt very cold. His arms had grown heavy; he could hardly hold them up. He caught himself nodding off, and blinked. Tears oozed from his eyes.

"F-Father? Father w-wake up . . ." he sobbed.

His father did not hear him, just as he had not heard him fall down beside him, or the water splashing in the river. His mind was submerged in a deep-weaving sleep.

Despair took him; and in that moment, he heard Tashira's high-pitched hissing. The kaara crouched in the grass, watching him with piercing eyes, holding back a little, cautious, her teeth bared. She came closer and pressed a wide paw on Miriethal's chest.

The keeper's eyes flickered brightly open.

There was a flash of light.

Father's arms wrapped around him, pulling him into a fast embrace. Relief washed over him.

He wiped his tears against Father's chest, swallowing his frightened sobs. "I'm . . . cold."

"I know, child. But have no fear now. The danger has passed."

He grabbed the dampened fabric of Father's silvery robe and held on to the embrace. Miriethal pulled back enough to gaze into his eyes. Because he had allowed the power to fade from his sight, he saw his father's form as it was in the stillness of things—his small eyes white and dull with tiny black pupils, his mouth unsmiling but wrinkled with kindness.

"You did well," Father told him. "Now lie in the sun for a while. You will soon feel warm."

Without protest, he lay drowsing in the heat of the sun.

They set out for home well before nightfall, riding fast on Tashira's back. He did not complain of the early departure—he did not feel like talking, anyway. He leaned against Father's chest and clung to his strong arm, shielding himself from the cold air that seeped under his clothes. It had never occurred to him that riding on Tashira's back was such a strenuous and uncomfortable thing. By the time they reached home he was chilled to the bone. The day had grown dark, and he felt sick and exhausted.

For the next three days, he ailed with fever. He spent the hours sleeping or listening to his father read the stories of old. When at last he was deemed on the way of recovery—his favorite meal of coconut bread and pumpkin soup devoured as proof of good health—his father sat down solemnly beside him and told him, then, of the nature of darkness.

"The unlife, we call it, although what its true name is, we do not know. It is by curse of knowledge that our people are sworn to do battle against it, and protect the world from its cold grasp. For darkness is the ender of all life."

Father talked of how, hundreds of centuries in the past, their ancestors had tamed the powers of light, and with them, had secured the Haven from unending night. They had built the city of Irieth very near that passage between this realm and the one beyond, where this evil resides. And ever since then, they had kept watch.

In the silence that followed, he thought for some time. Presently, he asked, "What happened to the darkness I took from the snake?"

"I cast it out of our realm," his father said, "and shut the doors behind it."

"Will you teach me?"

"I cannot."

"Please?"

"I would teach this to you if it were something that you could learn. But you cannot learn this."

"I can learn! I promise!"

"You are strong," said Father; "I know your power. You are the guardian. But you cannot cross the borders, and so you cannot cast out darkness. It is beyond your skill. The task falls to the keeper alone."

He knew his father spoke the truth, because in the presence of the unlife, and for the first time in his life, he had felt defenseless. The memory upset him.

"But I fought it! Alone! I saved you, Father!"

"That you did. You were brave, child. But you must be braver still. You must wield courage even when your power fails you. Your strength must come from your mind, as well as your heart. Never let one rule over the other."

He pondered his feelings for a while. It was fear he felt beneath the frustration. "What do I do if more darkness comes?" he asked.

"Bring it to me. And I will cleanse the world of its taint."

"But what if I can't, Father? What if you're not with me?"

"Then you must slay it."

He stared in bewilderment. Father had taught him the value of all living things, Alassians, kaaras, the creatures of the forests, skies, and waters, the plants, trees, and flowers, the grass that crowns the earth and the insects that crawl in it. Slay it, Father said now, slay it—he did not think that darkness could be slain, for it was emptiness, it was coldness—slay it, the creature, slay the creature it wears.

"The unlife cannot thrive in this world without a living body," said Father. "A creature infected by it may be slain, and darkness trapped inside it for a time. But not forever. Eventually it will escape the body, and seek a new servant. That is why the Light exists. That is why I am its keeper. I am the vanquisher of darkness. It is my duty to cast the unlife from our realm. And your duty—when you are old enough to take it upon yourself—will be to watch the borders between the worlds, to safeguard the Light, and with it, the life of all things. Now you know."

"I am old enough," he said. "I can fight the unlife with you."

His father smiled, and there was laughter in his heart. He said, "No, child. You are still young. First, you must grow into a strong falyn. Only then will you fight at my side."

"But I am ready!"

"You are ready to learn how to defend yourself. And that, I will teach you. I will teach you the art of combat."

An art that to him became a passion.

Father taught him the stances and movements, the foot positions, how to feel for his center and find balance. He was a perseverant student, driven by the rigorous practice. Fighting was a fascinating dance, slow and graceful at times, fast and fierce at others. In the training he found clarity of mind and learned to open his senses far outward, farther than ever before.

And so it was that one sunny day in his thirteenth year, his mind came upon something odd, an indistinct noise, like a buzzing. He was sparring with his father and became distracted. Dropping his stance, he shone his gaze eastward, where he could see the jungle's living light for miles, a confused blend of colors and movement. He saw no darkness. Yet, what he sensed troubled him.

"Someone comes," he said.

There was a flicker of fear in his father's heart. "How many, and where?"

"Twelve," he counted, "far beyond the great waterfalls."

"Alassians?"

He gave his father a questioning look. "No."

Miriethal, too, gazed to the east, although he would not see past the tree-walls of their garden.

"Father? What are they if not Alassian?"

There was a long silence; then at last, Father said, "Human."

2
THE COMING OF OTHERS

KEEPER MIRIETHAL GATHERED a party of twelve to ride east. The guardian waited at home, sitting cross-legged on the grass facing the pond filled with duckweed and the wide green leaves of water lilies. His gaze was lost on a hollow gray rock which was part of a wall crowned by blooming red bushes. His mind was absent, soaring eastward ahead of the twelve.

Deep in the heart of the Sa'dalia rainforest, human explorers had come upon uncharted waterfalls. The slow and wide Uwano River, which they had followed for miles, thundered down from towering cliffs, foamy white into a pool of glistening water. Overhead, the sky was a half-circle of bright blue, a splinter of daylight in the dark canopy roof.

Laboriously the humans descended to lower ground where the sun shone hot and the grass grew wild and tall. Here they made camp. They erected green tents with roofs firmly stretched and held by tense ropes. They gathered wood and built a fire inside a ring of flat stones. Well before nightfall, they turned their gazes to the west where twelve pale figures emerged from the jungle shade, noiselessly as ghosts.

The humans jumped to their feet bracing guns, shouting and baying. The pale jungle people stood in a silent line and watched them.

Keeper Miriethal studied the intruders through eyes hard and careful. He had seen humans once before, though not these humans. He had seen simple creatures, half-naked and nomadic. These in front of him now, were men and women from a far more advanced society. Their tools were fine and intricate: big packs with strings and buckles, perfectly shaped flasks and bottles, neatly-built tents. They wore identical garments in brown and green blotches: long trousers, long-sleeved tops, vests covered in pockets, small hats, and thick boots.

Unlike the humans of nearly two thousand years ago, who had looked like one people, these humans had skins of every shade, from fair to very dark, and their hair was brown, blond, red, or black. They each held a bulky black tool—a weapon—with tiny metal parts, a small handle, and a long tube whose hollow end was aimed at Miriethal and his people.

The humans scanned the jungle people from behind the protection of their guns. Alien creatures stood before them, ghastly-pale, with long white hair and monstrous eyes that had no iris but only the small pupil. They wore loose-fitting clothes from another era, and each of them bore weapons. Slim wooden longbows, quivers filled with feathered arrows, and sheathed swords tucked into sashes at the waist. One of them spoke first. From the center of the line, he said in their foreign tongue, «Nuhina liavn te, alannen.»

«We come in peace!» replied one of the soldiers.

Silence.

«Sélia,» said the same pale one, bowing his head slightly. «Miriethal se'nuyhiéleh.»

«We're friends!» cried the same soldier, gazing from over the barrel of his gun. «You understand?»

A longer silence.

The soldier, a stern weathered man, searched his comrades. His eyes settled on a young woman with deep ebony skin and kinky black hair. He said to her, «Talk to them.»

«Me?» The woman gawked.

«Now!»

«Yes, sir!» She lowered her gun and addressed the jungle people, projecting her voice, a hand to her chest. «I . . . aaam . . . Looomaa,» she said.

The pale people exchanged silent glances. Someone among the soldiers sniggered. Then a pale hand rose, copying Loma's gesture.

«I . . . am . . . Tawori,» said a pale male at one end of the line.

Loma stared. «We come in peace,» she blurted.

The pale one shook his head.

«Keep talking,» encouraged the weathered soldier.

«Uh . . . This . . . » said Loma, «is Sergeant Jonson.» She indicated the man, who lowered his gun and signaled the others to do the same. Loma continued, «This . . . is Andra. And Devid. Hanah . . .» She named all twelve soldiers, then looked at the one called Tawori and waited hopefully.

The pale one turned to his companions. He spoke in a blur of soft sounds. «Ashe nur, ihn, nimvn eth luhila?»

The white eerie gazes went in unison to the person who stood in the center of the line and who had spoken first. He nodded.

Tawori walked to him. «This ... is ... Miriethal Alaire,» he said. Then from left to right he named the others one by one from Theidrin and Aruhin, to Omoin and at last Gwendier. They each nodded as they heard their name.

«A pleasure to meet you,» said Sergeant Jonson.

The pale one refocused his attention on him, but did not reply.

«Come,» said the sergeant, «sit at the fire. Make space for them, make space.»

The soldiers moved back, clearing the area around the fireplace. The pale people didn't move.

«Sit down, please. Come,» repeated the man, beckoning.

This time the pale one walked forward, confidently and with the bearing of a warrior treading among warriors. His companions followed him. He stopped and they stopped, across the fire from the humans. They did not sit.

«Do you live around here?»

No reply.

«We came a long way,» continued the sergeant.

The pale one shifted his silent gaze back to Loma, and the woman tensed.

«We ... come from Terica,» she said, and waved

vaguely to the east.

«And you?» asked the sergeant, gesturing for the pale one to speak.

Tawori looked at him, and said, «Lur ven'gornvn nuhina tisa veiahm.»

Beside him, Miriethal Alaire nodded.

«We...» said Tawori, «come... from Irieth.» He pointed westward.

«We came here for you,» the sergeant said, extending his open hands. His gesture was met with a frown. «We came to meet with you.»

At that, the pale one cast a sharp glance about him, as if noticing only now the other soldiers standing around him in the firelight. He said, «Lur dedvn veiahm pre isi nuhina.»

His companions all began to speak at once. They chattered over one another like a flock of hungry seagulls, all but Miriethal Alaire—he was quiet, his gaze moving slowly from one soldier to the next. After some time, he spoke; then the others fell silent.

That day and long through the night, the pale people of the deep jungle sat with the humans from a land far away, learning of their culture and their journey. When they parted ways, long after nightfall, the woods were pitch black.

«We come back,» Tawori told the soldiers. «You wait. Here. After tomorrow.»

The pale ones called to the night, and something, or some things, in the trees beyond the fire-lit circle moved with rustling noises. Eyes burned in the dark. The Alassians walked into the trees, and were gone.

...

IN THE MORNING, the boy set out breakfast on the kitchen table: dried mango, boiled goose eggs, and coconut flatbread. By the time his father came into the kitchen—little more than a closed fireplace and a wide wooden table with four chairs—the eggs and bread had cooled.

"What of the humans, Father?"

Miriethal slumped into a chair and began to peel an egg. "They have come looking for us and our city," he replied.

"Will they find it?"

"That is yet to be decided."

He watched Father eat his egg then reach for a piece of dried mango, change his mind and take instead another egg.

"Are they to be feared?"

"I should ask *you* that question," Father said. "You hear their hearts, whereas I only hear their words, and I do not understand their meaning." He chuckled, shaking his head, and cracked the eggshell on the table with a knock.

He had already eaten while Father slept, but the taste of dried mango was still sweet on his tongue. He took a slice and chewed it absentmindedly. He had been thinking hard on his own question, but had found no answer. The humans' hearts and minds were unfamiliar to him and unsettling. All the previous day and again this morning, he had listened to them and still was puzzled. At first, he had heard a bitterness, which he had thought was mistrust, then he had felt a distinct richness, like satisfaction. But everything was clouded in a chaos of fast-shifting emotions; the constant buzzing of it was dizzying.

"I fear what I don't understand," he said when Father

was leaving.

"So do we all," Miriethal replied.

That day, the keeper summoned a council of the people. A crowd of hundreds gathered to hear him talk. He stood before the Temple of Congruence, at the foot of moss-covered stairs, low easy stone steps flanked by square granite poles. Behind him was a gateway, a stout square arch of rock toppled with dense moss over which sat two great stones shaped like drops. On them were carved runes of the ancient tongue: *ire*, the light; and *ànwi*, the equilibrium. Past the gateway, and to the left and right of the stairs, were broad trees, their bark rough and ancient. Round boulders circled each tree, and flat even earth lay about them. Everything was blanketed in green and white moss. This was a place of meditation, learning, and training. Here, the keeper spoke of the coming of humans.

Not for the first time a group of nomads or lost travelers had found their way to the city of Irieth and learned of its people. Alassian history was scarred by such occurrences. The race of Man was young and short-lived, ruled by passing desires, and prone to extremes. Once, the humans would exalt the Alassians as gods, once, they would wage war on them with swords and shields. The occasion of their latest coming was most troubling. A decision must be made as to whether these humans should be welcomed or turned away.

From a place of silence, sitting in the grass near a quiet pond, the guardian heeded the council. Throughout this day and the one that followed, he listened to the worries and discord of the people, their hopes and curiosity, until the keeper with his party rode to the far waterfalls, where he welcomed the humans into the city.

In the solitary confines of his home, the guardian listened to the humans' astonishment at the sight of Irieth and its inhabitants, and in the days that followed, he kept a watchful eye.

The Alassians found their visitors to be of great interest. Little they resembled the primitive species remembered by some. They carried with them knowledge of the faraway world, of lands unseen by the Alassians for millennia, and possessed tools that replicated images and sounds, voices of things and people from those far-lands. They showed the Alassians a world they had long forsaken and forgotten.

But while the Alassians learned of the humans, their technology, and their lands, so too, the humans of those far-lands were learning of the Alassians, their strange city, their uncanny appearance, and their centuries-long lives. And they, if only by intuition, began to glimpse a mystery surrounding these pale jungle people, an unseen mysticism that filled their being and their everyday life. It was in the way they walked, in the way they spoke, and in how they communed with the flora and fauna of their habitat. For when the Alassians spoke to wild animals, these seemed to listen, and when the wind shook the leaves of tall trees, its voice appeared to answer them.

IT WAS THE TENTH night since the coming of the humans when the guardian awoke from sleep gasping for air. He sat up trembling, feverish and cold. The bed sheets, bright in his Alassian night sight, were wet with sweat. A dreadful fear was in his heart and he thought perhaps a dream had caused him distress, but thinking hard, he could not remember to have been dreaming. When at last his drowsiness dissipated, he remembered the humans.

He fixed his gaze on the wall where a knot in the wood drew a darker shade in the light blue tinge of his night vision. He silenced his mind and let his consciousness seep out of his body and into the world, outside his room, outside his home, to the south, a mile or so through Irieth, to the house where the humans had been lodged. There, he found the unmistakable sharpness of fear. Dread. Despair. Heavy and suffocating grievance. The humans waited, awake in the night. What were they waiting for?

He threw off the sheets and barged out of his room. The wooden floor felt warm beneath his bare feet. Cold night air snatched at his naked torso.

He banged on his father's door shouting, "Father? Wake up! Wake up, Father!"

The door swung open. "What is it?"

Father stood dressed in his day clothes, his ivory-sheathed sword secured at the waist, his robe creased, and his face showing signs of slumber.

"The humans! They fear for their lives!"

Father made no reply; his mind was slow with sleep.

"They are waiting! Awake. All of them. I think—" He shone his gaze to the sky, and in the distance he saw an object, dark in the flow of the world's energies. His eyes could not glimpse the object per se, for it was too far, but he discerned its shadow in the force that propelled it forward, a force that gleamed bright as fire, leaving behind a vaporous wake that far, and farther, dissipated into darkness.

"Something comes," he said. "I don't know what it is. It's falling toward us."

Miriethal stepped onto the stairs, from where he could look at the night sky.

"Father, I think that's what the humans fear."

"I see a falling star."

"It's not a star."

For an instant an overwhelming fear gripped both their bodies. Then it was gone, suppressed by his father's will. "Come with me!"

They ran down the spiral staircase, stopping near the quiet pond at the garden's heart where the sky was open and vast.

"You must share the guardian's power with me" said Father, "and with as many Alassians as you can. Those who are adept will know how to use it to defend themselves and others. I will do the same and give them my protection, but you must open the way for me."

He looked at his father, confused. "What—"

"There is no time! Do as I do."

Through the guardian sight, he watched as a thread of light stretched from his father's belly and reached out to him, white, unwavering, and pure—his father's light, the keeper's light. Heat filled him from within as the power wholly surrounded his body, a blanket against the chill of the night.

"Hurry, child!"

He understood what was asked of him, only he had to find a way to do it.

He held the inner flow of his life force steady, as his father had done, and reached deep within himself for the essence of his being, the core of the guardian's power. He began to pull it outward. At once he felt sick. His instincts screamed at him to stop, to let go, let the essence fall back where it belonged. He was hurting himself.

Yet his father's gaze was upon him, strong with determination. He must do what was asked of him, because now, in this time of need, he was the guardian, and that who stood in front of him requesting his aid did not do so as his father but as the keeper of the world's light.

He did not understand what danger was upon them, but that mattered not. He was called to fulfill his duty, and this he would do.

In his mind he envisioned the essence of his being take shape in a thread of red light. He willed it to spiral around the white strand that joined him with his father. Then his own ruby essence enveloped Father's body, and through it the keeper's light pierced here and there like beams of moonlight.

Father's eyes shone red. "Yes," he said gazing at the sky, "now follow my light." At once, a myriad of white rays stretched from Father's luminous form and went in all directions. Fast, far, and sure. They sought Alassians in the city, touching and surrounding them with light and with power. They went farther and farther. And the city began to awaken.

He stared at his father in awe. Long had he known Father's power to be great, but never had he imagined such manifestation of mastery and intensity. Not only did Father wield the keeper's light with skill, but while they shared in each other's essence, he was able to look at the flow of the world through red shining eyes and open his senses to all of Irieth. He heard in his father's mind the chorus of countless Alassians, and in his heart felt their distress.

He understood, now, his own insignificance. What was the mere decade of his young life compared to his father's long centuries of wisdom and training?

And yet the guardian's power had been entrusted to him and him alone. Akihalla, the guardian who had preceded him, had chosen him among all people to protect the world at the keeper's side. This he would do even in his inferiority, in his childhood inadequacy. He would prove his worthiness. He would be the Guardian. He would protect Irieth.

He began to stretch his ruby essence in the wake of his father's light, but found he could not follow all threads by sight—they were too many and went too far. He shut his eyes and focused on the hearts and minds of the people, willing his essence to them with every fiber of his being. The guardian's power pierced him through a thousand times, straining in all directions. He groaned and gasped, but kept at the task. One after another, he enveloped all Alassians in his radiance.

Then the entire city was under his and his father's protection.

"Ready yourself," said Father.

He opened his eyes.

The world thundered with a deafening blast. Almighty currents came crashing from east to west, brighter than the sun and blinding to the eyes of the living. Through the guardian sight he watched the flow of energies hasten by. He saw the earth dig underneath his feet and the trunks of ancient trees shred like desiccated leaves. Splinters spewed into the air like water from hulking buckets.

Rocks and boulders flew up in the sky and shattered one another like pottery.

He pushed against the mighty forces and, in them, split an opening where he and his father stood bent against havoc. It took all his strength and concentration to do so, and to keep the tear in place around them. The debris of the physical world, he moved aside. Some slipped through his guard, his father caught it. Some they both missed, it stabbed their flesh, digging deep and sharp. A scorching heat washed over everything. It burned everything. It hazed the sight. It set fire to their lungs. Limbs of it slipped past his will and brushed against his flesh, hollowing the fabric of his trousers. They did not burn him, for the keeper's shield was at work.

In the midst of chaos a new awareness awoke in him. While he fought the harmful energies, he learned of a falyn who was on the verge of losing his own battle. He saw through his own eyes what the falyn's eyes saw, and it was, then, as though he were in two places at once. Instinct guided him. Without hesitation he subdued the falyn's life force, bound it to his own will, and used it to shape the world of chaos. He pushed against the currents; he caught the debris before it stabbed the living body; he protected the life.

He sensed other frightened hearts, overwhelmed minds, and came to their aid, unbound and unyielding. Time stretched endlessly as he battled on. Then the thrusting force ceased.

The heat vanished. Silence lay still.

Fire rose from the earth with the violence of a storm.

He let his essence withdraw. It snapped back and

struck him with a blow to the stomach.

He dropped on all fours, vomiting a mouthful of bile, coughing, and gasping for air. When the fit passed, he fought to quell his panting and trembling. His body hurt as if it were scraped all over. His strength was spent. The light faded from his sight and he saw scarlet blood stream down his arms. Thick drops dribbled from his face and chest, dousing the ground beneath him. All he could sense now was pain. Great, overwhelming pain.

He shut his eyes and concentrated on breathing, gathering his life force, shaping it into threads of vitality in his belly. Wearily and with great effort, he sent them prodding into the far reaches of his body. His flesh prickled and heated with healing fever. The ringing in his ears eased, and he heard the sputtering and whooshing of fire.

The bleeding stopped, then he sank back on his heels.

His father was kneeling a step away from him, covered in blood, his eyes closed in concentration and his breathing puffing with effort.

He wanted to reach for him, help him heal, but he couldn't. His body wouldn't move.

Around them were ash, cinder, and fire. Nothing stood where it had once existed. Their home was a deformed ring of blazing debris. There was no shape to it but for a hollow where they had withstood the forces of chaos. The soil was scorched black. There was no water left in the pond—there was no pond left in the earth. The sky above was dense with smoke.

From a fiery pile of rubble came a movement and a growl. Tashira emerged with her fur matted with dirt and blood. He watched her stupidly as she plodded to Miriethal and licked his cheek once with her wide tongue. She began cleaning her wounds. She licked her right front paw. With it she cleaned her muzzle and ears. She licked her belly thoroughly. Then she licked her left front paw. She went on licking and washing, and her fur slowly turned black. Suddenly her snout snapped toward the sky, and she snarled.

There was a swooshing sound, like a flapping of vast wings.

Black and sharp through the smoke's haze, a powerful body took shape, two legs thick and muscly, four hooked talons on each foot. It flew on bat-like wings, long, wide, and with scales like thorns. The neck was serpentine and rugged, the face like that of a snake or a crocodile. It had long spikes and horns bent back. Thick membranes stretched between the spikes. It flew downward, writhing a little in the air, as an eel would in water. It was very near already.

It landed atop the circle of burning detritus and crouched forward on its taloned wings. Even so shrunk, it loomed enormously. It turned its neck to one side and watched through a shadowed black eye.

"Lenthieh?" came Father's voice.

Almost in reply, a dark figure leaped from the creature's back, light and agile, a cascade of long white hair dancing with it, waving behind a black robe and stroking the ground. A second figure followed, heavier, slower, less graceful. Both dashed forward.

He had not moved, still sitting on his heels, puzzled by the apparition. Father's grip seized his arm and snatched him onto his feet and to the side. He heard the clanging of metal against metal and the sliding of blade against blade. He bumped against his father's back and tripped;

then the steely grip shoved him face-first into a pile of waste and ash, and lost him. He yelped as hot dry dirt scorched him.

He scuffled blindly out of it. Grains of dust burned his eyes and forced him to blink, and squint, and peer half-blind at his father, and the black-clothed stranger, and the winged creature, and—where had the second figure gone?

He saw Tashira bite and tear at the ground beneath her.

Father slipped and reeled backward. The stranger pressed after him. They paused, immobile, Father almost kneeling, the stranger towering above him. It was a falyn—that much he could discern despite the burning tears blurring his vision. He was muttering something. His voice, sharp and rough, echoed in the vastness with a chanting, hypnotic rhythm that was ominous to hear. All else had fallen silent, as though the world awaited answer.

In that stillness, Father spoke words of the ancient tongue. His voice rang loud and bright. "Nuykaara! Fàiwon'nàlanwih ônnihìmmara!"

Tashira's roar crashed like ocean waves. She moved like wind, rushing past Father and the stranger, and bouncing to where he half-sat on one foot, baffled and slow, unable to do anything but watch the fight take place around him. She bumped her snout against him, and he floundered forward, catching himself with unsteady hands on the ground.

"Go with her!" shouted Father.

All he could do was blink back at him.

"Redien! Go with Tashira!"

He turned his gaze to the kaara. She had bent her legs, her belly on the ground. He climbed onto her back and squeezed his thighs around her flanks. At once she sprang up. Fast and slick, she climbed over the wall of burning rubble and wood, down the other side, away from the battle, and into blazing desolation. She ran.

Fire and smoke burned his eyes and filled his lungs with fitful coughing. Trees rushed by—broken, bent, turned to cinder on one side and to flame on the other; they crackled, snapped, came crashing down. Leaves of ash fell like hot snow in a blizzard.

He put his arms up to shield his eyes and mouth. The wind howled hot in his ears.

A sudden pain in his abdomen squeezed the breath out of him. The echo of a scream stabbed at his mind with the sharpness of a spear, wrenching his vision black. He bent over, pressing his face in Tashira's fur, clinging to her with one hand, and with the other clasping his belly where a searing pain burned him from within. He panted, slobbering in the dark.

Father's anguished cry wailed on, and on.

He screamed along with it.

Stop! he thought. Turn back! Turn back!

But Tashira kept on running. She kept running.

He kept on screaming, screaming. Screaming.

Until it all ended.

He drew a lungful of smoke. He coughed it out.

There was silence. In his mind there was silence. Emptiness. In his heart there was a hollow. Death. There was death. He was dead. Abandoned. He had abandoned him. Left him to die. He was running away. Not turning back. Not doing anything. Not knowing anything. Not seeing where he was going. He was empty. Full of cowardice. He was weak. He was nothing. He was dead.

He was no longer aware of the passing of time. He did not notice the coming of rain. When Tashira staggered and collapsed, he made no effort to stop himself from falling along with her. She did not get up. He did not get up.

3
UNDONE

HE STARED AT HIS left hand in the short grass. It was daytime, and all was silent. He was flat on his stomach on soggy turf. The right side of his face had sunk in mud, and his nose was full with the odor of it, a pungent, acrid smell—although perhaps it was the smell of the air. There was something in the air—or was it in his throat and lungs? Something that tightened his breathing.

The mud was cold. He felt cold. There were raindrops on the back of his hand.

He stirred. The fabric of his trousers stuck to him, soaked and heavy. His right arm was pinned down by a weight; when he tried to move it, he couldn't. But the left arm, the one he looked at, he could move. He dragged it slowly toward him and propped himself over it enough to pull his knees under. He felt utterly exhausted and had to pause to catch his breath. He panted, pressing his forehead in the mud. When his breathing eased he looked to his right and saw Tashira, her head resting on his forearm, her mouth ajar, her eyes open and still.

"T-Tash—"

He stroked her damp fur, and his hand came back red with her blood.

"T-Tashi—" He tried to call her name, but the word would not come out. She lay still. He sobbed and shuddered closer, his face in her wet coat, his weight over hers and his arm crushed beneath them both.

He shook her. "Tashira!" he called.

She didn't move.

"Tashira! Tashira!" he sobbed. He won his arm free of her weight so he could better shake her awake. He called her name again. She did not answer. She was dead. Her eyes looked at him and did not see him. She did not move except from his shaking of her, which stirred her only faintly. Her mouth lay open, the tongue out on the grass.

He thought how foolish he was. How foolish! He placed both hands on her body and called her life force to his will. But there was no life to obey his command. So he poured his own energies into her. He could heal her if he healed her wounds, if he healed her body. If only he could heal her body, if he were strong enough. If he could bring her back, if he could—

He collapsed over her cold body and sobbed helplessly, uselessly.

The wind howled over him.

When he came back to awareness, he was drooped over Tashira's body and breathing shallowly.

He was hungry, and felt sick.

His legs threatened to give in, but he managed to stand.

Around him was a small glade encircled by tall half-charred trees the leaves of which were scarce and blackened. Dense, gray fog filled the sky, and the gleam of day pierced through, casting shadows over the sodden grass. He did not know this glade; he had not been here before.

A gush of wind brushed the tree branches, carrying the niff of burnt wood and a smell of decay. He shivered. His body was stiff and seized by tremors.

He hugged himself, but found no comfort in his own arms, wet with mud and blood, the blood of Tashira.

He looked down at her, she looked up at him.

It was a long while later when he turned his gaze away from her dead yellow eyes. He watched the jungle loom with grayness. The branches of the trees were half naked and sick, and when the wind blew, they moaned. He staggered forward. One step after the other the mud swallowed his feet in loud gulps. He reached the trees, where the earth turned hard and dense with roots. Sticks and leaves and little plants bent and cracked beneath the soles of his feet.

He treaded on warily over no path and in no particular direction. He was going nowhere he knew, and did not know why he was going there. He was going somewhere, somewhere that wasn't here.

He stumbled, and recovered. He stumbled and fell. He got up, and kept on walking. His labored breathing was all he could hear—Why was it all he could hear?

He stopped to listen.

His breathing quieted slowly. Then he heard silence. Dead silence.

He hugged himself in his bruised arms, shifting his

gaze to the world of energies. He could not quite see. His vision was blurry, and he was weak, hungry. The cold had eaten his strength away, and the long walk, and the run, and before that the explosion, the light, the heat, the debris. The black creature, and the strangers, and . . . his father . . . his father was . . . was he—No. He had not seen what had happened, only felt it. He'd felt his suffering, so terrible, and his cries and fear . . . the anguish. Then it had all stopped. All at once. He remembered that. He was sure he remembered that. Unless . . . unless he remembered wrong. Maybe he'd lost consciousness—he had done that a lot in the last . . . hour, was it? Had it been hours? Or maybe . . . maybe he'd gone too far to hear him . . . Perhaps he should go back. Yes, go back. But which way was back?

He had been walking away from Irieth, he'd thought, though perhaps that wasn't true. Perhaps he had been headed toward it after all, toward the battle. Maybe his father and the falyn were still fighting. If he hurried, he could do something. But which way? Which way? Which way!

He did not know this place, this empty place, this deathly place. There was no one here, not even animals, gone, all gone. Maybe they were all dead, all dead like Tashira, like his father. Dead. They were all dead.

His legs gave way and he fell to his knees. What little power had brightened his sight, now faded. The light of day had waned. The trees crowded about him, black and naked, like grasping hands in the fog. The jungle was ill. The day was ill. Maybe the world was dying. What was he to do? He was lost and alone.

He tried to get up but his legs wouldn't hold him. His

body was trembling. No matter how tightly he hugged himself, it kept trembling and shivering. He had found no food and no water although he had walked a great distance; slowly, but he was sure that he had walked a great distance, heading away from Irieth or maybe toward it—he wasn't sure of that.

His head ached, and he was hungry. Painfully, he crawled to an old tree with wide, fanned out roots, which offered little protection from the biting cold. He curled into a ball with his back against the trunk, and listened to his own weak whimpers, like a lost pup without hope, bound to die alone, helpless in the growing gloom of dusk.

When he opened his eyes it was night. The trees, the leaves, and the ground were a dark shadowy-gray tinged with yellow and blue; the air was a whitish murk. His heart beat fast, and he was panting. He was afraid. Something had woken him.

He sat up and stretched his inner senses, listening. There were six—no, seven of them. One was the falyn his father had fought. He recognized him by the malice in his mind and the hunger in his heart. The other six he'd never heard before; they were like Alassians, but wrong.

He cowered against the tree, making himself small. If he hid and didn't move, he would make it harder for them to find him—because they were here to find him. He had no doubt about that. He knew what they were after; it was obvious.

He had understood a long while back. Thirteen years was a long time to be kept hidden from the world and be lied about why. One day he'd seen it clearly, as though a blindfold had been lifted from his eyes. He had never spoken of the matter, because he remembered too well the day he had disobeyed his father, the fear and misery he'd caused. He'd had no wish to bring those feelings back. So he had kept his knowledge to himself, pretending not to know. But he did know. And now, his father's most dreaded fear had come true at last. It was very near.

A screech filled the silence, making him start. He pressed his back harder against the tree, feeling the rough bark pry his bones. He heard wood snapping.

Something was nearby, something big and clumsy that made noise in the undergrowth. Yet he sensed no creature close by; and still he heard it sniffing, like wind rasping in a cave. There was a thudding, heavy steps, more snapping higher up in the trees, another screech. Something slammed down near him. He did not look at it, but sprang up and ran, bolting left and right through the trees. A thump beat the air out of him and hurled him forward chest first, his feet gone from beneath him. He plummeted to the ground blind with pain, his body frozen. With a desperate effort he stirred his focus to the pain. There was something cold, metal, a sharp point, a shaft—an arrow, stuck in his chest. It had gone a few inches in, pierced a lung, and cracked a rib. He dared not to breathe. He begged his life force to gather at the wound, to form into a sphere of energy and heal him. But the flesh could not mend while the weapon was inside him. He couldn't make his body move. His consciousness was slipping away.

A weight slumped on his lower back and crushed him awake. He drew in air; with it came a stench of death that filled his throat and nose. He saw dark-green scales, a jagged nostril, and a bloody black eye staring at him at arm's reach. The draconic creature blew out foul air and made a low grating purr.

He heard a voice speak, but the words were swallowed up by shrieks. The beast snapped its head outside his vision, and the weight lifted from over him. Hands seized him and bound his wrists behind his back. Then the arrow was jerked out of him, and he screamed and forced himself to breathe through the pain.

He was left lying on the ground, facing down. The globe of energy he had assembled stopped the bleeding. His flesh heated, mending slowly.

The falyn, the enemy of his father, had begun chanting a droning rhythm. His voice, barely a murmur, shook with power, reverberating beyond the audible. Over his own struggling and panting he could not make out the words. Wrestling the ropes that bound him, his forehead kissing the ground, little by little he got to his knees.

Then the falyn said loudly and very clearly, "Ickh akaenn'ahk ishieh uwa ek'anmah. Ickh akhbenn'ahk ingnah'ihk. Ackh ekka u ishjish'ehk!"

There was a silence. A deadened thump. Then a blood-chilling bellow.

He straightened himself up and half turned, only to be trampled belly up with his arms crushed beneath him. A wide, heavy creature shuddered and slobbered on top of him in a frenzy. Its slimy secretions stung him, burned him. A spasm clutched his gut, and he gulped in air as fire flooded his body. The agony seared at his navel, going deeper, sinking inside him, widening a hole. His very essence jerked and warped, writhing him, mangling him, while life was sucked out of him.

His father's scream echoed in his ears, but it was his own voice howling now. Loudly and jarringly it screamed, and wailed, until his own cry was all he could hear. And then he could hear nothing at all.

Silence.

Darkness.

A presence in his mind.

He opened his eyes and for an instant saw his father's face above him, the high canopy of sickened leaves looming overhead.

"Stubborn little leech!"

It was not his father.

The stranger crouched over him, looking down on him, eyes filled with hatred, hair hanging like drapes at the sides of his face. With both hands he was pressing his head into the ground, pinning him down. And through that touch the falyn's mind was entering into his.

He urged his life force to brighten his sight and he saw the keeper's light glow, white and strong, within the falyn's form.

Grief drowned him.

In sudden desperation he pushed against the light.

"I will break you!" the falyn yelled, his face full of anger, the teeth bared and the nose wrinkled. "I will crush you! I will leave nothing of you! You will be nothing! NOTHING!"

A wave crashed through his mind. He tried to stop it, but it forged ahead growing oppressively, spreading like rot, stabbing everywhere, ruling him. His nose filled with blood. Heat leaked from his nostrils and ran down his cheeks to his ears. His tongue bathed in thick, bitter bodily fluids. His breath drew gore into his lungs, choking him. He could not breathe. He could not think. He could not see.

Twisted things raced before his eyes. He did not trust them to be real. Images and sounds took shape in fast succession. He heard his father's voice and saw his kind, dimpled face turn into a grimace, screaming in agony and begging for him to stay, to not abandon him. He wondered whether what he saw was real. He thought it was a dream. It was a nightmare. But it was real. It happened as it had happened before. It hurt him as it had hurt him before. He died. And his father died. Yet they both lived. His father laughed and his face shifted, becoming the glowering face of a stranger bent over him, eyes shining red. The eyes had the guardian's power, and as they watched him, they scorched him from the inside out. Then he awoke.

He was lying on the ground with his hands tied behind his back and his feet bound together. His father knelt beside him, looking down, a grin on his face, a blackened hand descending to rest, hot, on his naked belly, and it slid inside, resolute and unstoppable, going all in, and the fire made him scream.

He cried out in terror, but there was a gag in his mouth, so he heard only a muffled sound. He was awake, and everything was black. Cold and darkness pressed around him. His arms hurt; he was slumped over them supine. His breath came in labored heaves. For a while he listened to his breathing and the silence in between. He was alone. Alone with his hunger, his thirst, his pain, the cold, the darkness. He could see only darkness.

He waited.

When he thought nothing was going to happen, he

tried to turn to one side so that he might relieve the pain in his arms and breathe more easily. The irons at his feet made this an arduous task. It seemed his whole body was covered in scabs, and the more he stirred, the more the wounds reopened and burned. The hurt made him mewl through the thick cloth in his mouth. At long last he managed to roll to one side. By then his nose was stuffed with snot, which made it somewhat harder to breathe, but it was less painful this way, for a moment. Then his arms began to prick and burn so hard that he had to lash out kicking and screaming and knocking his head on the floor.

When the torment eased, he lay still, panting through his wheezing nose and with a hot sore on his temple.

He did not know how long he lay alone, but it seemed a very long time. He fell asleep and had nightmares. They were the same nightmares as before. When he woke, he was biting hard on the gag and the right side of his body, the side he lay on, hurt badly. He didn't sleep after that.

He began to feel thirst above everything else. Water was all he could think about.

Then they came out of nowhere. He did not sense their approach or hear their steps; he could not see them in the dark. They removed his gag and drowned his mouth with water. He tried to drink, but they poured too much too quickly, choking him. He coughed, and that displeased them. They smacked his face, then gave him more water. He was careful not to cough, nearly ran out of breath, gasping when it was over. He was thankful for the water and thankful that it was over. Before he could speak, they stuffed his mouth with something like sand. It was most likely food—he wasn't entirely sure. He tried to swallow it; he choked; they beat him on the nose. It hurt and bled. He swallowed the blood, and the sand-that-was-food with it.

After he'd drunk and eaten, they forced the gag back into his mouth and left him alone. He lay on his back as they had left him, afraid they might still be watching. When after long, nothing happened, he toiled to turn to one side. After a while he succeeded. Eventually he fell asleep. He awoke screaming in the gag, with nightmares racing through his mind.

His body shivered in the cold.

He crawled over the stone floor—it must be stone, for it was smooth, hard, and cold. Too soon he found a wall, and sat up with his back against it.

When his buttocks ached, he lay down again.

Like so, the days passed. In the dark there was nothing to see and nothing to hear. His eyes were blind and his other senses were deaf. His focus was sick and would not obey his will—he had not much of that, in truth, will. There was something in the darkness, something hefty and intrusive. It confused his mind; it made him see and hear things that weren't there—because there was nothing there. There was the floor, six square feet of it, give or take. There were four walls, tall enough for him to stand; but with the chains at his feet he could take only a step or two, and very short ones. Then there was a metal door that opened only when they came to give him food and water and to beat him if he coughed or tried to speak, and sometimes when he did neither. At first he thought they might eventually stop coming, and let him die. He spent the hours pondering whether he'd rather they never returned. But whenever he felt he was closing in on an answer, the thirst would take his mind; then he would think only of water. They always returned, but never before the thirst had dried his thoughts. In time he stopped wondering if they would come again: he knew they would. It was one of the few things he knew, the others being darkness, cold, hunger, thirst, pain, and the nightmares. He had countless of those, and they were all alike. He died in them; and sometimes he watched others die too—like this falyn, whom he thought he knew. He had chalky-white braids, thick and long to his feet; his mouth had deep laugh lines, though he never smiled, and he never spoke. There was something about him, a light of sorts. This falyn must be lost in the darkness just as he was, and perhaps, one day they would find one another. One day, perhaps, they would emerge from this place of darkness and meet. There was no harm in dreaming of the day, was there? But it never seemed to come, the day of his freedom. Not today, not tomorrow, not ever. Yet, he thought, time could not hold still forever. Something must happen, something other than hunger, or pain, or nightmare. There sure must be something else besides those things. A light, perhaps. At times he remembered a round yellow light. He did not know what this was but he remembered the heat that emanated from it, remembered his body bathed in its heat. Yet his body had never felt warmth, and his eyes had never seen anything other than darkness. Still, he remembered the light. He remembered the warmth.

AT THE EDGE OF the Sa'dalia rainforest in the far north of Sa'dar and a thousand miles from Irieth, lies a vast cave with cold tunnels, a dungeon under that mountain the

Alassians call Seligor and the human people of Sa'dar call Mount Valdu, for it is a mountain with jagged naked peaks that pierce the dry sky.

When the Alassian War began, the Sa'dari were the first to be caught in the conflict. The Alassians emerged from the Sa'dalian jungle like a tidal wave. They came to kill and burn all that was human: the population, the farmlands, the cities. For hundreds of miles they went unhindered until the human army met them on the plains of Ka'len, and it seemed, there, that the pale jungle people would meet their end. They retreated back under cover of the trees. But from the jungle, then, came swarms of monstrous demons, beasts unknown to humankind, frenzied horrors of brutality. With them came darkness and desolation, a disease of the mind. The humans called it a weapon of mass destruction, but the Alassians know it as the unlife. It is an evil that dwells in a realm beyond, beyond doors that near Irieth had been guarded for millennia, doors that had now been torn asunder by the Alassians' new leader, Lenthieh, he who wields the Light.

Yet there were those among the Alassians who would not forsake their sworn duty to safeguard life against the powers of darkness. They would not serve this new keeper on a path of violence. Instead, they sought peace with the humans, and by their own people they were marked as traitors. Much occurred between these Alassians and the humans before trust came to be and an alliance was formed.

It was the Alliance of Ydalon that at last brought light deep underground in the belly of Mount Valdu. In a small, dark cell, a young Alassian was found lying on a stone pavement coated in years of blood and filth. He was very thin, scarred, and disfigured, his face a mask of pain and dirt, his eyes half-opened and staring into nothing. His hair was a snarl of muck; it was two inches long, for he was now seventeen.

The falyn who found him put his weapon away. He kneeled by the ruined body, and holding a finger over the thin mouth, felt a warm, shallow breath. He sighed. He bent closer and whispered in the youth's ear, "Hear me, little one. I have come to save you."

There was no answer. No twitching of a finger, no fluttering of an eyelid. No sound came from the dry, broken lips.

"Leave him, Tawori," said a husky voice. "The youth is spent. He will not survive the night."

Tawori's gaze snapped to the newcomer, a bulky figure in the torchlight, bent to fit through the narrow doorway, his mane of alabaster dreadlocks filling the opening.

"Since when have you no mercy, Beriun?" Tawori said coldly.

"It would be a mercy to end his suffering here and quickly."

"Why, if he can live?" Tawori began to, very carefully, lift the young Alassian from the dirty floor. "Help me with him. Help me save a life, Beriun. We have ended many today, but this one will live. Help me with him."

"You alone have ended more lives, today, than all of us together," said the other, but he came to help the falyn place the dying youth onto his back. "What has gotten into you, my friend?"

"It is the smell of this place," Tawori said, "the stench of darkness. Do you not feel it?"

"Aye, that I do," said Beriun. "I do feel it."

From the belly of Mount Valdu the Alassian Tawori of the Alliance emerged covered in the blood of many enemies and with a waning life on his back. The youth was taken to a house of healing in human lands across the sea, at the place of the Alliance. For many days and nights the young Alassian lay on a hospital bed, his head resting on a soft pillow, his face cleaned, his short hair pristine white. Little by little his features eased. His injuries healed, and his thin lips came to rest together in a soft line. But beneath his low brows, white as snow, his misty eyes remained half open and fixed somewhere in the distance, unseeing, and oblivious of the world.

Doctor Alfrit Bash, a man with olive skin and a square, hard jaw, had said that the youth was in a state of unawareness, and though he slept and woke, he was never conscious. Nothing more could be done for him, but wait for the brain to heal itself if it could.

Yet Alassians know more about the workings of the mind than humans do. So at last, it was the selyn Aruhin who brought the youth back from oblivion, sitting for long on the blue sheets of the hospital bed, her hands gently holding the youth's face, her fingers in his hair, her eyes closed in concentration. The young Alassian stirred, his lips twitched, he moaned, and then his eyes closed. Then he lay still, breathing softly as one dreaming peaceful dreams.

Aruhin drew a heavy breath and wiped the sweat from her face. She tucked a stray lock of long ivory hair behind her ear and stood up. «He rests,» she said smiling. She spoke the human tongue, for there were humans in the room. «I believe when he next wakes he will be with us.»

«He's been with us for over a month,» Doctor Bash observed, shaking his head. He began to check his patient's pulse and breathing.

«Of course. You are right, doctor. My apologies.» Aruhin lifted her brows at the falyn beside her. He was taller than she and wore his ash-white hair in two long braids that from his scalp hung thick and heavy past his waist. «I did as you suggested, Theidrin,» she told him. «I hushed the nightmares, and his mind quieted.»

«Will he wake then?» Theidrin asked.

«I think he will, yes. Though there is something... I may have found memories within his nightmares. It is hard to tell the difference. His mind is terribly twisted. If I may, Captain?» She looked at the man with ginger hair, a friendly wide face, and bright blue eyes, who at once smiled at her. «He should be watched when he wakes. He will be confused, and he could be dangerous.»

«I have that covered,» the man assured her. He tilted his head toward the entrance where, seated comfortably on a soft green chair and with his face widened in a gaping yawn, was the one who'd brought the youth back into daylight.

«I wondered why you were here,» Theidrin said sourly. «You were asleep when we walked in, so I couldn't ask.»

«Was I, really?» Tawori replied, clearly fighting the urge to yawn again. «I would never. As he said, I'm on guard duty.»

«There is nothing to guard here,» Doctor Bash complained. «When, and *if*, he regains consciousness, he'll be lucky if he can lift his head from the pillows. I told him days ago to make himself useful somewhere else.»

«Thank you, doctor,» intervened the captain. «Really, no. But thank you.» He smiled. «If there's one thing this war has taught me, it's to never, ever, underestimate the strength of an Alassian, no matter how helpless he or she looks. And I mean no offense to the lot of you.» He beamed at the Alassians. «So, Alfrit, let *me* worry about my men's usefulness.»

The doctor snorted.

«Tawori is here on my orders, and he will remain here until I say otherwise. Especially when I'm told that we can expect this one to be dangerous.»

«A trapped animal is dangerous,» said the selyn Aruhin, «and even more so when afraid. There is much fear in this young one. It was terror that held him suspended between sleep and wakefulness, nightmares of the worst kind, those born from memories. I glimpsed some, though I couldn't tell truth from nightmare. It all seemed nightmare. Doctor, why do you try to wake him?»

Doctor Bash had pinched the sleeping Alassian, and with a groan, the youth had moved his hand an inch. The doctor pinched him again, and again the youth shrunk from the touch.

«I'm not waking him. I am checking if he's responsive.»

«We've all seen that he is,» said the selyn. «Or have you missed it? Please, do not pinch him again.»

«Enough, enough,» said the captain. «I'm sure the doctor knows his medicine.»

«Precisely! And if you are done with what you came here to do, you should leave. Let my patient rest.»

«Yes,» agreed Theidrin. With a hand at the small of Aruhin's back, he led her outside the room. Captain Liu

Logain went after them. Doctor Bash busied himself at the bedside for a time, then he, too, left.

Tawori remained seated in the green chair. Once alone he retrieved a thick book from beside him on the floor, and began to read. Now and then he raised his gaze from the pages to see that the youth still slept. At times he stood and paced about the room with his hands in his pockets. He went to look outside the small square window at the land: a dry desert of hard earth and distant mountains. Groups of men and women dressed in gray and brown camouflage went about on foot or in trucks. Tawori removed his military hat and looked at it pensively, stroking the short visor with his thumb. Then he sighed. Putting the hat back on, he returned to his book.

4
WAKING

THE CREAM-WHITE SKY was flat and even. There was in it a round bulge that was whiter than the rest, and was glossy with reflected light. On this lustrous bulge were painted darker shapes, sharp but crammed together, difficult to distinguish. He watched them patiently, blinking slowly. On the leftmost side of the bulge was a wide rectangle brighter than the rest, with straight dark shades at its two vertical sides. Inside the rectangle were other smaller forms, some dark and some bright, all white. He guessed this rectangle was an opening in the sky to some place with light. It could be a door or a window, or perhaps it was a gate; he did not know. He studied the opening for long, thinking that in doing so he may be able to see where it led. The more he stared at the shapes inside the square on the glossy bulge which swelled out of the otherwise flat surface of the sky, the more the shapes seemed to slip off suddenly, sliding downward. Yet always they remained in place. They stayed where they were and did not fall down.

Across from the bright rectangle, on the other half of the smooth bulge, nothing could be seen. With the passing of time, the shiny white surface became gray; it was still shiny, but turned darker; and the sky became darker.

However, it was not a sky, but a ceiling: a white, even ceiling.

From the corner of his eye he caught a movement, and with a gasp, he turned his face to look. There was a falyn, there. Sitting on a chair. Gazing toward him.

He held his breath, and kept still.

The falyn remained still.

So he made to get up, and his muscles tore all at once. The pain forced a groan from him and crushed him back down.

He stared at the falyn in horror. His body refused to move; he could do nothing but wait. For the falyn. To come to where he lay helpless and hurt, and beat him.

He waited and watched the falyn; and the falyn watched him.

A moment passed, and still the falyn watched him: he was not coming to him; instead, he was just sitting there watching.

"You are safe now," the falyn said.

Was he talking to him? Why would he talk to him? No, he wasn't. No one talked to him.

Again he struggled. His body felt heavy. Terribly, terribly heavy.

"You are among friends," the falyn said, looking at him—there was no doubt that he was looking at him. Though why would he look at him and speak? Speak to him? Was he speaking to him? "We have rescued you," he said. "Your captors are dead. You are among friends now. You are safe; you have nothing to fear. Don't try to get up, you are still weak. Your body needs time to recover. Calm, now. You are going to be all right. There is no need to fear. I am just sitting over here, see? I will not harm you."

He fell back aching all over, huffing and puffing. He kept his eyes on the falyn, who had yet to move from the chair, a strange chair with thin silvery legs and fat green pillows. His clothes, too, were odd, colored in gray and brown shapes and blotches: a squarish top with short sleeves, long trousers, an outlandish hat, and clumpy, brown boots. He was warrior-built with strong shoulders, a lean body, and tone veiny forearms. His pure white hair was tied at the back and the thin tail rested over his left shoulder, dropping down into his lap. His face was sharp, his expression calm. The tiny pupils of his ivory eyes were intense and watchful.

If he looked into those eyes, they looked right into his.

The falyn did not speak now. He was sitting in his strange chair, displaying no intention of doing anything but simply continue to sit there.

Propped against the chair were two beautifully crafted swords sheathed in black wood, slender and gently curved, one a little shorter than the other. Their guards were thick bronze disks with polished small figures carved in relief. The hilts were of the same polished metal, with sharply raised lines that spiraled and crossed. The guard's carvings depicted small trees with miniature figures underneath, difficult to discern. He stared at them until he saw, beneath the bronze trees, forest cats with bronze furs, sit and lie and stand and run, slim and wild-looking with a familiar grace. Had he seen them before? The same wild cats, beneath the same small trees?

He squinted at the falyn. Why was he sitting there? Who was he? What was this place?

He looked around in alarm. He was in a small room with bare walls, a closed door, and opposite it, a window with open brown curtains filled with empty, gray sky. He was lying in a bed covered with white sheets and a blue blanket. Nearby were strange objects, white and metallic, with bumps and cords. The cords went from the strange objects to the bed and under the covers.

He pulled back the sheets and from the back of his hand wrenched a long needle—a drop of blood rushed from his skin.

"Don't do that!"

From his chest he plucked four threads with sticky round heads. Then in horror he clasped the thing that was digging a hole in his belly. He was about to pull it out when the falyn took his hands and wrestled him down on the mattress.

He fought to get free, but the falyn's grip was steely. "You'll hurt yourself if you do that. Stop struggling! Look at me—hey! Look at me!"

He looked. Then a second voice spoke, hard and crisp. What it said was a jabber of inarticulate noises. Behind the falyn appeared an ... not Alassian ... human. A man-human with black hair and full eyes. The falyn snapped his head toward him and barked something in the same incomprehensible jabber, his eyes narrowed to slits. The man backed away. "I will let go if you stop struggling," the falyn said looking down again. "But you will not touch that, or you will hurt yourself. Look at me.

Yes? Show me that you understand. Nod, if you understand. You will not pull that out, because that would hurt you. Do you understand? Good."

Then he was let go. He tried to lie very still and be quiet, but he was out of breath and could not stop panting.

"I know it looks frightening," the falyn said, "but it is nothing to worry about. That is how we gave you food because you would not eat and needed help, you see? It will be gone when you are able to eat again. Soon. You will be all right. Do not worry about that now."

The human said something; and the falyn turned to speak with him.

He watched them talk, and in time got his breathing under control.

The man left, and the falyn said, "Are you thirsty? There is water." He lifted a blue pitcher from a small table half-hidden by the strange objects, and poured water into a brown cup. "I have to raise the head of the bed so you can drink. This is a human device; they have many strange things. Yes, it moves, but it is harmless. Here, drink. I'll hold it for you," said the falyn, lowering the cup to his lips.

With a jolt he pulled back, turned his head away, shut his eyes, and waited for the beating.

It did not come.

His heart felt suddenly swollen. It made his breathing quiver.

After a moment he heard water pouring, and dared to take a look. The falyn was emptying some of the water into the pitcher. Then again he held out the cup, though not as close.

"Take it," he said, "take the cup."

He remained still.

"Are you not thirsty? Take the cup."

He was thirsty.

Was the falyn really handing him a cup with water? And was he being asked to take it? Was he really supposed to take it?

He lifted a hand—it was very thin, and trembling—and reached for it. The falyn let him have it. It felt heavy. He looked inside and saw a little water. The inside of the cup was white—was it made of paper? He looked at his hand, and then raised his other hand. They were scarred, and jagged purple rings were carved in both his wrists; but the ropes weren't there. There was a cup, there, in his hands. Inside it was water, and he could drink it.

He took a sip, then another; then the cup was empty.

"Do you want more?"

The falyn poured more water into the cup.

He drank it.

"Are you hungry? I will ask for some food."

The falyn walked to the door and there spoke to someone in a language that was not Talassian. When he came back, he said, "My name is Tawori. If you have questions, I can answer them. That is, if you feel like talking, of course. I will be here until you are well . . . or I can leave if you'll want me to. Just, for now I'm here, I mean. H'm." His face hardened. He walked away and went to sit in the green chair, put his elbows on his knees, held one hand in the other, and looked down. He was blurry, as was everything else in the room.

His sobs forced him to breathe in gasps. The tears dripped down his cheeks and onto the sheets like raindrops. Was he really out of the darkness? Was he truly somewhere else? How did he get here? Where was he? Was he going to stay here, or was he going back into the darkness? Could he stay here? Could he? He didn't want to go back. He didn't want to go back into the darkness. He didn't want to be cold and to be hungry and to be thirsty and to be beaten; he didn't want his wrists tied and his ankles tied—he couldn't breathe . . . he hurt. He was afraid, drowning. Darkness pressed around him. It was heavy, and he was sinking . . . He wasn't alone. Someone was with him. He could hear a heart weeping . . .

He opened his eyes and glanced at the chair. The falyn was crying, his eyes red and filled with tears, his mouth wearing a scowl as if he were angry.

For a moment they looked at each other, the falyn weeping silently, and he shaking with hysterical sobs. Then the falyn bent his head, hiding his face.

His sobs began to abate, and he dried his cheeks.

He felt cold. His hands went to the blanket with a familiarity that was notable, and pulled it over his chest and shoulders. A blanket. A bed. Warmth and comfort. And somehow, these weren't unfamiliar things.

He turned to look at the light that came through the window, and listened. He could hear the falyn, his heart quieter now; and he could hear a human at the door, bored, perhaps, or sleepy. His senses stretched no farther. He felt nothing else. What he did feel was comforting—not the human, for he was alien, but the falyn, the one called Tawori: his heart was warm. He closed his eyes and listened to it, turning a deaf ear to anything else.

. . .

A mouthwatering scent reached his nostrils, he opened his eyes. He was in the white room of the human place. He had forgotten that he was there. The falyn, Tawori, stood by the bed, offering a cup half filled with a creamy orange soup that smelled of carrots and poultry.

"Drink this."

He took the cup and slowly sipped the hot food, sniffing the vapor anxiously. The warmth, the smell, the taste, they made the tears come again. He didn't know why he cried, gasping silent sobs between sips. He felt better after he'd emptied the cup, though he wished there had been more. Perhaps the falyn heard his wish, for he produced more of the orange soup out of a gray, metallic bottle, and gave it to him. He had two half cups and then a full one. Then he put the cup on the small table, which had been moved nearer the bedside. He lay back against the pillows and watched the falyn open a book on his lap and begin to read, glancing up at him every now and then.

He woke up. It took him some time to understand where he was. Before he did, he sat on the edge of the bed with one foot on the floor. It was a cold floor.

"It's all right," said Tawori; the falyn stood in front of him with a hand raised toward him. "You are safe, remember?"

He remembered.

He sat still. The day had darkened, and a soft light encased in white glass shone from the ceiling. There was a human in the room, the same man from before. His skin was a bizarre olive tone that glimmered golden in the soft yellow light. His hair was black and oddly short for the years he looked, and a thick beard, also black, covered not only his chin, but his jawline, cheeks, and upper lip. From beneath his black brows, two brown eyes stared sourly.

"Will you let the human examine you?" Tawori asked. "He is a healer, and has been tending to you in the time you have been recovering here, although you might not remember him."

He did not like this human. He did not know if he liked *any* human. He liked the falyn, because he was kind. The two spoke for a while in what was likely the human tongue. Then the man began asking questions, and the falyn translated his words into Talassian.

He did not like the things being asked. They made him feel uncomfortable. What was his name? Where was he from? What was the last thing he remembered before waking up here? Did he remember anything at all? Did he know where he was? Did he feel any pain? Did he understand Tawori's words?

He looked into the falyn's eyes, and nodded.

The falyn smiled and a flicker of amusement touched his mind. He spoke to the human, then the questions stopped.

He was asked to sit back, which he did. The human shone a light in his eyes; the light blinded him, so he turned his face away and for some time avoided looking back. He was asked to move his legs and feet and other parts of his body. When the human tried to touch his face, he recoiled with a jolt and felt his eyes go wide with fear. After some time he was told to press his hands against the man's hands. He would rather not do that. He kept his hands in his lap and looked down at them, waiting for the request to be forgotten. When it was forgotten, Tawori asked if he would like to have the thing in his belly removed. The falyn called it a tube. He had thought it to be some kind of living parasite and was relieved to learn it wasn't so. Tawori said he would have to lie still for it to be done, and would have to let the healer touch him. He, himself, was unsure whether this was wise, but he kept feeling the thing, hard under his clothes, and was afraid of it, even if it wasn't a living parasite. He wanted it gone. So he nodded. He lay down with his eyes fixed on the human above him, waiting, and breathing through fear.

The man rubbed a wet cloth on his belly, cut with one light motion, and pushed down gently—he saw, crawling over his half-naked body, the black mass of something wide and heavy. He felt it poke at his navel, widening a hole and rummaging inside him. He heard a piercing scream and sat up gasping, looking at a square dressing on his scarred abdomen. He stared at it stupidly.

"It will heal quickly," Tawori said. "You did well. Breathe."

He let air escape his lungs, then sucked in a shallow breath, numb with relief.

When he could think again, he realized he was being asked to stand up. "I will catch you if you stumble," Tawori was saying. "You won't fall."

He was confused, but had time to think. He decided he wanted, very much, to stand up. He got his legs out from under the covers and sat on the side of the bed with his naked feet on the cold pavement, looking down at the brown tiles, looking at his feet, looking at his thin legs in the light, blue clothing covering him. He was unsure as to whom he was watching.

The man who had healed the hole in his belly sighed.

He remembered he had agreed to stand up, so he promptly put his weight on his feet and stood tentatively, very slowly.

His legs were weak. He did not fall, but felt as if he might. He was asked to take a few steps. He slogged to the foot of the bed and back. Then he was out of breath, and sat again.

Nothing more was asked of him.

The human spoke with the falyn for a while, then left.

"I shall take you to the washroom," Tawori said.

He froze. His gaze went from the falyn, to the door, to the falyn, to the door.

He did not know what was outside this room. If he left it, he was unsure whether he could return to it. He liked this place. He wanted to be here where he knew there were safety and comfort. He didn't want to go anywhere.

He lay back on the bed and pulled up the sheets, keeping an eye on the falyn. Tawori watched him in silence for a long moment. Then he returned to his chair.

Sometime later he was given food, green soup and a bit of plain rice, which he ate with appetite. Afterward he rested his back against the pillows and sat drowsily.

"Should I turn off the light? It is nighttime. Are you sure? If you want it off just point at the ceiling, and I will turn it off so you can sleep."

He never did point at the ceiling, though he did fall asleep.

He slept in the dark place with his wrists and ankles bound in thick ropes and irons that tightened if he tried to move. He could see nothing, hear nothing. He was utterly alone.

When he awoke, he found that his body was free and painless, and that he could see the night-room around him in shades of gray, tinged with yellow and blue. The light in the ceiling had gone out, but the world wasn't as dark as he'd thought it would be without it. Maybe only the cold place deep underground was pitch black to the point of blindness. This darkness here wasn't so dense, it wasn't so frightening.

He did not wish to see the nightmares again, so he lay awake listening. The falyn slept slouched in the chair, his mind busy with dreams and his heart silent.

When dawn broke through the window, he carefully stood from the bed to find his footing safer than before. He stepped unsteadily on the cold floor until his hands clasped the windowsill. Outside, the clear sky was slowly brightening. Twenty feet below, the ground was covered in dark-gray pebbles and patches of beige sand. A short walk away was a metal fence with a brown barrier, and beyond that was desert earth freckled with clusters of grass, and barren mountains in the distance.

What a queer land. Where were the trees? Surely there should be trees, but he saw none. Where did the wildlife find shelter without them? What manner of creatures could live in such emptiness?

He watched the quiet, still world with one hand pressed against the cold window and his breath painting fog over it. When he saw the sun rise in the east, a globe of red fire piercing the crested horizon, his heart beat in elation and a thrill coursed through him. His eyes were drawn to the sun. He watched it rise in the bright blue sky. Then the world went black. A dry pain stabbed his eye sockets, cutting deep into his skull and tearing a groan from his chest. His hands flew up to hide his face. At once he stopped the flow of energy rushing to his eyes, then concentrated on calming his breathing. The pain began to subside.

He dried his tears and looked up. Outside the window the world remained unchanged, though its beauty had diminished.

He was unsure of what he had done and why. He thought that something should have happened but didn't. The hunch tugged at him like a hefty emptiness. He stood there awhile looking outside on cold feet. He could not remember. What, he did not know. He should know something. Anything. There was an emptiness inside him. The sunlight whispered to him of things he should know, but he did not know them. There was something wrong with him, with his mind, with his eyes.

He stood still for a long time, unaware of himself if not for the cold beneath his feet. When a cloud moved in front of the sun, dimming the morning light, he turned away and walked to the bed. He crawled under the sheets, curled into a ball, and slept. He never noticed the falyn watching him.

When he next awoke, Tawori asked that he follow him outside.

He stood at once from the bed, but at the door he hesitated. He had the vague notion of some worry which had troubled him not long ago, though now, he did not remember what that had been. Tawori waited unhurriedly, his white gaze watching him.

They walked through a lighted corridor lined with open doors. The falyn led the way to a bright room furnished with strange objects of polished ceramic and metal, with bottles, brushes, and towels. This was a washroom, he guessed, but it was very strange. He could not tell what most of the things were for. The falyn showed him how to use some of the items, to produce a paste for the toothbrush from a colorful glossy tube, to squirt liquid soap from a rounded bottle, to start and stop a stream of water—"It will come out heated if you turn the knob like so," Tawori said. "I'll leave you to it. I shall be just outside. If you need help, make yourself heard."

He stood under the hot rain for a long time. It was pleasant. His fingers traced the scars on his arms, his torso, his legs. Feeling the raised damaged skin beneath his fingertips made him pant with the expectation of pain. But the scars didn't hurt, and eventually his mind caught up to the present moment. His body stopped shaking, and his breathing relaxed.

He dried himself with a blue towel, then put on the soft white-ash cotton clothes the falyn had left for him. They fit his thin body loosely and covered the length of his arms and legs, long arms and legs, he observed. He wasn't nearly as tall as Tawori, but surely, he was tall. Somehow that was strange. Yet even stranger was the face of the young falyn who looked at him from the square mirror on the wall after he had wiped off the steam. His bony cheekbones, his right brow, the bridge of his nose, and his thin lips were scarred with deep ragged lines, darker than the pale undamaged skin. His nose and mouth were small, and his eyes were sad.

He asked himself whether he felt sad. He did not think so, not right now. It was stillness he felt in his heart, and in his mind dull emptiness. There had been fear—it kept coming back, suddenly and unexpectedly—but when there was no fear, there was nothing—

The door of the bright room slid ajar and a cautious utterance came from outside. "Are you well in there?"

—or perhaps there was a relief, perhaps a longing, a yearning for something he had forgotten.

On their way back, a short walk down the lit corridor, the falyn paused twice to wait for him as he steadied himself with a hand pressed against the wall, fighting a sudden dizziness that blackened his vision. He was exhausted and out of breath by the time they returned to the room.

A plate with food had been brought in their absence: fish, potatoes, and cooked vegetables. He ate quickly, wholly immersed in the rich piney flavor. Then he lay back dozing.

Later, he stood by the window with his feet tucked in a pair of white laceless shoes. He watched the coming and going of humans outside. There were many of them, all with their hair hidden beneath small hats and wearing identical gray and brown clothing, the same as Tawori's.

When the sun reached its highest point in the sky, the falyn told him they should take a walk in the *hospital's* corridors—*hospital* was the name of this healing house. It was a vast building with three floors. His room, like many others, was on the middle floor. All the rooms had the same wooden doors that opened to the same white walls, small windows, and brown polished stone floors; the same blue sheets covered the same thin mattresses in the same metal bedframes.

There were no Alassians about, only humans, men and women. Most of the men had very short hair, he noticed. If he met their gazes, the humans turned their faces away, although not their minds—those stared warily and followed his passing closely. He felt out of place, like the spiky grass that poked the dry land outside. He made sure to stay close to his guide, keeping two steps behind him at all times. The falyn stopped often to let him catch his breath, as he tired quickly. A few times they sat to rest on the small chairs that lined the hallways. To the busy corridors, he preferred the quiet calm of his room, and he was glad when they returned to it at last.

The following day in the late afternoon, a man he had not seen before came to the room. His face was pink and puffy, his hair was thick and copper red, and his eyes were like the blue sky. He wore a friendly smile, but his mind was tense and preoccupied. He spoke with Tawori in the human tongue, and the falyn grew anxious.

The man came to stand by the bed and said that his name was Liu. He spoke Talassian with a graceless, slothful accent and mispronouncing some of the words, though well enough to be understood.

"I know you don't want to talk," he said, "or maybe you can't. I need you to try to communicate with us. Will you do that?" The man waited a moment, then continued. "We need to know who you are. Do you know what your captors were doing in that place? Seligor, you call it, right?" Liu glanced at Tawori, who nodded stiffly.

"Do you know why you were there? Do you know what they wanted from you?" There was a long silence. The man's blue eyes studied him expectantly. "Can you write?"

He did not know whether he could.

The man spoke the other tongue and walked to the door. He came back to the bed holding a small book and a pen, and offered them to him.

He took the pen with his left hand and knew that was his writing hand. It was an odd pen made of a transparent hexagonal tube filled with a thin black straw and a metal tip at one end. The book found its way in his lap, open to an empty page. He held the pen suspended above it, metal tip pointing downward.

"Can you write something? Can you write 'Hello'? Or draw, anything? Can you at least try?" Slowly, the man's hopeful gaze turned into a frown. "We need to know if you are a target. Do you understand what I mean by that? Is there someone out there looking for you?" He said something in the human tongue, quickly, and impatiently. Tawori replied briefly. "I didn't mean to scare you," Liu continued. "You're safe here. We want to protect you as best we can. That is why we need information. Do you understand? Do you understand what I'm saying?"

Liu left the room unsatisfied, leaving behind the notebook and pen. Day turned slowly into evening. He was offered food, and ate it; he was led to the washroom, and went there. After the lights were put out, he sat in bed awake, book and pen still at hand.

It was the darkest hour of the night when he slipped his feet into the laceless shoes and stood up. He gazed at

Tawori, who sat awake in his chair. The falyn replied with only the utmost silence. He took that for consent and walked to the door, opened it, and stepped outside into the soft light of the corridor. A human was standing there—there had been many over time, all standing, waiting, and feeling bored. The human looked at him nervously, puzzled by his being there with an empty hand lifted in an obvious gesture of asking. The man took some time to react, but eventually lifted his own hand in the same way.

He took the man's hand in both his own, slowly, so as not to cause him alarm. Through the warm touch, he felt the human's life force flow steadily and strong, and with a swift, backing movement of both hands, he wrenched that strength from him. The man collapsed. But his body never hit the ground.

For an instant he thought Tawori had moved to attack; instead, the falyn caught the falling man and lowered him safely to the floor. He pressed two fingers on the human's neck for a troubled moment, then looked up, and said, "Are you sure that you are ready for this?"

He did not reply. He turned and headed down the corridor toward the stairs. The falyn followed him a moment later.

He had walked these corridors for two days and knew his way about. He noticed, now, that no room besides his own was guarded, and vaguely pondered that matter as he listened for the sleeping minds beyond the closed doors. Walking as quietly and as quickly as he was able, he descended the stairs to the empty corridor below, pulled open a heavy door, and took left. Then he froze.

A wakeful mind was approaching.

One of the doors on his right was ajar. Behind it, two people slept. He hurried inside and pressed his back to the wall. Tawori squeezed beside him. Soon, a woman walked past the door. He waited until she moved out of sight, then slid back into the corridor. He turned a corner into the long hallway leading to the entrance, a wide glass door with white vertical bars. Through it he could see two humans standing a couple of steps from the building with their backs partly turned to it, conversing. Black weapons hung from their shoulders and onto their chests—he had seen other humans wield the same weapons and by now knew them for what they were, though he did not know what power they held.

"They will not be fooled by childish tricks," Tawori said quietly beside him. "We have to be swift. I will deal with the one on the right. The other will intervene and be distracted. You do with him as you did upstairs. Quickly, and nothing else. Do not harm either of them." The falyn cast a hard glance at him.

He nodded.

They reached the door unnoticed. Tawori put both hands on the bar that would open it, then pushed, dashing forward like a jaguar. His arms came up around the right man's neck in a chokehold. The second man reacted, but Tawori turning his victim to one side kicked him in the shins, making him stumble and drop a knee to the ground.

That was his cue. He hurried for the kneeling man, a tap on the shoulder, a tug at his life force, and unconsciousness.

In Tawori's hold, the other human struggled a moment longer, then became still. All was silent.

Ahead of them, gray, empty ground extended for a hundred feet to a shielded fence with a closed gate. Light from the hospital reached as far as the fence; beyond that, was only the dark of night.

"This way," said Tawori, taking a step not toward the gate but along the hospital walls.

He hesitated. He looked at the falyn and then at the gate.

"Come, Nillith. Come this way."

He followed.

They walked around the building to a place where the fence bent into a sharp corner close to the wall. The falyn helped him climb and get over the spiked lines at the top; then he pulled himself up and down the other side with ease.

"This way. We must be quick now."

They went sneaking, walking, then running, and walking again, trailing on slowly. Sand and long-leafed spiky bushes covered the ground as far as the eye could see. He turned once to look behind. The hospital was nowhere to be seen.

"How do you feel? Can you go on a little longer?"

He trudged ahead with growing fatigue, watching the ground pass unchanged beneath his feet. The night air chilled him.

"Walk next to me," said Tawori; "I don't want you falling unconscious."

"We are going to the sea," he continued after a while, pointing in the distance. "Look, it isn't much farther."

He looked and saw a flat expanse beyond the sand and dry vegetation, dark water fading into black sky.

They were going to the sea. He would walk for a while longer and he would reach the sea.

He kept on walking, eyes fixed on the water, one heavy step after another.

At last they came to a group of houses, no lights, small paths between the houses, then a tiny beach. Three small boats were lined up near the water.

"Climb inside," said the falyn. "You'll have time to watch the sea as we go. We are ... h'm ... borrowing this without asking. So we want to be quick about it. Yes. Sit down there where it's safe."

The water sloshed against the boat's hull as the falyn worked the paddle and the coast moved away.

"You should rest. Sleep, if you can. They won't know where we've gone. We are safe for now. You can trust me."

He was nodding off with exhaustion, curled up against the hard wood of the boat. He forced his eyes to open and met the falyn's gaze.

"Sleep, Nillith."

He slept.

Far from the coast, Tawori drew in the paddle and turned the motor on. His passenger did not stir, and his sleep, for once, appeared to be dreamless and calm, perhaps thanks to the sea's embrace, or to the watchful stars of the night sky.

In the early hours of the morning, back on land where the Alliance base of Oxwish stands obstinate against the cold, dry desert, a nurse found a man unconscious on the floor of a small hospital room. He was alive and unharmed, but the patient of that room was long gone. On the bed, a notebook lay open to the first page. On it, written in black ink, were three words of the Alassian tongue:

Nur envn ruhira.

Thank you.

5
A DREAM

"GOOD, YOU are awake."

The sky above was blue and cloudless. The air was filled with the smell of salty water and the flight and cries of white seabirds. He could hear the rolling of gentle waves on a sandy shore. He turned onto his front and propped himself on his elbows, sitting up. A coat slid from over him and crumpled on the boat's floor. The little vessel was ashore on a small beach surrounded by high craggy walls. A narrow path led away from the sea and disappeared behind tall dunes. He turned to watch the line of the horizon, blue below blue. The sun shone strong, but the morning air was cold. He could see his own breath.

"You can come out now," Tawori said, "we continue on foot."

He climbed clumsily over the side of the boat, feeling cold and stiff. His shoes sank in the wet sand.

Tawori stood fastening the two belts that held his

swords in place above his left hip. He wore a short-sleeved shirt and his arms were roughened by the cold.

Retrieving the falyn's jacket from the boat, he offered it to him.

"You wear that," Tawori said. "You have no energy to spare for the cold. It is still a long way to where we are headed."

He wondered where was it that they were headed.

"I need a weapon to hunt for food, and you need warmer clothes. We will go to where a human city used to be, some twelve miles east of here. There are still valuable things there, but there is danger too. We will be careful. We will be fine. We should go, now."

He slipped into the falyn's jacket. It was too big for him, but it shut out the wintry chill.

Beyond the sandy dunes, the arid land was speckled with gray rocks and scattered evergreen shrubs. They walked in the light of the distant sun rising over rocky hills. The creatures of the wild watched their passing undisturbed, with only the stirring of a fluffy ear, the raising of a snout from dry pastures, a glance, then indifference. They walked on black-paved roads, unbroken lines inked over creased brown parchment. Now and then they came across the wreckage of a building or a small group of buildings, deserted, crumbling, burned-out.

At mid-morning they stopped at a narrow brook that cut deep between rocks underneath a low bridge, wet stones green with moss. They drank from its icy waters and rested for a while before hiking on.

They had set off walking side by side, but now, he was falling behind. His legs felt stiff and heavy, and his breathing came shallow and quick. He kept his gaze on the black pavement passing beneath his feet.

"This land is called Ydalon." Tawori's voice chimed silvery in the light breeze. "It is surrounded by sea, and it is closest to the shores of our homeland. It has seen much conflict. Many battles were fought here in the second and third year of the war. Now it is almost deserted.

"The humans of this land mostly lived within their cities. They built houses upon houses, tall buildings that climb the sky so high that between them from the ground, one sees but metal and glass and only a glimpse of blue. They liked to live in crowded clusters, all together, safe, and noisy, and awake in the nights they turned bright with lights.

"War came to their cities first, but the humans stayed anyway. They stayed until it was too late to run. They were used to a life unlike our own, you see, surrounded by their inventions and constructions. They did not hunt the wilds or till the earth with their own hands. They did not know how to survive outside their cities. That is why they stayed. They hoped to be saved by their fighters and their weapons of war. But Lenthieh's forces were too great—Do you need to stop? We can rest for a while."

Tiny, pointy pebbles jabbed his palms as he slumped onto the hard road, barely stopping himself from falling backward.

"You look like you have a fever. And you need to eat. If we are lucky we will find food in the city."

The light of the sun was warm. He opened the jacket.

"You ran, but I wonder where you would have gone without me. I think not far."

Tawori sat down beside him.

"I don't think it was time for you to leave. I think you should have stayed and rested longer, get your strength back."

He looked at the falyn, whose gaze was fixed on the road ahead.

"But what's done is done."

They were silent for a while.

"We should go, now. It is only another mile or so to the city, beyond that hill."

THE CITY OF TIDFYL was a porcupine of derelict skyscrapers, shattered windows, and broken roads. It was rubble upon rubble, rivers of wreckages and steel, and crumbling bridges. It was empty buildings, and silence. They walked unnoticed, stepping silently over cracked roads. Above them towered ghosts after ghosts of human homes. The things of mankind lay scattered and damaged as far as the eye could see, and between them, hostile, grew shy grass and thorny brambles. The city was empty, yet the humans lingered inside buildings and wreckages: they were only bones now, dead and decayed. The edifices were time and times taller than the highest of trees; they pierced the sky like swords raised to wage war against the laws of nature.

Road after road the maze grew denser—always gray, always motionless and unwelcoming—until in some areas the buildings lay crumbled in fields of debris and litter. Of these areas they steered clear, making wide circles around, lest the ground give way beneath their feet and swallow them.

This large building sculptured in black tiles stood seemingly untouched by the passing of time. He followed

Tawori inside, although he disliked the idea of entering such a massive construction. The heavy doors flew shut, blowing a squirt of dust in the air and cutting out the light of day. For a time his eyes saw near darkness. He stood by the door, his throat turning dry and his nose growing stuffed. When he could see the jumble of broken shelves and smashed boxes that littered the place, he flipped an empty crate upside-down and sat on it. He coughed and watched the falyn go about the place.

Tawori went from box to box, opened the many cabinets, and searched through piles of junk on the floor. Once, he cried out in triumph, speaking a word in what might be the human tongue; then he spent a while longer rummaging through cupboards and rubbish. When at last he came to stand by his improvised seat, the falyn had gained a sturdy cloth quiver on his back, poorly stocked with three black arrows. Secured to it was a short square rod of a black material.

"I was lucky," he said smiling, "I found a bow on the floor."

He did not see a bow with the falyn, nor did he see one on the floor or anywhere else.

"It is folded in three and looks like a broken thing. It is this, you see?" He turned partly to point at the square rod on his back. "But it is intact. It will do. It is quite the ingenious thing. I had no luck with fishing lines or hooks. No knives or anything else of use. But this was lucky." Tawori sighed and frowned. "Should we search the houses? We'll find clothes, surely. I doubt there will be food. We'll get what we need and go. There's plenty of animals to hunt. Lucky I found this bow."

He didn't feel hungry; on the contrary, he felt slightly

nauseous and his stomach ached. He paid it no mind, though, for it was only a cramp and he'd had food the evening before; he was far from starved. He was tired and feverish, cold with chills, and he wished to sleep. But Tawori was leaving the building, so he stood up and went after him.

The falyn led the way heading back the same roads whence they had come.

He began to wonder which house Tawori wished to search, for the falyn entered none, keeping to the road, not searching but going somewhere, heading in one direction as much as the broken city would permit. He followed along with growing fatigue. They would arrive, eventually, wherever Tawori was headed—only, he very much hoped that "wherever" wasn't far. The falyn knew the human world, whereas he, himself, did not. All he knew was the falyn, and so all he did was trail after him, even though he'd much rather find a corner to lie down and sleep. His head throbbed, and his mind was hazy, so much so that he felt as if he were drifting.

His foot caught on a piece of metal that poked out of the black pavement, and he stumbled. He got his balance back, then stopped. He looked behind them scanning the silent houses. Nothing moved, but he was sure he'd heard something.

"Keep walking," Tawori said.

He hurried after the falyn.

"Beside me."

They walked side by side.

"I saw them when we left the building. They are following us. That is why we are leaving. The city belongs to them. We are intruders here. I only hope they let us leave."

As the falyn spoke, a hefty feeling of malice grew behind them. More waited ahead, hiding in the buildings. He took Tawori's arm and held him back, but something else had the falyn's attention. Then they were running. Tawori dragged him by the jacket through earsplitting bangs. In two strides they passed the entrance of a dark building and were racing up a staircase. Human voices raved behind them, bouncing off the cold, echoing walls. Half-dragged by Tawori, he stumbled up two sets of stairs, down a corridor, and through a doorway to a room with tall windows and wooden shutters with gaps and cracks through which shone swords of sunlight.

"Hide!" Tawori yelled, his back to the entrance wall.

He would have hid beside the falyn were it not for a wide cabinet taking up space there; he made due flattening against a side wall.

The humans' voices grew closer. The metallic tip of a weapon winked through the doorway, and Tawori's hand slapped it upward. It thundered at the ceiling tearing a hunk from it. Tawori struck the wielder's face, and the man toppled sideways into the room. Already the falyn was fighting a second human, holding him by the jaw. This one cried an unrestrained howl before dropping like a stone in the doorway. There was a second ear-splitting bang and a yelp, and Tawori took half-a-step back. A third human trampled through, but the falyn pushed forward again, jabbing him in the temple. The man's head hit the entry-wall with a thump, and he began to fall. Then his weapon was in Tawori's hand, the tip pressed against the man's ear as he kneeled onto one knee, with a hand in the air and the other pinned behind him, the falyn holding him fast.

Tawori's words brimmed with menace. He yelled in the human tongue, glaring into the corridor through the doorway. The assault came at a standstill.

From his hiding place by the side wall, he had watched the brawl unnoticed. Now he saw the man who'd fallen first into the room regain his footing, dive a hand into his pants, pull out a knife, and bolt at Tawori.

He pushed himself off the wall, got a grip on the man's clothing, dodging the retaliating blade, then reached for the man's face and thrust his sharpened focus into his mind. He heard the man's squeal of pain, and Tawori's shouting: "Wait!" He crushed the man's will, flooded his mind, and ended his life. "Nillith, DON'T!" The dead body struck the ground, eyes open wide and blood leaking from his nostrils onto the floor.

Panic hazed the senses like fog. The echoing walls clamored with commotion as the humans began to flee.

Tawori let his hostage go; the man cast a terrified glance into the room, then ran. Tawori's glare refocused. He kneeled by the dead body without looking at it, two fingers feeling the neck for a pulse. After a moment he spat out a word in the human tongue and stood up, towering tall with wrath. "What have you done!" he barked. "Why did you kill him? Why take his life? Don't look away, look at me! You had him helpless. Why didn't you stop? This is wrong, killing is wrong! We don't take a life without need. The humans are weak. They know nothing! They *are* nothing! They don't deserve to die. They would have left. They were going to leave. It's wrong to harm the weak, it isn't right! I thought you knew—Nillith?"

His vision turned black, his head spun, and his legs came unhinged.

"Nillith!"

He knew Tawori had stopped his fall, then he knew nothing else.

HE LAY SHIVERING, his furrowed forehead burning hot, his eyes tightly shut. His chest rose and fell hurriedly, paused, then hurried again.

Tawori tucked the blankets over him and sat on the bed, which squeaked once, then was silent. He propped his elbows on his knees, and burying his head in his hands, let out a deep sigh.

It had taken Tawori a while to find a bed with its covers intact. He'd latched the shutters at the windows and pulled the curtains closed. Now the bedroom was dark, and dusty—everything was dusty in this wretched place.

The only furniture in this room was the bed and a tall brown wardrobe that took up the length of a wall. He would look through the wardrobe first, then search the rest of the house. Hopefully he would find warm clothes, maybe a bottle for water, some strings or threads. He wouldn't mind finding a lighter or two—those were handy—and a saucepan, at least one saucepan.

He sat up straight and looked at the sleeper. He should get water for him; if he found that pan he could boil it, give him something warm to drink, maybe something to eat. They had not eaten in nearly a day, and they had walked way too much.

He should not have brought him to the city. He should have asked him to hide somewhere; then he could have come here alone. It would have been quicker, safer. But Tawori had been too afraid of letting him out of his sight, not knowing whether he would stay put, not knowing whether he fully understood their predicament. Now the only option was to let him sleep; if he slept the night, in the morning he might be well enough to walk a few miles. They could leave at the first light. Until then, Tawori would keep watch and make sure the humans did not find them, because he knew they were coming back for them, sooner or later. When that happened, they better be gone. But for now they could go nowhere. For now, all Tawori could do was wait.

BENEATH THE HEAVY blankets of this bed inside a room filled with years of dust, for long hours the boy slept and dreamed. He dreamed that he stood staring at a door of dark wood. It was a huge door, and it was shut. From behind it came the sound of muffled voices.

With small hands, he reached for the black knob some distance above his head, and pulled the door open. He stepped with bare feet onto warm grass. The day was bright and the air cold, and he did not know for how long he had been walking. He was out of breath and exhausted, but the pond, green with duckweed and waterlilies, was not getting any closer. He had to reach it. He was sure that he had been walking toward it, but now, he could no longer see it. What he could see was a square mirror on a white wall, and he must not look into it. He must not see his reflection in it. He must not wake. Not yet.

He was searching for something and mustn't wake before finding it. Yet there he was, standing in front of the mirror, peering through the hot moisture covering it. A vague, distorted image was all he could see. But that was he, beyond the moisture; it was he, and now he wanted to see. He wanted to see himself, what he looked like. He needed to know.

But he must find what he was searching for. It was important. He had been very close to finding it before; then he had come to the wrong place. It wasn't in this room with the hot steam and the mirror that he should search. It was outside, by the pond.

He saw it from atop a spiral staircase: a pond green with weeds, surrounded by grasses and tiny white flowers. Standing near the pond was Tawori, dressed in gray and light brown patterned clothing, a bright red line painted over his eyes. He was not alone, a second falyn was with him, tall and gracious, with long chalky-white braids, a dimpled smile, and sad eyes. This was whom he had come to find. This was his father. His name, he remembered, was Miriethal.

They stood face to face, Tawori and his father, speaking quietly.

"Where is he?" Tawori asked. "Where is Nillith?"

His father gazed toward the staircase. "He has gone with the humans," he said, though he was staring right into his eyes. "Can you find him for me?"

"The humans are weak!" Tawori barked, suddenly angry. "They know nothing! They don't deserve to die!"

"You must be kind to the weak," said his father, his white gaze probing. "You must not use your power for evil."

"I'm . . . sorry . . ." he sobbed.

"I thought you knew!" Tawori yelled. "Look at me! Why did you kill him?"

He looked up at Tawori, and saw him tower above him with eyes full of tears.

"I'm . . . afraid . . ."

Tawori kneeled down in front of him; his voice gentle as he asked, "What are you afraid of?"

"Darkness," he whispered. And he looked down at the hole in his belly. It was dark and swirling, wringing his whole being in that motion. He screamed, gasping for air, and pushed against the darkness that pressed him on the icy floor, suffocating him. He fought for breath. He bawled, and he struggled. He kicked, and he screamed. And then he saw Tawori's face—"Shhh!" the falyn said, "shhh! It was just a dream, Nillith."

He stopped fighting.

The falyn was pushing him down flat. "Be quiet," he hissed; then he let go, and in a moment was gone.

He lay immobile, listening to his own panting and to the whisper within it, ". . . just . . . a dream . . . Nillith . . ."

When later Tawori returned to the room and quietly asked questions, there came no sign of acknowledgment. The falyn kneeled by the bed, looked into his eyes, and saw him stare right through him. He said nothing else, but stood and left him alone.

It was two hours later, and the first light of dawn crept through the curtains, when Tawori came into the room again.

"Nillith . . . ? I brought you food."

He had to blink a few times before he could see Tawori clearly. He sat up and looked around confused. He was in a dark bedroom with a huge wardrobe and a comfy bed with warm blankets. Outside, it was daytime.

Tawori offered him a plate with food: half-burnt flatbread, and a skinned mouse on a stick. The scent of cooked meat made his mouth water.

"Here, eat," Tawori said, "and drink this. We should go soon. It isn't safe to remain here any longer."

There was a burning pain in his left arm—although it was not his own arm, it was Tawori's. The falyn had wrapped a bloody bandage around his shoulder.

". . . I can heal you," he said with the voice of a stranger, little more than a broken whisper.

Tawori stared at him wide-eyed. "You . . . you must eat, first. You need to eat."

"It's painful . . ."

"Right. It is, yes." Quickly the falyn untied the reddened bandage, then paused looking at him with a worried frown. Finally he sat down on the bed and waited, preoccupied.

The wound was a narrow lesion half an inch wide piercing the falyn's arm from side to side below the shoulder joint. It was swollen and dark with coagulated blood. He placed his hands around the falyn's arm, and beneath his touch he felt Tawori's flesh burning hot and the flow of his energies hustling chaotically. He began to guide it toward the hurt. It was slow, tiring work, for he felt weak, and his focus was hesitant.

"I am not a healer," Tawori said, "far from it. I am not good at patience and concentration. I am too impetuous, they tell me. And I think that's true—I can feel it healing now."

He kept at the task. When the wound was fully healed, he took his hands away.

The falyn searched his gaze.

"Thank you . . . Nillith."

He nodded.

"Eat now, please. You must be hungry. We'll leave as soon as you are ready."

He turned his attention eagerly to the food. He devoured the roasted creature and guzzled the warm tea; then he started on the burnt bread.

"I found clothes that should fit you. This isn't our warm land; it gets much colder here. What you are wearing is too light."

The bread was dry and hard to chew. He got out of bed and changed into the clothes the falyn had procured for him: a sturdy pair of gray fleece-lined trousers; a chunky, knitted woolen jumper the color of chestnut jam; a dark-green down coat long past his hips and with an odd fluffy hood; a woolen hat; a red scarf; thick socks; and a pair of heavy brown boots. He was chewing the last bit of char when Tawori returned wearing his gray and brown jacket and carrying a sizable backpack.

They walked through an empty corridor that descended three flights of stairs then went a way to a door and out onto the black paved road. He stopped; and Tawori paused to look at him.

He stared at the dark entrance across the street, recognizing the building they'd run into the day before.

"I do know it," he said, turning to the falyn. "I was wrong to take his life."

Tawori sighed heavily. "We have to go."

6
LITTLE WOLF

THE COLD SUN OF autumn was low in the east. It cast through the silent city long shadows and yellow spears of bright light. In the empty roads walked two Alassians, pale figures in a sickened land. They went quickly and without looking back, as though fleeing from something. They were unlike any visitor the city was accustomed to, strangers belonging to someplace else. The first was tall and surefooted; a thin stream of white hair mooched behind him in the wind. The second was shorter and loosely clothed; he walked hurriedly to keep up. They departed the city of man and headed south into open lands, under the golden light of the rising sun.

"We will find shelter in those hills."

He followed the falyn's gaze far in the distance. Beyond a stretch of dry earth, rocky hills rose tall, crammed against the blue sky.

"We can hide there for a while, until you are well."

The sun brightened the land, yet it did not warm it.

The earth was dry not because of heat but for lack of rain; and the vegetation was scarce. It was the kind of flora that holds water within, little green plants with thick leaves and small needles; and the kind that endures thirst, prickly shrubs, and hard pointy grass. The fauna, here, was silent and shy.

They were still a long way from the hills when they spotted a herd of small deer grazing the pale grass. Peculiar chubby creatures, with short legs and dense shiny fur. Tawori stirred their course toward them. When they had neared but were not too close as to alert the animals, the falyn stopped and set down his pack. He took the folded bow and assembled it swiftly as if he had done so a hundred times already. Once built, it was a sturdy bow with gently-bent black limbs. The falyn nocked an arrow and stood up, his stance sure, his gaze fixed on one of the deer, his breathing deep, his arms relaxed, and the bow pointed at the ground. In one swift motion he raised the weapon, tensed the bowstring, and let the arrow fly.

Swoosh!

The animals started in alert. Some paused very still; some took a step or two, their heads snapping briskly left or right. Then one by one they returned to grazing the dry grass.

Tawori stood with the bow along his side and his gaze sure. It was a minute or so later when one of the deer lay down sleepily on its belly. It placed its small head on the ground and closed its black eyes.

The falyn folded his bow and stored it away, then picking up his pack began to walk.

The deer scattered and hurried away, all but one.

The arrow had pierced through its victim's shoulder and dived tip whole into the arid earth. Tawori pulled it out, cleaned it, and put it back in the quiver. He kneeled beside the lifeless deer and caressed the length of its snout with the back of one finger, murmuring a whisper in its furry ear. He lifted it onto his shoulder and stood.

"I can carry it."

"No, Nillith. I will carry it. You are tired, and I am not."

The sun was high above them when they began climbing the rocky hillside. Soon they found a cold rivulet where they stopped to drink and fill a pair of metal bottles. Then they ambled on, up the first hill and down the other side then ahead a while longer through rocks and along crags. They stopped when the sun was beginning to descend. Tawori put down the deer and the pack and asked him to wait while he went to gather what wood he could find.

As he sat watching the soothing wilds, a great sleepiness came over him. He caught himself nearly nodding off. Tawori had asked him to remain watchful, and asleep wasn't watchful, so he stood and paced about. When he spotted the falyn heading back, he wasted no time. He lay down on one side, tucked his forearms beneath his head, and let sleep take him.

He awoke to the smell of roast meat and the light of a fire that burned brightly against a darkening sky. He sat and opened the front of his coat; he was hot and sweating.

The deer had been skinned, impaled on a stick, and propped over the heat; it had been cooking for a while already. He watched Tawori spin it slowly, distractedly. His swords were laid beside him over gray rocks, and the firelight danced on their bronze hilts. The fire's pops and frizzles echoed with words from a faded past. *Why are you doing this to me? You are hurting me!* A feeling of anger, fierce rage. *Is he? Or is he not? Answer me!* A sword thumping on soft grass. His father's voice saying, *He is, but no one must know.*

He stood. He went to search the pack and took a long drink of water. He kept the bottle with him and sat back down, gazing into the fire. When he began talking, he felt Tawori's eyes study him.

"When I was a boy... when I was very little... maybe five or six years old... a falyn came to my home." Tawori's undivided attention was on him. "He was angry. Shouting things, demanding answers. He had asked a question of my father and was threatening to fight him." A strain filled the falyn's heart, tensing his body with anxiety, excitement, hope. "Were you that falyn?" Regret.

"I was."

Inside the circle of rocks the fire crackled and jiggled.

He met the falyn's gaze and held it. "What question did you ask of my father?"

Tawori looked away, peering into the depths of the flame. It was some time before he replied, looking up, staring determinedly back at him. "Is he my brother?"

"Brother?"

Hot tears ran down his cheeks. They were not entirely his tears, they were Tawori's, too. The falyn didn't cry, but his heart was full of a dark weight, a grief, remorse.

"But I remember... my father, that day"—his throat

was taut as he swallowed—"he said to me that you were no son of his."

"And by blood, neither were you."

His breath was shaking. He stared at the burning campfire, struggling to make sense of the words.

The falyn's heart was true, and so, too, were his words. He did not question them. Very little he knew of himself and of his own childhood. None of it he could trust. He wiped the tears off his face and met the falyn's gaze resolutely.

"Then whose son am I?"

"Your father was my father," Tawori said, "and your mother was my mother. They are no more. Our father died in battle before you were born. And our mother, I believe, died giving birth to you. But Miriethal never told me the truth of her passing. I do not know. I do not know the truth."

Silence. The campfire burned brightly between them.

"Did I know you? Before, I mean . . . before . . ."

The falyn's brows rose in thin arches. His face wore a pained questioning look as he replied, "We have not been in each other's company outside the day you spoke of. If that is what you are asking."

The fire's soft crackling filled the empty silence.

"Is Nillith my name?"

"Your name? Have you forgotten your own name?"

"I have forgotten many things."

"I . . . I'm sorry . . ." Tawori said. "I'm sorry . . ." He hid his face for a moment. "I do not know your name. Miriethal never spoke about you, and I knew not to ask. Our parents had died. I thought you had died. But you lived, and Miriethal had you hidden from your own people. I knew that your life was in danger. I kept the secret. I asked no questions.

"The other night, when we ran, you trusted me with your freedom. I wished that you felt safe. In your eyes I saw the eyes of the wild wolf, and so I called you Nillith. Do you speak our ancient tongue?"

He shook his head, no.

"In Matál, Nillith means 'little wolf'. I thought the name suited you." Tawori smiled. He poked the fire with a stick, and the flame bounced lively.

"Why did my father—why would . . . Miriethal . . . will us apart?"

"You should call him father," said Tawori, "if in the past that has been your way. He considered you his son; I know that he did. And to answer your question, he did not will us apart. He wished to protect you. He believed that only by hiding you, he could keep you safe. And perhaps he was right. But you weren't always hidden. You were seen once. I learned of you, and perhaps I was not the only one."

"Lenthieh . . ."

Tawori sighed. He spent some time turning the meat over the crackling fire. The night was dark about them now.

"He leads this vile war against humankind."

"And he is looking for me."

"Maybe," said the falyn. "Probably."

"You are in danger if you are with me."

Tawori shook his head. "I have spent years searching for you. Not knowing, but hoping that you lived. Now that I have found you, I do not intend to leave your side. Besides, where would I go? I have betrayed my friends' trust. And I have betrayed the humans'. They have many rules and do not forgive transgression. I would not be welcomed among them if I returned. My fate would be grim. My only place now is with you. But I must ask. What is it you planned to do after you ran from the humans? Was your sole desire to run? Where to?"

"I . . ." He looked down at his hands. "I know I had power, once. But I . . . I don't think I do any longer."

"You are the guardian." The word rang in his mind full of an ancient meaning. It sent jitters to his gut. "For as long as you live, you are the guardian."

"Yes . . ." he whispered.

"I have watched you," said Tawori, "I know what you think you have lost. But there is more to the guardian's power than the shine of your eyes. You sense the minds of others and what is in their hearts, do you not? I know that you do, and that you listened to what is in my heart since the moment you first awoke. You would not have trusted me otherwise. Back when our journey began, you took a man's senses from him with the touch of one hand. And this morning you felt the pain of my very flesh. Your senses are keen, and you have fine control of your focus. But you have been hurt. You need time to heal. Your mind needs time to heal.

"If I may, I have given it thought. I think we should go someplace where you can feel safe, where you can find peace. In the northernmost part of Ydalon, the mountains are covered in snow this time of year. I suggest we go there. The cold will be our protector. And the snow, well, it is marvelous to look at. I think you would like it. We could make our way there when you are well and have some of your strength back."

Hot tears welled up in his eyes, tears of relief and gratitude. This time, they were his tears alone. "Thank you, Tawori," he said.

"I am glad I found you, little brother."

A single tear trailed down his right cheek, following along a ragged scar. He closed his eyes and, hugging his knees to his chest, he listened to the crackling of the fire and to the warmth of Tawori's heart.

"Aha!" the falyn said a little while later. "It is ready! Let us eat to our fill!"

They ate by firelight under the dark, open sky. Tawori chomped his venison eagerly, as a hungry lion, and said nothing more until, later, he declared that he was full and could not take another bite. Then he spoke softly in the silence of the wilds, his soothing words fading into the haze of drowsiness.

He was staring blindly at the fire when he noticed Tawori handing him a blanket. He wrapped himself in it, lay down, and slept.

When he woke, the darkness was tinged with the yellow and blue of his night sight. The fire was out, and the embers were red and hot. He sat up and cast his gaze about in search of Tawori. The falyn stood a short distance away looking north and west. As if aware of him, he turned and came to sit close by. "If you are awake, Nillith," he said, "I will sleep for a while. We must keep watch tonight, we are too visible here. Will you stay awake? I have not slept in three days." Without waiting for an answer, he lay with one arm folded beneath his head. "Thank you," he said accepting the offered blanket. He fanned it out over himself and fell asleep at once.

"I want to scout the area," Tawori said in the morning, "find a place for us to stay comfortably for a while. These hills, they are hollow in places. I hope to find caves. Will you wait here? I shall not go far. If I find nothing, we will move farther south. Stay alert, and watch the skies."

He returned not long after with a tale of caves he had found near a small stream—towering overhangs casting long shadows; inside, tall, spacious chambers went deep into the belly of the hills. They would settle in the widest of them, dry and homey, according to Tawori, a single chamber that curved slightly to one side and would hide them from sight.

They headed there slowly and with great effort on his part, his feet catching on rocks, his breathing puffing with exertion.

He took in the majesty of the cave, the dry musky smell, and the babbling of a rivulet outside; then he found a place to lie, between two rocks and a wall, and slept.

He rested peacefully for many days, sleeping, or sitting with his back to the shade and looking out at the silent hills. Tawori took to being away for long hours, exploring, hunting, gathering. Always he brought back food, wood, stones, and other things.

One time, returning from a day-long excursion, Tawori showed him the content of his pack, beaming with satisfaction. It was filled with small apples.

"A rare finding in these lands," Tawori said, dropping four into his lap. Then he was busy stripping the bark from the twigs he'd collected, chipping stones, working pelts, and plucking feathers from a dinner soon-to-be.

He watched the falyn absentmindedly from where he sat, his mouth full of the sweet juicy taste of apples.

When a little strength returned to him, he began practicing the stances of combat. In the cave's entrance, barefooted on the cold earth, he patiently taught his body to listen and find balance, and to move with what little grace and control he could muster, his gaze relaxed and his inner senses turned to the surroundings. His body was clumsy, his punches and kicks weak, and his balance poor. Nevertheless he took great delight in the exercise, and day after day he found his body loosening and following a flow that carried him more surely, more swiftly.

When not away in search for things or busy crafting, Tawori practiced with him. The falyn taught him a number of motions that he did not know, or that perhaps had forgotten. He was a knowledgeable teacher, precise and passionate.

In turn, he took to helping Tawori in preparation for their journey to the mountains, though never did he venture far from the safety of the cave.

Neither of them kept count of the passing days.

Then one morning Tawori lit a fire although there was no food to be cooked. He made it small and hot with cinders before extinguishing the flame. Near it he gathered all the wood, stones, and other things he had collected, and sat down among them.

He watched the falyn work the wood, passing a thin, skinned stick back and forth before the cinders, pressing it between his fingers, bending it softly. From time to time Tawori held one side of it close to his eyes and looked down its axis, then he returned it to the cinders, again and again, until he was satisfied. He studied the falyn till he was sure he understood the task, then took one of the sticks and began to do the same.

After a shaft was straightened, Tawori used two flat pieces of sandstone to smooth its surface. Once he had learned that technique as well, he alone carried on with the straightening and smoothing, while the falyn melted a mixture of yellow pine pitch, charcoal, and dried dung, forming a hard black glue. He used that to fit the stone arrowheads into the groove at the end of each shaft. At the place where rock met wood, Tawori wound a string of thinly chewed deer sinew, patiently and precisely.

"Will you teach me to hunt?"

The falyn looked up from his work, puzzled for a moment. "Oh, you mean archery."

He nodded.

Tawori brought the arrow to his eyes and inspected it, revolving it slowly and passing his thumb over the tendon he'd just wrapped. Satisfied, he placed it on the growing pile of head-fitted shafts and took the next one to be assembled. "I will teach you," he said. "It is a useful skill to have."

"When do we go to the mountains?"

"I think the day after tomorrow. I planned to finish these arrows before we set off. Careful not to burn the wood."

He pulled his stick away from the cinders and inspected a spot blackened by the heat.

"Why don't we stay here? It's safe."

"It has been, in this cave," Tawori replied. "But we cannot spend our days inside a cave. The land outside is bare. There are no woods in which to hide, no cover for miles. We would be easy to find, if someone came searching for us."

"With 'someone' you mean 'him.'"

"Not only. I might have people on my trail, too. For helping you escape."

"What would they do if they found you?"

"It is best they do not. But don't worry. I imagine the war has the Alliance far too busy to spare the men for the chase of a mere deserter such as I." The falyn applied a bit of glue to the shaft and inserted an arrowhead.

"And this war? Where is the fighting now?"

Tawori let out a sigh. "Lenthieh's forces have pushed past this land," he said, "Ydalon is no longer a concern to him. It is mostly deserted. The human survivors have all but fled to the lands east of the water, and Lenthieh, too, is focusing his efforts there. He does not come to conquer and rule, you see, he comes to destroy, to 'rid the world of the human plague,' he says. But the Alliance has its base on this continent, and there are a few settlements here that still support it. Less than six months ago we fought a battle on the coast of Ydalon north of here, near the place where you first awoke. We faced Lenthieh's army on the battlefield, his Alassian fighters, and his creatures of darkness."

"Creatures of darkness! The unlife answers to him?"

"It is Lenthieh's most powerful weapon, and how he wages war against humankind. With demons and creatures tainted by the unlife, beings and forces from the Realm Beyond."

"But how? Who is he to command . . . the nothing?"

"How he commands the unlife, that I do not know.

He is . . ." Tawori paused his work. He rested the arrow in his lap and looked at him with the hint of a scowl. "Lenthieh is nineteen centuries old, and he is Miriethal's son. By blood and by birth."

"What? No. He . . . but he killed . . . my . . . my father his . . . father?"

"Nillith, did Lenthieh kill Miriethal?"

He stared numbly.

"I'm sorry, I shouldn't have asked," Tawori said. "I'm sorry, Nillith. Miriethal loved you as if you were his own son. I know he did. He wished to protect you above all else. I believe this in my heart. It was because of his love for you that I heeded his wish and stayed away after learning of your existence and who you were. Because I knew that in him you had the family you deserved. You had a father, which was more than I could give you. I do not wish to take that away from you even now.

"But it is also true that Lenthieh is Miriethal's son, firstborn and only child. The keeper and his beloved never had another—at least not one I know of. After the secrecy he kept around you, it would not surprise me to learn that they had another; but I think not."

His hands still held the thin wooden stick, light and smooth to the touch, fair in color, but for the spot darkened by the heat.

"I knew Lenthieh in my youth," continued Tawori. "He was kind, as his father was. But unlike Miriethal, Lenthieh was a free spirit, a traveler and lover of the farlands, a seeker of adventures. He is much older than I am. I have yet to live half his years. When I was young, I looked up to him. Our parents were close friends, and he was someone I knew well. Or so I thought.

"I do not know what he found on his travels or what occurrence befell him, but he changed. Some years ago, long before you were born, I went to see him one day after learning he had returned to Irieth. I expected to sit in his company and hear of his adventures. But on that day he was cold, disgruntled, almost violent. He threatened me with harsh words and told me that I should not approach him again. I feared him. I was a warrior then, although only a junior, and he was not one. Yet I feared him. I felt ashamed. I said nothing of it to anyone. Soon after, Lenthieh left Irieth, stating that this time he would not return. I put the matter aside. It was easier to forget than to face my cowardice. Yet he did return. And to do more than threaten with words. He fights a war now. And he is keeper."

"He is not!"

"He has the keeper's power," Tawori said softly. "But how he acquired it, of that I am unsure. I and others who joined the Alliance struggle to believe he was entrusted with it by Miriethal, although that has always been the will of the world. Some wondered if, perhaps, somehow he has taken the power from Miriethal. By force."

" . . . he has."

"Did you . . . witness that?"

He did not reply, but rubbed his thumb over the black spot on the arrow shaft.

"For how long was I . . . in that place?"

"In Seligor," Tawori said, "I do not know when you were brought there, but the day Miriethal died, that was over four years ago."

"Four years . . . ?"

He stared at the burnt spot on the wooden shaft

without seeing it. When he spoke again, his own voice sounded frail. "I remember you carrying me out of there. I heard you talking. It was the first time I'd heard anyone's voice since . . . No, I had no memory of ever hearing anyone speak before. You said, 'I have come to save you.' I thought I was dreaming. But I had never had good dreams before. After that, I forgot. When I woke in the humans' place, I remembered only the darkness, and the silence, the cold, and pain, and . . . the nightmares. Visions. When, the man . . ." He raised a hand to touch his hair.

"Liu? Ginger hair?"

He nodded. "After he asked me things, I began to remember Lenthieh. I remembered how he . . . what he . . ." He forgot for some time that he was talking, until he heard Tawori stir. "I was in the forest," he said then; "there was fire everywhere. I wasn't with Father. I was running somewhere. Tashira, she . . . Tashira . . . she wouldn't stop. I could hear him scream in my mind. I felt his pain like it was mine. But we kept running. And I felt him die. I . . . I think I . . . abandoned him."

He tried to stop the tears, but they kept coming. Loud sobs shook him, and his throat turned tight and sore.

When he could control himself somewhat, he said, "When Lenthieh found me, he . . . he . . . something, a-a poison . . . it . . . it burned"—his hands clasped his belly; he had not thought to put them there and could not move them away—"it devoured . . . it pulled . . . my life essence from my body, j-just like it had with Father's. He . . . he died . . . because his life essence was wrenched out of him. I know. I know. But mine, Lenthieh, he couldn't. He . . . he was angry. He was very angry. He'd killed Father and taken his power, but mine, mine he couldn't take it. I . . . I don't know why."

A long silence followed his words. He kept his gaze on the ground, unwilling to hear the world around him. He wanted to be alone in his mind, his senses closed and deafened.

When next he heard Tawori speak, he was oblivious of how much time had passed.

"I believed," the falyn said, "when I first saw you, you know, that day of many years ago—you were only a child but with so much strength in you—I believed perhaps you were born with the power of the guardian inside you. Given to you by our mother, you see?"

He met the falyn's bright gaze.

Tawori's voice was silvery and vibrant as he added, "Because our mother was the guardian of her time. Oh? Did you not know?"

" . . . I didn't."

"But you do know of her?"

"The guardian Akihalla."

"Yes," Tawori said smiling. "You look more like her than I do, even with those scars and that gloomy mien of yours." He chuckled lightly. "She was quiet and composed, after all; so perhaps you resemble her a little in that too. But when she smiled, it was unfeasible to hold her a grudge, and when she fought, she moved and danced like a dandelion fluff in the wind. She was powerful and beautiful, our mother. And you remind me of her."

Tawori's love filled both their hearts. The joy of recollection was sweet, washing away all pain and self-pity.

He sighed, and his breath quivered only slightly. He picked up the blemished wooden shaft and returned it to the cinders, moving it carefully back and forth, back and forth.

7

DOWN BELOW

THE CAVE WAS DARK and desolate, disconsolate, sad, although of course the cave was just a cave and the gloom lived in his own heart. He looked out at the sloping hills covered in jutting rocks, wishing he weren't about to depart from the only home he knew. He was standing with a heavy pack on his shoulders and his feet tucked in stiff boots, listening to the familiar voice of the clearwater rivulet babbling endlessly cheerful; he would miss its voice dearly.

"This too," Tawori said emerging from the cold shade of the cave.

He took the offered quiver made of coyote pelt filled with their crafted arrows, and secured it to his pack along with the human-made quiver and the folded bow. On his part, Tawori carried a back-piece of wood and twine to which he had tied their pelts, two rolled up mats made of thin sticks, the human blanket, and the two green cloths from Tidfyl of a rigid material impervious to water.

It was midmorning under the clear blue sky, and the air was chilly. They walked with the sun rising on their right. Soon it settled above them, far in the distance ahead and gleaming in their eyes. The land was rocky and hilly, changing quickly from hilltop to hilltop, passing by them effortlessly. But after midday, when they entered unending fields of dry earth and clumped vegetation, the scenery slowed to a near stop.

They trekked for half the length of a day, and at evenfall, they found shelter beneath a lonely acacia tree with dense leafy branches like the cap of a giant mushroom. They wrapped themselves in pelts and ate a cold meal in silence. Then they took turns to watch the open sky in the coldness of the sunless time.

They journeyed north through desert landscapes, every day hiking a little longer than they had the day before. They encountered many animals, but no people. The sun shone distant and frail in the sky, and the wind blew tediously uninterrupted. The land unrolled before their eyes mostly unchanging, sloping frequently and carelessly.

On the tenth day, they saw the shape of a vast and somber city to the east surrounded by sea.

"That one's name is Methyr." Tawori stopped to point at it. "I was there once with the Alliance in the aftermath of Lenthieh's assault. We rid the place from the creatures of darkness left behind and took the human survivors across the waters to Terica, a land northeast of here many leagues by sea.

"Methyr was their greatest city, their most prized, the last to fall. They called it a 'medie,' which means 'center of the world,' in Taelic, that is. Taelic is the tongue spoken by the humans of this continent, but it is known widely elsewhere too. It is simple and pleasant to speak, although not so pleasant to hear at times. It depends, I suppose, on who speaks it." The falyn smiled, amused by his own words, and began walking again.

"The humans have many languages," he went on, "some are young and some much less so. Many share rules and words, and are easy to grasp. But some are old, complex and stiff, difficult to pronounce and alien to the ear. I speak Taelic the best. I learned Majunderin because it is a melodious language, but I haven't had much chance to practice it. Same goes for Sa'dari, which may well be a lost language now. Odenic I know not too well. I can read it and understand when it is spoken, because it is similar to Taelic. Awdalin and Hashi I know only a little; I could ask a man for food and directions, if the man were to let me close enough to speak . . . which I doubt he would." He sighed and was quiet for many steps. "I haven't had much time for studies in these years, but languages come easy to me, and I do like to read."

His words fell into silence, and the wind blew howling.

That evening dark clouds filled the sky. It drizzled in the morning and then again in the early hours of the night. The clouds stayed with them for three days. On the fourth morning the weather began to clear and mountains crowned the horizon. This range was called the Caerphil, Tawori explained, its slopes were dense with evergreen woods, but some of the peaks climbed as high as twenty thousand feet and were covered in ice and snow all year long.

They walked well into the evening and by sundown

reached the shelter of a pine forest. There, they lit a fire and ate their first hot meal in many days. At night they both slept soundly, trusting in the wilds and the grove.

In the days that followed, their pace became relaxed and wandering. No longer preoccupied by the empty sky stretching above them, they ambled aimlessly in the safety of the woods. They began to pass the time training in the art of combat and practicing archery. To Nillith, bow and arrow were delightful to hold. There was much in this discipline of balance and focus. Tawori taught him that breathing was as important as taking aim or tensing the bowstring: inhalation brought the target into focus, and exhalation sent the arrow flying true—though not often did it fly where he hoped it would. There was peace of mind to be found in the nocking of an arrow, its seeking of a target, its flight through the air. Soon, archery became a preferred pastime of his.

THE FIRST TOUCH OF SNOW filled his heart with excitement. Soft, white flakes danced in the immensity of the sky, gathering on tree branches and bushes, forming a spume of frost that sparkled in the sunlight. He stomped his feet on the earth's frozen white coat, listening to the crunching of his boots. He picked up handfuls of snow to melt in his mouth or squeeze into hard chunks that turned his fingers red and stiff.

Tawori looked at his brother's smile with delight. He let the little wolf walk ahead of him, free of thought and light of heart.

That night they made camp amid a sea of white. They dug the site a little into the snow, making deeper trenches all around to sink the freezing air. They spread one of the water-dry cloths onto the hardened snow, laid the wooden mats and pelts over it, and topped it with the second stiff cloth forming a roof.

He lay with his eyes closed, listening to the cold silence. Near him, Tawori's mind floated for a while on the surface of wakefulness, then submerged into deep slumber.

He opened his eyes to the glow of reflected starlight, and stirred. Carefully he crawled from under the pelts, minding not to wake Tawori, and put on his day-clothes, his hat, and boots. He walked quietly like a leaf in the wind, fifty steps or more over the blanket of snow that shimmered brightly in his sight of night. He stood with his gaze fixed on the icy expanse, the cold wrapped around him, his body relaxed, his senses alert.

He began to move. Slowly at first, shifting his balance from foot to foot. He lifted his hands stretched out in front, pulled them back, elbows in, hands into fists, left foot to thigh, hands open flat, left arm feeling his center, low step to the side, body close to the ground, punch, then kick, twist, then jump. He moved faster and faster, his feet lifting splashes of snow. White flakes drizzled around him and danced in the wake of his motion. Soon the cold was unfelt. He went from stance to stance, his senses focused outward in the stillness of the night.

There was a sudden flash of light. His hands shone of his life force; the air around him filled with sparkling motion; and the floor of snow turned obsidian black, glossy as the most precious of stones. He gasped, and the vision vanished.

His breathing fluttered.

He sank to his knees, sweating palms deep into the shimmering snow, and began to chuckle. He had seen the world's energies! He was himself! Truly, he was. He had doubted. Doubted his mind. Doubted his heart. Doubted his very existence. No longer. He was, if not whole, a true remnant of his memories. Hot tears burned his cheeks, fell like steaming pearls, and vanished into the snow.

It was some time until his sentiment eased, then his body shivered with the bitter cold. He paced quietly, hardly leaving footprints. He stripped off the wet clothes and slid under the pelts. Still smiling, he let sleep take him.

He awoke with the high-pitched call of a bird soaring in the bright morning sky. Tawori was sitting on a bench of snow, nibbling on a handful of nuts, a bushy pelt tightly wrapped around his figure.

He got dressed and went to him. "You were right that we should come here," he said.

The falyn looked up in surprise and seeing him standing there smiling, said, "Oh." Then that was all.

He sat down beside Tawori on the snow bench and took a few nuts for himself from their little twine pouch.

THEY WALKED FROM SNOW to forest, to snow, and forest again, up and down the snowy mountains, leisurely and aimlessly for days. Around them, above them, and below them, were only the wilds. Then one day as they hunted the lower Caerphil for food, Tawori with bow at hand and he padding quietly behind, the green mountainside revealed itself to them suddenly dotted with fluffy white drops of clouds, and they heard faraway cries.

"Baa-ah! Ble-eh."

"Sheep!" Tawori exclaimed, grinning. "Humans farm them for food and wool. See the pink smears on their backs? It means they belong to someone. But I wonder . . . finding so many roaming the land free is most peculiar. Animals such as these became rare during the war. The humans value them highly." He folded his bow and fastened it to the quiver behind his back. They were traveling light to hunt and did not have their packs with them. "Indulge me. I wish to satisfy my curiosity." The falyn strolled ahead; and he followed.

These sheep-creatures seemed easy prey. If they belonged to no one, then they would be theirs for the taking. The animals looked odd with their bodies round and fluffy and their legs white and skinny. Their faces wore silly expressions, as if the chewing of hard mountain grass had emptied their minds of all thought. Once or twice he found himself giggling aloud as, close by, one of the creatures paused, looked his way with its mouth half open and grass sticking out of it, then said, "baa," and ran away.

It was nearly an hour later when they spotted a gray wooden house, worn and drab against the pasture.

Tawori stopped a fair distance from it. "It seems they still belong to someone," he said. "We'd best leave and find other hunting grounds."

Right then there was a movement outside the house. A mass of something brown-black and wide ran downhill and came to stop in front of them. A bush of tangled dreadlocks hid all features from sight but for a thin, pointy snout. The bush barked and whined once, then sat down. Its black nose pointed up at them.

"Is it . . . a dog?"

"Looks like it," Tawori said.

"It does?"

"Well, no." The falyn's lips crooked up in a smirk. "But it is a dog. Domesticated. Trained to herd sheep."

The bush whined, skipping its nose left and right between the two of them. "It's hungry," he said—he could feel its distress, "and thirsty. And it's afraid, anxious . . . sad, I think."

Tawori looked at the house and without a word began walking toward it.

They peeked through the windows. Inside was dark and nothing moved. The dog barked at the door and whined, scratching the floor, sniffing it. Paint had been completely scraped off the door near the bottom.

"I think something has happened to the humans who live here," Tawori said. He watched the animal for a moment. "Make a cup with your hands, Nillith."

He did so, kneeling near the dog, and Tawori poured some water from their bottle. The dog drank it, licking his hands thoroughly. They emptied their bottle, and the dog drank again, then proceeded to lick his face with its warm, wet tongue. He winced and petted the animal on the head to abate its sudden enthusiasm.

The handle clicked, and Tawori opened the door. «Hello?» The dog ran inside. Tawori spoke a few more words in the human language and waited.

No answer came besides a single bark. They entered.

The air smelled stale. The house was cold but looked to be lived in. The floor and all the furniture were made of wood: a wide dining table with chairs, a smaller and pretty table, a three-legged stool, a long sofa, a low, wide bookcase, cupboards and chests, and, in a second room, two beds, one wide, the other small. There was a fireplace, unlit, and a rusty, old square thing for cooking that stood on four sturdy legs. On the dining table there was a plate with dry bread and a piece of bitten, moldy cheese.

"Could they have left?"

Tawori looked back at him thoughtfully, then turned to watch the dog who was intent on sniffing the entire house. He bent a knee to the floor and began speaking soft words in the ancient tongue, his voice like a singsong, mellow and warm. "Sàrnahuòn, tanîn'nuyhèsq."

The dog went to him whining.

"Nurihànne hìro'nuydàlnh hiélsu. Suymàlan, fàrilnu hiéllua."

The dog barked, and ran outside.

"We must follow it," Tawori said.

The old sheepdog, who proudly wore the name Snoot, ran through the cold pastures that belonged to him and his masters, down to where the mountain steepened into a ravine and the air was made humid by a noisy, frigid brook. He stopped to wait for the stranger who'd asked about his masters. Snoot had not returned to the place since running in fear. He had stayed away from the cave, away from the ravine, and away from the river. He had been afraid. But now, with the aid of this stranger whose words unraveled meanings in his mind, he felt again loyal and valiant.

They followed the dog down the mountainside, running fast and agile over the uneven terrain. The dog stopped three times waiting for them, each time resuming the sprint as soon as they caught up. Then suddenly it slowed to a cautious pace. Sniffing about scrupulously, it led them to a place where high boulders shadowed the sunlight. There the air was wet and smelled of mud, and the ground was slippery. Whimpering, the dog took one small step and another, then stopped and sank to the ground. Its nose poked over a dark hole among rocks, wide enough for a person to slip through.

They gathered round and peered into the hole. Darkness, and silence. Their eyes accustomed to daylight could not penetrate the pitch black below. At first all was still, then they heard a sound of scuffling and a bleat. Beneath the earth, a life, feeble and hurt, struggled to survive.

He crouched down with a hand on the ground, closing his eyes and focusing his senses. Tawori caught his shoulder, squeezed a moment, then relaxed.

He could feel the sheep underground, cold and cowering. He searched the space around it and felt nothing. Too much nothing. He could not feel the air or the earth. Nothing lived in them—not a worm or a fly.

Looking into the darkness, he lowered his body.

"No," Tawori said, and pulled him back.

"I want to help it."

"I fear this place, and so should you."

"I'll be careful."

"Careful? This dog is careful! It has more good sense than you do."

Belly-flat in the mud, the dog whined. The bushy brows lifted revealing round brown eyes, big with worry.

He smiled at the creature, then returned his gaze to the hole. "It'll die alone in the dark."

Tawori's fingers bored into his shoulder. "I will go first."

"I think I should go—"

"Brother! Little brother, I will go first."

Tawori released him and climbed into the hole.

He followed after him slowly, taking care not to slip. Cold, damp air crept under his clothes. It was perhaps three yards to the bottom. He could see Tawori's shape crouched nearby, besides that, darkness. He concentrated on the feeling of the hard ground beneath his feet, the beating of his heart so loud that he could almost hear it echo in the emptiness of his other senses. As he stood there, the walls and ground gradually lightened from pitch black to dark gray with a faint yellow tinge, revealing a natural passage with rocky walls and a rocky, muddy floor. The sheep, like a vague puff of whitish smoke, was a few steps down the way. It bleated, and its voice rebounded around them. They stepped forward.

Tawori halted at arm's reach of the animal. "*Stop!*" he hissed. "*The humans . . .*"

He peered ahead from behind the falyn. Some distance away, the yellow tinge of the walls was hidden by a dark shape, perhaps two dark shapes propped against one another.

"*Stay back.*" Tawori took a step forward and kneeled. He perhaps stroked the sheep; clearly he murmured something to it, though the words were lost to silence. Then he gasped, hunched down, and let out a groan.

"Tawori?"

"Get back!" the falyn yelped, shuddering, breathing loudly, bent over the sheep as if under a heavy load.

His own body tensed with fear, he reached out a hand,

and Tawori swung a fist at him striking him hard in the chest.

He stumbled back, tripped, and landed on his butt and elbows.

"Leave!" Tawori yelled. He towered over him, glaring down in anger, a hand on the sword's hilt at his hip. "We should not have come here! You should have listened to me!" He pulled out the blade and brought it down on him.

He dodge the cut by a graze, pushing himself off the floor and to the side, hands and feet slipping out from beneath him as the sword clanged against the rocky ground. His back hit a wall, and he immediately pushed off, hurling himself away. The sword slashed the air a second time; then Tawori slammed into the wall at full speed. He turned with a snarl, a bloody gash on his temple, his eyes rabid with rage. He stabbed his sword again, yelling. "Run!"

This time he felt the blade cut the air an inch from his face as he recoiled. Again the steel reached for him; again he twisted his body out of the way. One more swing came flashing in front of his eyes, and he snatched his head back, whacking the wall behind him. The impact shook his skull. He lurched forward, dropping into a squat, stunned, knowing only that his back was to the wall. He heard the tip of the sword stab the rock above, resonating loudly.

"Why won't you run!"

Tawori's knee struck him under the chin. His head bashed the wall a second time.

"I told you to run!"

He was hammered hard on the scalp and began to fall

sideways, his vision blurred; he grabbed for Tawori's clothes and kicked at his shin as hard as he could. The falyn went down falling on top of him.

Half blind he sought Tawori's exposed skin before the other could pull away, he brushed his fingertips on his jawline and tugged at his life force. Tawori yelped, coming down heavily on one side, thrashing him hard in the ribs as he did, breaking free, rolling out of reach.

The stolen energy pulsated in his palm. He held his fingers bent around it like hooks. He could not see it, though he could feel it. It was muddled with cold emptiness.

He got to his feet, gaze fixed on Tawori who was struggling back up. He brought the focus to his eyes, and they scorched with fire. Tears came. His vision turned black.

He shut his eyes.

"You are weak!" Tawori shouted. "You cannot defeat me!"

The falyn's hand found his throat, choking him, pushing him, pinning him against the wall. Pain jolted through his body, and his muscles tensed in spasm.

"All you do is cry!"

The current intensified, thundering ferociously through his flesh. He fought for control of his inner energies, but he could not outwill Tawori's might.

In desperation he rallied his life force, sharpened it, then all at once, he pushed. There was a static noise. The blast of their colliding energies crushed the wind out of him and flung Tawori against the opposite wall.

He gulped a breath of air, his twitching hand searching the wall for support. His focus still sharp, he forced his life's strength to light his sight. Through the burn, he saw Tawori's inner energies sparkle like liquid diamond, and the unlife's taint writhe through him like veins of black blood, pulsating, breathing, stabbing.

He stretched out his free hand and willed the dark essence still.

Pushed up against the wall, Tawori grunted trying to break free, hissing and gritting his teeth.

He plodded forward, limping from the pain in his ribs. With the right hand he took hold of Tawori's arm, and the life force within him, and the left he put at his throat. Then he wrested the unlife from him.

Tawori's body arched and his chest rose as he cried a heart-aching wail of misery.

He tightened his grip and kept on tugging. A sphere of coldness amassed in his palm. He held it firmly and let his brother go, watching him sink to the ground.

His left hand felt heavy and stiff. Already he was growing weak. The cold had spread past his wrist to his forearm. Yet unless his senses deceived him, the globe of darkness was contained in his grasp, beating time to the throbbing of his heart's fear.

He looked away. The cave was lightless in the guardian sight. The humans were dead—lumps in the murk. His own body was filled with life's radiance; Tawori's faint luminance huddled on the floor at his feet; and the sheep they had come to rescue was but a feeble, quivering glow where it had lain all along—weak, but clear of darkness. His brother's sword, a clear gleam of pale light, lay abandoned. He limped to it and picked it up. Then he limped to the sheep.

The animal looked at him and bleated. He kneeled by

the helpless creature and brought the sphere of darkness close. The unlife reached out, hungry, avid for life's warmth, eager to break free. He let it. The animal kicked and jerked. He clutched the stiff wool at the nape and slid its throat. The sheep blinked slowly twice, then it lay still.

Tears poured down his cheeks. His eyes burned with dry pain. He let the flow of his inner energies quiet and his sight returned to the stillness of the cave, its walls, and its muddy floor.

Tawori was groaning and panting, trying to sit up, and failing.

He helped him lean against the wall.

"S-sor-ry . . . N-Nillith . . . a-am . . . s-sor-ry . . ." He shivered violently, and his teeth chattered.

"It was my fault."

". . . s-sor-ry . . . s-sor . . ."

He took his brother's icy hands in his own and brought their foreheads together, infusing his life's energy into the touch, feeding him a little of his warmth.

"Can you stand?"

His brother just shivered and mumbled.

He passed Tawori's arm over his shoulders and stood up, lifting his full weight with great effort. Tawori was taller and heavier, and unstable on his feet. Slowly he led him to the faint light beneath the opening.

"Hold on here," he said, "I'll help you from above." He watched Tawori find a grip and hold it with intent concentration. The effort seemed to cost him great determination. Then he climbed up and into the open. "Give me your hand," he said, leaning back into the hole. "Tawori! Give me your hand!" He clasped his brother's outstretched hand and pulled him up.

There was slipping and grunting. At last, Tawori crawled out of the narrow opening and lay down in the mud.

"Come on." He tugged at him again. "Get up, Tawori."

"Just . . . rest . . ."

"Not here." He pulled him to his knees—"Stop it!" The dog was leaning against Tawori, rubbing its body and head against him, wagging its tail. "Not now, dog!" He shoved it away. He picked up the sword he'd laid on the ground to help Tawori out of the hole, the shorter of his two swords, and sheathed it in its scabbard at his brother's hip. Then he got him to stand. "Hold on to me."

Tawori clung to him, and together they plodded toward the sunlight. It was the frail winter sun of late afternoon, hiding behind thickening clouds. It offered little warmth. Around them the mountain stood silent. The air was cold and still.

"Where . . ."

They had been walking uphill. The path was brittle beneath their feet. Little rocks skittered from under their boots.

"To the house," he replied.

" . . . water . . ."

"I'll find you water when we are there."

The dog now led the way, strolling three steps ahead of them, pausing to wait if they stumbled or fell behind. The sun dived behind the western peaks, painting the heavy clouds gold and black.

At long last he saw the gray house in the distance.

The night closed around them, and Tawori collapsed.

They fell down together.

They were close, now. So very close.

He crawled to his feet. His chest hurt from Tawori's thrashing; his head ached and throbbed where he'd twice hit the wall; and his legs trembled with exhaustion.

But they were very close, now.

Tawori lay still. He rolled him over and slid both arms under his shoulders. One arduous step after the other, he hauled him the rest of the way.

The air in the house was nearly as cold as outside, and the night was denser. His Alassian sight scarcely availed him. He found the fireplace by touch, an arched alcove in a stone pillar within one of the walls. Some half-burnt wood was on the hearth. He searched for more, remembering having seen a crate with logs and paper. He found it and arranged the fire at best he could. Then he searched his brother's pockets for the silver box. He'd seen him use it, he was sure he could do it. He flicked the top open and rolled the little wheel a few times with his thumb. There were sparks, and the flame leaped to life.

By the light of the fireplace, he stripped the smaller bed of its covers and dragged the mattress in the heat. He took off Tawori's boots and muddy clothes, pulled him onto the mattress, and tucked him under the blankets. Then he went in search of water. There were empty glasses and cups in the cabinets, an empty bottle, and an empty kettle on the stove. There was no water.

He returned to the bedroom to find the dog settled on the mattress and intent on licking the mud from its fur. It paused and looked at him guiltily.

"Where can I find water?"

The dog blinked and stared.

"There must be a well or something."

There was indeed a well at the back of the house, with a small stone shed built next to it. He drew a bucket full of water and carried it indoors. Then he sat on the wooden floor, glass of water in hand. Tawori lay asleep, motionless, cold. The fire burned hot.

The dog finished cleaning itself, then snuggled close to Tawori and slept. The fire crackled and popped.

Late into the night Tawori began tossing and turning at the mercy of nightmares, mumbling a name, whispering incoherently. His breathing became unsteady, his heart quickened.

He placed a hand on his brother's burning forehead, and beneath his touch he felt Tawori's energies whirl chaotically, casting the mind into an abyss of hopelessness and torment. He concentrated, taking deep breaths in and out, his eyes closed, his touch infused with his life force. He focused on the soothing whisper of the fire, luring their minds both to a place of stillness. Little by little, Tawori's strain eased, and at last, a deep slumber came upon them.

He lay in the darkness unable to move, blind and mute. Tawori was beside him, cold, bound, hurt. They lay immobile side by side, their breathing overlapping, their heartbeats racing, converging. Everything else was silent. About them, emptiness.

They came out of nowhere and gathered around. He saw them. Shapes disfigured and tainted, spoiled, warped in darkness, red eyed, bright eyed. They had the guardian's power, his power—defiled, stolen. "I will break you!" Lenthieh's voice yelled, "I will leave nothing of you!" They bent down over them, over his brother and him, one body, two minds, two hearts beating as one, and worked their agony; they made them scream. He heard screaming as he woke. And he sat up hurriedly, greeted by daylight.

Tawori was watching him from the pillows with glossy, feverish eyes. He had a hand up toward him but let it fall back on the mattress, smiling wearily. "It was just a dream, Nillith," he murmured. He swallowed with difficulty, and his eyes went to the glass of water.

He helped his brother drink, and felt him shiver. Tawori took two shallow sips before pushing the glass away, mumbling, "Something warm would be nice."

And so he went to fill the kettle for him and lit the stove. He stepped outside in the chill morning air and went around the house to the stone shed he had noticed the night before. The door was locked. He forced it open with a hatchet he found thrust in a wooden workbench. Inside the shed, he found an ample stash of dry food, cured meats, cheeses, dry herbs and spices, chopped wood, and all about, mounds of white wool. He took what food he could carry, then stopped the door with a heavy stone.

He brewed a tea of thyme leaves and chamomile and brought it to the bedroom. Tawori was dozing with an arm wrapped around the dog. As the animal stirred, his brother woke and sat up, pulling the blankets tightly around himself.

The scent of thyme leaves filled the room. They sipped the tea slowly.

"I should have listened to you. I'm sorry."

Tawori stopped petting the dog and raised his gaze.

His voice was tired and hoarse. "We were both misguided," he said.

"You were right, and I was wrong. I didn't listen, and you got hurt."

Tawori shook his head. "You wanted to save a life. That is noble."

"I killed the sheep. It doesn't matter what I wanted."

"It does matter. It always matters. You have a kind heart. *That* matters."

"You're hurt. And it's my fault."

"But I will be all right. And it is not you who hurt me. Besides, I agreed to go in there. As I said, we were both misguided." He took a long sip of tea, then scratched the dog around the ears. "Is there anything to eat?"

"There's plenty."

"Have you fed the dog?"

"No . . ."

"Nillith, look at him, how gloomy he is. All night he has given me his warmth; and he is hungry. Fetch him some food. Hurry, now."

He sprang to his feet and saw a little smile on Tawori's lips, felt a spark of amusement in his mind. Last night's suffering was fading into memory.

He entered the kitchen and heard Tawori in the other room speak the ancient tongue. A moment later the dog came running, barking and wagging his tail. He fed him and gave him water, then brought cheese, meat, and dry fruit to the bedroom. Tawori took only a small bite of cured meat and nibbled the dry fruit unenthusiastically. He, on the other hand, was famished, so he ate quickly and eagerly. When his hunger was sated, he tended the fire.

"Do you think the humans fought as we did?" he asked afterward.

Tawori cleared his throat. "I don't think so. I think they sat in the dark and waited for death. That is what the unlife does to humans. I have seen it before. They do not fight it. It takes them quickly, a day at the most. They lose their will to live. They are not like us." His gaze hardened, and he looked to the flame. "We fight it, but as we fight it, it feeds on our greatest flaws. In my case, that would appear to be anger." Tawori's hands clasped one another in his lap. "I was angry at you for putting yourself in danger. I was angry that you wouldn't run when I told you to do so. I was infuriated because you couldn't stop me from hurting you. And all the while, I believed I was helping you, I was convinced of it." He fixed his gaze on him and pleaded, "I did not mean the words I said. You are not weak. *I* am. I have seen others resist the unlife's touch. I have trained as they have. Yet I succumbed to it. I failed you."

"You failed me?"

Tawori's gaze was repentant. He did not reply.

"But you did help me, Tawori. You helped me see again."

His brother made to speak, but instead looked down in silence. They said nothing for some time.

"I don't understand why the unlife ignored the sheep. Why it didn't feed on it until I made it."

"Ignore it? No," said Tawori. "The creature could never have left that place. It was bound to die there; the unlife had no use for it. But I think the humans came there looking for it. Perhaps the unlife knew others might come if the animal lived; with me, it found an able host. Had you not stopped me, through me it would have spread chaos and death. I would have served it to my last breath."

"We should seal that place."

"We will. We shall go back and make sure that nothing can stumble into it by accident. Though most wild creatures will have sense enough not to go near it willingly."

"More sense than I do."

"You and I both, it seems." Tawori flashed him a weary smile, then set his food plate on the floor. He lay down and tucked the blankets to his neck.

"I'm going out for a while. I'll collect our packs."

"No, please. I would rather you didn't go anywhere alone. We'll fetch them together. Tomorrow."

He nodded. "Or the day after that."

"I could sleep until then."

"I'll be just outside, then. The sky is clearing."

"Don't go far."

"I won't."

In the cold morning sun, he sat gazing eastward at the sloping grassland. The sky was open and weightless, and the snowy peaks of far mountains enclosed the landscape in ancient beauty. He had grown accustomed to the silence of these wilds, their openness and stillness, so different from the vibrant liveliness of the homeland he remembered; although in truth, his memories of home were little more than the vague remembrance of a dream once dreamt—dense luxuriant woodlands, and a cacophony of sounds—and he, in turn, was no more than a faint image, a fragment of whoever might have lived those dreams.

Red, sunlit grass waved in the white winds, and the far snowy peaks glowed with obsidian luminescence; then the vision faded. He wiped a tear off his cheek, stood up, and took a fighting stance.

Hours later, after the sun's warmth had waned, he gave his body rest and went inside. Tawori was asleep, not on the floor but in the bigger bed, pillows propped against the wall, a thick book open beneath his right hand, the dog curled up at his feet. The fire, lit only by cinders, gave little warmth. He fed it thin wooden sticks and watched the alcove fill with flames. He took off his boots and placed them with his brother's at the entrance, then set the room in order. He returned the mattress to its bed-frame, folded a little pile of muddy clothes neatly over one chair, hung the quiver and folded bow on the back of it, picked up his brother's swords and paused.

He sat cross-legged on the small bed with the longer sword on his knees and the shorter in hand. He pulled the blade from its sheath: it was about thirty inches long, one edged, and gently bent. The metal hilt was smooth and cold to the touch, with sharply raised lines that spiraled and crossed making the grip feel steady.

"I call that one Shie," Tawori said; he was sitting up on the bed. "It means 'shortest of two.'" A crooked smile brightened his face. "The longer one I named Wanninh, 'bringer of lightning.'"

"Will you teach me to sword fight?"

Tawori chuckled hoarsely. "Twice you've asked to learn from me, twice you've asked to wield a weapon. You know, there are other things I could teach you. How to read the human language is one of them; their literature is unending and oftentimes amusing." He held up the thick book he'd been reading. The cover depicted a green landscape with valleys and mountains, a tall, bearded figure in gray robes and a pointy hat carrying a long stick, and behind him, several shorter figures with backpacks and walking sticks. "I searched the bookcase," he said, "and I saw you practicing outside. I read half of this already, and took a lengthy nap. You were out there a long time.

"Tell me, why are you so fond of the combat arts? It seems to me you live in a world of your own when you practice. You hardly hear me if I talk to you, yet I think that you are well aware of your surroundings."

"It gives me peace of mind," he said simply, but Tawori waited for him to say more, so he tried to explain. "When mind and body are one, and the body moves without thought, there is no chaos and no fear, only the present moment. The flow of the world becomes a part of me, and I a part of it. It's harmony."

"Now you speak as the true guardian," Tawori said smiling. "In the darkness of the cave, your eyes shone bright red. They were magnificent. You have regained your power."

"Some of it."

"You wield it with skill. I owe you my life."

He shook his head. "I owe you mine. My life and my freedom. I will never repay my debt to you."

"There is no debt, little brother." Tawori got up and took Wanninh from his lap. He unsheathed it with a swift, silent motion and cut the air once. He ran his gaze along the blade, then looked down, smiling broadly. "In truth, you see, I searched for you these long years only so I would have a younger brother to pass down my wisdom to. For I know many things. I am a master of the sword and of the bow, a musician, woodcrafter, and scholar of linguistics, among other things. I am eight centuries old, after all—eight hundred and forty-three years, to be exact. I intend to teach you all I know, beginning with the sword skill that you just so happened to request I teach you. Because I am your older brother, and that is what older brothers do, I think. Yes, I think that is what we do." He sheathed Wanninh and handed it to him. "I will teach you to sword fight, so long as you continue to practice your archery, for you have yet to hit your target in the center if not by chance, and you will catch no prey unless you improve."

"Of course I will keep practicing," he said, accepting the sword. "I like archery."

"I know you do. But I think you will find sword-wielding even more to your liking. Which is why I'm striking a bargain now, before you have all the facts. You see, swords are no use for catching a meal."

"I'll practice archery every day you'll lend me your bow."

"I think I can accept that arrangement. But I imagine we'll soon need to make more arrows. You lost three already, and five are damaged."

"And I will help you craft more arrows."

"Now, now. You should not agree to everything I say; I am told I can become unreasonable when encouraged."

"I'm glad you're feeling better," he laughed.

"So am I. And the dog is feeling better, too. Dog? Where is he?"

A bark came from the other room; the dog followed it

wagging his tail. He hopped on the small bed and sat on his haunches.

"But I am sorry he lost his masters," Tawori said scratching the odd beast under the chin. The dog's pink tongue poked from his mouth. "How would you like it if we stayed here for some time? This house is welcoming; there is plenty to read. The dog will be happy, I think."

"I'd like that," he said. He petted the dog behind the ears. The beast yawned, making a high-pitched whistling sound. "Do you think we can bathe him?"

"Yes, yes. We should," Tawori said. "He smells awful."

And to that the dog said, "Woof!"

8
A KINDNESS

"THE SPACE BELOW feels hollow. I sense nothing at all." He was hunkered in the shade of a great boulder, a hand touching the muddy ground at his feet. "The earth and the air are empty. Not even the crawlers go in there." He despised the wet, stale stench of the place. The hottest sun of summer, bright in the cloudless sky, did not reach between the high boulders, cold and darkness lingered.

They had returned to check that nothing disturbed the heavy rocks sealing the grotto infested by the unlife.

Tawori sat outside the ring of darkness on a rock doused in sunlight. The dog lay belly flat at his feet. "It is uncommon to encounter the unlife in its true form," Tawori said, "and here, so far from our homeland, it is disquieting. Perhaps it came to Ydalon with Lenthieh's forces, or perhaps it is an older darkness, one that escaped our borders long before this war began. Either way it must have enslaved many lives before arriving here. It would have traveled the land until somehow it found itself trapped in this cave unable to get out."

"Why would it want to get out? Doesn't darkness wish for darkness?"

"The unlife wants nothing but to take and consume. Its sole desire is to blight the world. It cannot do that from inside this cave."

"I wish I could sense its desire, or anything at all. I don't sense thoughts, or feelings. It's almost as if . . ."

"As if it did not exist," Tawori said. "Because it doesn't. Not in this realm."

They walked slowly back, climbing the steep mountainside.

Following his brother's steps, he let his mind wonder about the nature of darkness and what little he knew about it. Words, fragments of memories, a cold touch lingering on his tortured body. For four years in the belly of the earth, under Seligor, in the prison his mind still revisited in his dreams, darkness had tormented him, watched him in hunger, longed to devour him. Back then he had known the unlife as a constant threat at the edge of his consciousness, although it had not been the same ungoverned darkness as this. He had not known it then, and only lately guessed, that the darkness of his imprisonment was one bound to obedience—Lenthieh's, perhaps, or his jailers'. It had not been a darkness free to do as it pleased, for had it been otherwise, it would have consumed his life.

His foot caught on a mossy root. He stumbled and recovered, his nostrils full of the metallic smell of fear and his senses tense in alert. A light breeze brushed his bare arms and legs. He looked about. He had been walking without paying attention and was now in the dense shade of tall pine trees. He could hear water babbling nearby. Ahead of him, the forest bed dived and hid behind a steep slope.

He walked as though in a dream through the earthly smell of soil and the snapping of twigs beneath his boots, and he came to a narrow stream of which shallow waters scuttled over rocks and pebbles. On its green banks, dense grass bathed in the heat of the sun. He watched the woods and the earth become aglow with myriads of lives. The sun's brilliance drenched everything red, it engulfed everything, filling all things with vibrancy and warmth, and life-giving strength. The water's currents pushed and split against rocks in a rainbow of swift-changing colors, weaving a symphony in the matter of the world. In it all, the echo of a slithering darkness emerged, unliving, intangible, direful. He remembered a place and a time gone by, another he, a jungle filled with the scent of familiar flowers, wet wood and earth, with a sun that shone hotter and brighter, and his father asleep on the riverside.

TAWORI STOOD BY HIS brother's side, gazing at his frowning face and the steady, ruby shining of his eyes. Nillith had grown taller in the past few months and would surely grow a while yet before coming into full adulthood, but he would never match Tawori's height—the years of captivity had scarred his growth as they had his flesh. Nillith's slight build, however, well complemented his nimbleness, for he possessed both speed and precision, agility and fine balance made him a skilled fighter.

The months of tranquility and zealous training had worked a great change. In him the guardian's power now flowed again unabated, and with it that quality was reborn, that inner charm which so powerfully had pulled at Tawori twelve years ago when for the first time he had seen the sobbing face of his little brother.

Tawori sat down cross-legged on the warm grass and watched the shallow stream go by. He listened to the birds call out to one another filling the forest with their songs. A squirrel came by and climbed the trunk of a pine tree; it searched the low branches with great zeal, staying for some time before moving on with its quest. Still his brother remained unmoving, the gaze fixed on the river and the sight turned to the world of energies. It was only after a long time, after white clouds had hid the sun and the summer sky, that he spoke, and his voice seemed to come from a place far away. "'I am the vanquisher of darkness,'" he said, "'it is my duty to cast the unlife from our realm.'" He looked down at Tawori, his eyes dull at last, white and doleful. "They were my father's words. When he spoke them to me, he also said that one day I would fight by his side. He told me that my duty would be to watch the borders between the worlds and to safeguard the keeper's light. Because the life of all things depends on it."

He sat down and looked at the river. "Tawori, why do our people fight for Lenthieh? He is not Keeper. Even if he wields the Light, he is not its keeper."

Tawori sighed. He did not answer right away, but found a pebble and threw it in the water, watching the splashes disappear.

"Because he is Miriethal's son," he said at last. "Because they believed him to be a loving, kind hearted son. And because he promised to be their savior. You see, Lenthieh returned to our people when they had lost all hope. On the night of the humans' attack, he came to them as if sent by the world's will. Our people needed salvation, and Lenthieh was there to give them precisely that. He came to them, to us, broken-hearted and in distress, carrying his father's body through the rubble and dust of our once city. He declared that Miriethal had died in the effort to protect us from harm, that he had given his life to save us all. He wept for him miserably.

"Nillith, this is what I *saw* then. Listen, now, you asked the question and there is only one way I can answer it. By telling you what I saw, what we all saw: a son grieving his father's death."

"Did no one suspect?"

"That he had killed Miriethal? No. Not then. Not for a long time. Not until he began unleashing the creatures of darkness, and by then our people were blood-bound in a war with humankind. It was too late to turn back. You see, Lenthieh told us his father had passed down the Light to him so that he may protect us from the humans. He swore to us that he would devote himself to that duty, and that he would make the humans see our ways. Most believed him word by word, and why shouldn't they? He played the part well.

"But I myself, I thought of you. What happened to you? Why were you not in Lenthieh's account of his father's death? You must have been at his side when the humans' weapon hit. I was sure of it, because then, I had been granted both the keeper's and the guardian's powers with which to protect myself."

"Granted our powers? What do you mean?"

"Well, I asked myself how could you have known to share your power with us. You were only a child. Miriethal must have guided you through it."

"Share my power? The guardian's power? With you?"

"With all of us. Do you not remember?"

He shook his head.

"How much do you remember?" asked Tawori. "Of the explosion, I mean."

He thought for a moment. "I don't."

"Nothing? But you know of what I speak. The humans' attack?"

"I know Irieth is destroyed and our forests have burned. I know humans are the cause of it. And I understand that's how this war you told me about began."

"But you do not remember this."

There were many things he did not remember. With the passing of time, some knowledge was returning to him. Fragments of thoughts, things said or heard, images scattered in such disarray that he could not piece together, except at times like today when something in the now would call out to him. Then a clear memory would emerge and become fixed in his mind. The memory of his father asleep by the river, the snake possessed by darkness, his father's teachings about the unlife.

The things he could remember, really remember, he counted on the fingers of one hand. There were other things he knew, or thought he knew—like the coming of the humans to Irieth and its subsequent destruction—but he had no recollection of them.

"Brother?"

He set his gaze on Tawori.

"On the night of Miriethal's death, the humans launched a weapon of great power on our city. If, as you told me, you remember our forests burning, then it is the aftermath of that attack that you remember. On that night, you and Miriethal stretched your powers to the limits of Irieth. You touched every one of us. You saved us all. If not for your combined efforts, no one would have survived. And well, if you do not remember this, I will keep on remembering it for you. From my point of view, that is. I know what happened. I know that you saved us."

Tawori smiled, but then his heart became shadowed and he frowned. "Our people already had their saviors. But Miriethal was dead, and you—only *I* knew of you. I approached Lenthieh and asked him whether someone else had been with Miriethal when he found him. At that, Lenthieh became angry. He said no, that his father had died alone, and had he not told me never to speak to him again? His tantrum did not go unnoticed. Others heard him, Theidrin, and Beriun—friends of mine—and few others. Then I was not the only one to see that something in the tale was amiss. But Lenthieh did not wait for us to spread doubt. He acted swiftly.

"He had not come to Irieth alone, others were with him, Alassians strangers to us. He sent them to hunt us. Few as we were, we were no match to them. We had to run. I and ten others escaped with our lives. Later, we sought to join forces with the humans. We had been the first to run, we were the lucky ones. Those we left behind did not choose whom to pledge allegiance to. Their choice was made for them. You see, our people are no longer free."

Tawori's heart was muddy with regret, his tone bitter. "I have asked myself whether things would have gone differently had I spoken about you then, had I told the others what I knew about the guardian. But Miriethal was dead, laid in front of my eyes with no breath in him, and I could not break his trust. For years I'd trusted his judgment more than my own."

They listened to the babbling of the stream, watched its waters flow by unconcerned with their presence and their troubles. He felt Tawori's heart harden under the weight of the past, but he himself looked to the future, for there lay his own struggle.

As he followed Tawori home, he pondered over their conversation. That evening they prepared their meal and ate in silence; then later, he lay sleepless in his small bed, thinking of what he must do, of who he had once been and who he must become. It was past the time he usually slept deeply when he voiced his thoughts.

"I have to go back."

There was no answer. Complete darkness filled the room; no moon or stars lit the sky outside.

He heard Tawori stir and turn.

He listened to the silence.

"You are not ready," Tawori said.

"I am the guardian... there's no one else but I. There's no longer a keeper. Darkness walks the land freely, and our people are lost. As guardian, I have a duty to—"

Stop!

Tawori got out of bed and moved about noisily in the dark, slamming the door on his way out.

He found him sitting cross-legged on the grass, a gray stone-figure immobile beneath the black sky, his gaze as hard as his heart and his sword, Wanninh, the bringer of lightning, unsheathed and beckoning on his knees.

He drew its sister sword from its scabbard. Shie's hilt felt familiar in his grip after the months of training, its weight light and balanced.

Tawori stood and took up a sparring stance.

That night he witnessed his brother's true strength. Tawori's mind was cold and unbending, and his bearing never faltered. It was as if a stranger inhabited him. Anger was his instrument of battle, a weapon at his command, as sharp and menacing as the sword. It was not blind rage but a stillness that filled his heart and mind. Tawori's attacks were unrelenting and savage, his defense impenetrable. Wanninh cut sharply, and soon it was smeared in blood.

He was granted no respite to mend his wounds. Time dragged on wearingly as he warded off his brother's attacks and fought to gain an advantage he never could attain. His body burned with lacerations, and Shie's hilt became slippery in his grasp. Breathing hurt his throat, and his limbs turned weak. Still, the blows came relentlessly.

He slipped and fell to his knees, panting. Dark, night blood dripped over the blue-tinged grass beneath him.

"Do not lie to me!"

He snapped his gaze up to meet Tawori's cutting glare.

"Or is it yourself you lie to, brother? With all your empathy, are you deaf to your own heart?"

He swallowed blood, and sat back on his heels, breathing hard.

"You speak of duty and obligation, but I will have you see the truth! If you are to defeat Lenthieh, you must know your heart. Should you refuse to see the truth of yourself, you will fail. You have not lied to me since I have known you, and yet you lie now, why? Why must you face him? Tell me, brother. I do not need to hear you say it, but you do. So, say it. Tell me why you must fight him. Why? You know the truth, so say it! Why must you fight him? Why!"

"He took everything from me!" he yelled. "He took my father, my freedom! He took my life! My place among my people! I won't let them! I won't let them bow to him! He is not Keeper! He is a liar! No one should follow him! No one!"

He panted harder than before, and his eyes burned with tears. The truth wreaked havoc through him. Tawori kneeled and squeezed his shoulders tightly, watching him with a spark in his gaze.

"Let your heart be heard, brother," he said softly, "and never again hide behind lies. Never. There is no strength in lies. See the world through your own eyes and stay true to your heart. You need not please my desires. You need not please anyone's desires. Whatever need drives you, I am by your side. As your brother, and as your friend."

"But I . . . I'm selfish."

"Yes," Tawori said, "so am I. So is everyone. Life is selfish."

"You, no . . . not you. You have done so much for me."

"And why have I? Out of selflessness, you think? I care for you deeply, yes. You know that. You hear it in my heart. But why do I feel the way I do, your power does not tell you, does it? Perhaps your smarts would, if you cared to question them. One day, perhaps, when you have found yourself again, you will see me for who I am. Will you still think fondly of me then, I wonder?" He smiled gravely and ruffled his hair affectionately; then he sat down by his side and watched the horizon. The first light of dawn tinged the cloudy sky orange and yellow. From behind the mountaintops, the sun rose fiery red and dense.

Tiredness weighed his mind and body. He sent his focus to heal the wounds of his flesh, reflecting on the truth of his confession and the burning ache he felt in his heart.

"It is a long way to the sea," Tawori said, coming out of silence. "And we will need more than a little boat to sail the Great Ocean. I do not have the knowledge to attempt such a journey. It cannot be helped. I know of a human settlement that supports the Alliance. My uniform and the rank it bears will tell them that I am not their enemy but a soldier and an ally. They are likely to trade with me if what I offer is substantial. We can buy passage there. It is a risk, for I was surely branded a traitor, and someone there might know this. But it has been many months now, and I can think of no other way to cross the seas."

A soft breeze whispered in the grass. His mind felt lighter now, easier. When he spoke, he said only, "What will you trade?"

"A hundred sheep. Two seasons have passed, and no one has come to claim this place and these animals. I do not think anyone ever will."

. . .

On the last day of summer, a hundred ewes, five lambs, and two rams with majestic down-curved horns descended the Caerphil. Wary of meeting other travelers, their shepherds kept a way off the roads, from the inmost Caerphil to the lower hills and then southwest, toward the rocky seacoast. At night, with their keen Alassian eyes, they guarded the flock from the predators of the wilds: coyotes, foxes, and many kinds of stray dogs. They traveled through mountains and hills for eleven days and came in sight of a castle that towered over a distant rocky cliff, its cream-colored stone darkened by the elements and the passing of time. Within its walls and towers, crowded against one another were old houses with pointy red roofs. This was the castle village of Kiolo in the midday sun of autumn, watching over miles of brown tilled earth.

Farmers stopped tending their fields to gape at the sight of a hundred sheep being herded along the North Road, and to shoo away the more daring animals. When they saw the pale skin and young faces, the white hair and eerie eyes of the two who shepherded them, they stared in horror. Some hid. Some called out insults. And some ran to spread the news of their coming.

On a signpost by the side of the road, thick, black letters read «The Madden». An arrow pointed to a conglomerate of wide buildings and pens surrounded by a high metal fence guarded by armed men.

Tawori stopped a short way from the gate at the sound of a man's voice shouting.

He waited uneasily a few steps behind Tawori, listening to the man's poisonous tone, enduring his accusatory glare. He did not understand human speech, but this man's contempt he could almost taste on his tongue. He did not like this man in the same way he didn't like the people who worked the fields and whose eyes were filled with hostility. He definitely did not like this place of metal, this prison for animals where, as he understood it, they were going to trade lives for wealth. His heart was heavy and full of guilt as he listened to the sluggish sounds of the human tongue, which his brother spoke quickly and fluently.

Some time went by before a small door in the gate opened and three humans walked out. They moved among the flock, counting and inspecting the sheep. One man spoke with Tawori. At last, resigned, Tawori nodded, and the flock began moving through the gate.

"Are you keeping that one, Nillith?"

He frowned a moment, confused by the question, then he looked at the lamb he had carried in a sling for many days. It had grown bigger and stronger, and now stood unsteadily by his side. He couldn't help but smile at the creature, although he was sorry to part with it. He patted its haunches and said, "Go on, little one, follow the others." Then with a heavy sigh he watched it walk away on its skinny white legs.

Tawori's sigh echoed his own. "Let us go, brother. Dog? Come."

The bushy dog stood a moment looking at the flock, immobile as a heap of hay in the sun, the snout high and dignified. Then his nose sank; he turned and plodded after them obediently.

"Would they not take him?" he asked.

"No. They said they have no use for an old dog."

They followed a wide black-paved road uphill, walking side by side quickly. Dark looks and angry words assaulted them time and again.

"Wear my hat, and hide your scars," said Tawori.

He took the offered hat, gray and brown like the rest of Tawori's uniform, and wore it low on his brows. In the distance, he saw the dark wooden gates of the castle close ominously; then he bent his head and watched the road pass beneath his boots. It seemed his poor attempt at hiding his scars made no difference. The humans' hostility accompanied them all the while, until at last, on a narrow stone bridge sided by the remnants of a once sturdy parapet, they found themselves alone before the gates. Nobody came to greet them, nobody turned them away. Tawori's hollers met no answer.

When it became clear that they would not be allowed inside, no matter their reason for being there or the promise of payment, they turned their backs to the gates, and disheartened, made their way down the hill, through sounds of scorn and mockery.

He kept his eyes on the black road beneath his feet, but with his other senses he watched the human's hearts and minds, from the castle hamlet to where the grass split in wide turns and the road slithered ahead past the fertile fields and into dry land. Loathing, contempt, envy. The feelings rippled through him like eels in a mud-pool, filling his heart, crowding his mind, ensnaring him. He saw a group gather and follow Tawori and him, drawing nearer step after step.

Abruptly he turned and sent the flow of his life force to his eyes. But Tawori's hand forced his head down. "Don't!" hissed his brother. "It would make things worse."

JOWANI SAW IT ALL from the window of his living room. Two Alassians. Very pale, as they say, skin whiter than milk. The one in camouflage, tall, young, but white-haired—hair that flitted like a kite's tail in the wind—stepped in front of the other, a skinny teenage boy in rags. Their dog, a fine sheepdog with dreadlocked fur, barked and bared its teeth at the scumbag Devent and his brats, handguns winking in the sun, about to play law again, but not if he had anything to say about it, and certainly not in front of his property.

«Oh, you are not doing that!» said his Moley in her loving tone of disdain, her thin, dark face shaking lightly with age.

He thrust the magazine into the chamber of his TM5 and clicked the thumb safety.

«Oi! You hear me?»

«I hear you, Moley.»

He opened the front door and stepped outside.

«What they done with 'em sheep?» Moley cried from inside the house.

Jowani made his way through the ten feet of weed-overgrown porch, his old junk of a leg threatening to give in under his weight.

On the road, trigger-happy Sani was yelling. «He means, Shut your shithole!»

«Get on your knees! Both of you!» barked Devent, but then he shut up an instant because the dog barked louder than he could. «Put your hands where I can see them!» he went on afterward.

«We only wish to leave peacefully,» said the Alassian in uniform, not raising his hands, not kneeling, calm and composed as soldiers come, or as they used to, back in the day.

The second Alassian, a good foot shorter, turned and looked right at Jowani in his porch—gun's muzzle pointed at the sky and a finger on the trigger. The scars... Jowani lost a thought looking at the scars—and at the eyes, white like they say, queer eyes, but smart: smart eyes, like he knew something. The scarred boy was the only one who didn't flinch. The others all jumped at the clamor of gunfire, ducking and pointing their guns, drawing a sword.

«Not on my property!» Jowani thundered, in the pungent smoke of his TM5.

They were stunned like idiots.

«It ain't it!» honked Devent—the scum couldn't keep his cool if he tried.

Jowani shot another fast string of bullets to the sky, then took aim.

«You lost it, mate!»

They cursed and spit on the asphalt in turn before leaving, the fine sheepdog barking after them.

The tall Alassian put his sword away. In very clean Taelic he said, «Thank you for your help.»

«That's not much use, son,» Jowani said, and he was nodding at the sword.

A flashing grin. Of all the odd things he'd seen in life, an Alassian grinning on his doorstep ought to make first place.

«Perhaps you are right, sir.»

Be damned if he started laughing, too.

Jowani cleared his throat. «Your uniform,» he said, «is the Alliance here?»

The Alassian shook his head. He wasn't smiling anymore. «It is only I.»

«You speak funny. Name's Jowani. I saw you go by with those sheep. And I said to my wife, Moley, that's not something you see every day, eh?»

«I am Tawori,» said the Alassian, «and my brother, Nillith. We came to sell the sheep and trade for passage. But we were not allowed in town.»

«Where're you headed?»

«Across the sea, to Sa'dar. We take the fight back to our homeland.»

«Are you with the Alliance?»

Private First Class, said the uniform. No gun. He did not answer right away, and when he did, he sounded cautious. «I was, but I am no longer. I was stationed at Oxwish under Captain Liu Logain for over two years.»

«Captain Logain, I know the name. Well, did you run?»

«Run?»

«Yes, run. From the fight.» The Alassians had come closer. Their dog was sniffing his fence. Tawori frowned, and his eyes went thin—the whiteness of them made Jowani feel uncomfortable. «Do you even know?»

«Know what?»—he could cut ice with those eyes—«I left Oxwish before winter,» he said, «to help my brother.»

Hideous scars. «What happened to him?»

«War happened to him.»

Jowani nodded. «Oxwish was destroyed, beginning of winter,» he said. «My son was there. He's with the Alliance. I don't know he's alive. We've seen no military since, heard no more news. You're the first uniform we see in what . . . nine months. I thought maybe you stole it, but you don't look like it. You all right? Come on inside.»

«Good lords!» Moley squealed. Her lips were tight, and her eyes had gone wide, just like the time he'd brought home that boa snake, fat as his own arm, the beautiful thing.

«Can't you see the man is shaken?» Jowani told her. «Bring him a glass of water or something. Sit down, son.»

«Good lords! Good lords!»—she was slamming cabinets' doors in the kitchen. «In my living room!»

The leather chair hunched under Jowani's weight. He put the gun flat on the armrests.

The scarred boy stood boots-on-the-rug in the middle of the room, silent, immobile as a painting, staring at the other, who'd sat down on the couch with his head in his hands.

They heard the kettle scream. The dog went to drink from Kimi's old bowl. When Moley came back, she set a tray with tea, bread, and butter on the coffee table. She took in a thin breath when the Alassian looked up at her.

«Thank you,» he said. He spoke a few words in his own language, and the scarred boy sat down beside him. The couch squeaked.

«Fine dog is that,» Moley said.

«And a fine shepherd,» said the Alassian. «We found him on the Caerphil last winter. His owners had died. It was their flock you saw earlier. We sold it at The Madden, although not for a good price. A hundred sheep for a hundred druu.»

«Worth five hundred if you ask me.»

The Alassian nodded.

They picked up their cups.

«Sir? Can you tell me more of what happened at Oxwish? I had friends there . . .» He had a wretched look on his face.

Jowani told him what he knew, which wasn't much. Third-hand news from a sailor at Junu beach who'd heard it down at Port La Gola from a truck driver who'd seen the place on fire, black smoke for miles—burned for three days, he'd said. People knew better than to go near the combat zones by now, so there was nothing else to tell, except that if someone had survived, they would have shown up somewhere, but they hadn't.

«Williem Hose . . . Williem . . .» the Alassian thought for a moment. «Bill? Bill Hose?»

«That's him, that's my son!» said Jowani.

Moley was leaning forward on the edge of her chair.

«I worked with him,» said the Alassian. «A brilliant pilot and a fine instructor. A brave man.»

«Brave and stupid,» Moley sobbed. She stood and went into the other room, no doubt to hide her tears from the scarred boy's doleful stares.

THE LIVING ROOM WAS growing dark. Old floors lined by the years, water-stained ceilings, worn leather, fabrics, and furniture. His brother stood up and shook the old man's hand. In the gloom of dusk, the man's skin was the color of charred wood.

When they were alone in the room, Tawori turned to him. "We will stay here tonight. In the morning the man, Jowani, will help us find passage. This was a good meeting." He walked to the small window facing the road and gazed outside, the weight on his heart growing again more painful. "The place of the Alliance was attacked," he said. "It happened nine months ago, shortly after we left. It was destroyed. If anyone has survived, no one knows."

The pain burned and throbbed. Tawori endured it in silence.

After a long while, he spoke again. "The base at Oxwish was well armed, but no human defense can stand against the unlife." He walked back to the couch and sat down beside him. "I feared a battle with you there. I could not risk your safety. I would not let you be taken again."

"He came for me. But I wasn't there."

"Running was the right thing to do," said Tawori. "If you had not acted when you did, I would have made you run soon after. Or at least I would have tried."

"I wish I could have warned them. I wish I could have told them."

"That you are the guardian? I am glad you could not." Tawori's tone was hard. "Had the humans known of your value in this war, I dread to think what they would have done to you. I know without a doubt you would not have kept your freedom. That is why I could not risk anyone learning your secret. That is why I had to be by your side. To make sure the truth was not discovered. I played with words, asked for a favor and got away with what I wanted, with guarding you.

"When we found and brought you here to Ydalon, you were trapped in some place of the mind between sleep and wakefulness. By day you lay with your eyes open, yet you were not awake. You were like this for a long time. Do you remember any of it? I did not think you would. A selyn tried to heal you . . . and succeeded, eventually. She entered your mind more than once, searching for a way to bring you back. Every time she attempted to wake you, I feared what she might see in your memories, what she might learn."

"I remember a presence in the nightmares," he said. "It was like a mist shimmering with light, a warmth."

"That was she. That . . . is Aruhin."

He could not bear the dread and grief of Tawori's heart. It made his own throat close up as he replied, "She couldn't have learned who I am, because I didn't know who I was. All the same, I have caused this."

"You? No, not you," Tawori said bitterly. "You knew nothing. But I knew all. You had no part in this. It was I who brought you to them. Without the humans' resources I never would have found you. Without the strength and numbers of the Alliance how could I have brought you to safety? And without their healing, and Aruhin's . . . I do not think you would have survived. I used them, all of them. In doing so, I brought Lenthieh's wrath upon them. This was my doing, and mine alone."

The light of a single candle gave heat to the colors of night as the two humans entered the room bringing food and beverages. Tawori looked away from him and turned his words to the human tongue.

9
DARKNESS

BLUE WATER STRETCHED to the horizon. Thin white clouds smoked in the sky. The hushed expanse glimmered with diamonds in the autumn sunbeams.

He was sitting alone at the bow of the boat, beneath the first and smallest of the Red Reef's three sails. The small fishing vessel would take him and his brother to the southernmost shores of Sa'dar. Tawori, as per his liking, was helping the humans with their craft, conversing with them and learning to steer and handle their boat; his brother had missed the company of talkative folk such as these, and among their deep voices, his laughter glided light over the wind and waves. They were three men of dark complexion with very short black hair, except for the oldest among them, Semuel, who had gray in both hair and beard, and blue in the friendly, bright eyes.

They had departed the coast of Ydalon two days before in the first light of a dark and ominous dawn. Their four legged companion had found new masters in the old couple and would remain behind, for they could not bear to burden him with the dangers and hardship that awaited them.

Bidding his farewells to the shores of Ydalon, he had felt the strain of fear in his mind, a dreadful pause. Now, however, with the endless ocean flowing beneath him and around him, something deep and grand was waking inside him. An urge made him restless. Clasping tightly the handrails, he looked ahead with fierce longing.

A splash of spume smooched his naked feet dangling over the cold water, sprinkling fine droplets onto his face. The wind blew strong and cool against his lightly clothed torso. The ocean held such great a power. The voices of countless lives filled its depths calling to him. He let his focus flow without conscious thought, and his sight shifted. The water's depths filled with a light brighter than anything he'd ever seen. He watched the chaotic energies of the ocean, the winds, and the sun, gazing into the distance and down below. There was so much to see. Brilliance and movement, innumerable life forms floating and surging, meeting and parting ways, singing in unison a song of creation. Great wonder filled him.

"The humans are watching you."

He summoned his mind from the depths of the ocean. "They are not afraid," he replied, "although they do feel awkward around us."

"Awkward?!"

He blinked the shine from his eyes, constraining his gaze to the world of things, and breathed deeply.

"They feel awkward?" Tawori repeated. "Nay! Not around me!" His brows rose in thin arches. "Well, surely only now that I am here with you." He sighed. "I thought

I had made good progress . . ."

"You have. They're not frightened of you anymore."

His brother sat down. His long stream of hair flew this way and that in the wind. "Awkward . . ." he muttered. He undid the sling of his ponytail and fastened his hair in an untidy bun.

"How many more days will we be at sea?"

"Why, have you already tired?" teased him Tawori.

"No, I could sit here forever," he said as much to his brother as to the ocean and the boat beneath his buttocks.

Tawori smiled. "The crossing may take six days, nine, or sixteen. The sea will decide."

For a time they listened to the wind blowing in the sails.

"What will we find in the south of Sa'dar? How far is Irieth from there?"

His brother thought about the question for a moment. "I suppose," he said, "we will find ruined towns and farmlands, empty roads, and of course the wilds. Farther inland there is a sandy desert that looks like a stormy sea, I read, and hollow canyons that twist for miles between walls of red rock—I saw pictures of them. And the woods, ah, the woods, each one different from the other. But I have never been in the south of Sa'dar. As for where Irieth is, that, I know. It is over a thousand miles to the north and then a thousand more into the deep woodlands of our domain. How far have you been from Irieth before all this?"

"Not far," he said.

Tawori watched him expectantly.

"I have been as far as the great river Sesa and the waterfalls," he explained, "and I remember looking often into the distance at a chain of high mountains covered in trees, but I never went there."

"Not far," Tawori agreed. "Many times I rode to the outskirts of our domain where the woodland begins to thin. On foot, that is as long as sixty days, if one does not get lost."

They watched the waves part and give way to the small vessel.

"What is our plan once ashore?" asked Tawori.

He glanced at his brother, puzzled. "Walk north?" he replied.

"And then?"

He shrugged and shook his head.

Tawori tapped a tune on the handrail with his fingertips. "I suppose 'walk north' is as good a plan as any."

On the morning of the eleventh day, land appeared on the horizon. An unbroken chain of soft mountains beneath which long sandy shores unraveled east and west. The Red Reef folded its sails and dropped anchor a short distance from the coast, to await the return of an inflatable lifeboat that under the cold blue sky paddled ashore and then back to sea.

They stood facing the sea and watched the fishermen's boat turn prow and sail away, then they began their journey through sand and tall grass.

Due west they could see a city with high buildings like gleaming needles piercing the sky. They made their way toward it for some time and came upon a wide black-paved road plagued by the remnants of human society. They paused before it in silent dismay. A spine of concrete divided the road in two halves. While the east side was empty but for little clusters of grass poking the blacktop, the west side was densely littered with vehicles and wreckages crammed against one another, like the skin shed by a giant snake made of steel. Broken windows, open doors, bones and rotting bodies. Nothing moved.

They walked the silent road a mile inland, heading north toward mountains that quickly grew nearer, until a passageway carved into a high wall of stone loomed in front of them. From within it, the breath of the earth came cool and foul.

He shone his gaze upon the darkness in the tunnel, and saw no end to it.

They chose not to enter, but traveled a long way back and east, before finding a narrow path that climbed the mountainside in an endless succession of turns.

He bore Shie at his hip, now, her black scabbard tied at his belt with a leather sling. He drew it quickly, echoed by the near-silent sigh of Wanninh. It was over in the gleam of a single swing. The creature lay dead at his feet, something like a small wolf with gray fur, slim and beautiful.

"It carries the unlife," he said.

"We shall not rest easy tonight," Tawori remarked.

Not that night, not the next. They slept in turns, and soon, day and night began to blur. The land changed from hilly to flat, from fertile to barren and dry. Wide canyons lined the earth like hollow snakes slithering for miles. The weather warmed, and the sun shone heating a thriving grassland till this grew dry and begged for rain. The rain poured abundantly one night and never stopped.

Dark clouds grumbled like the hungry belly of a beast.

All about, the outlines of broken buildings cluttered flat muddy ground. They had taken refuge one floor up, under a roof that barely stood, held only by two of its former four walls. Tawori sat with his back against one of the walls, his gaze turned to the evening dullness. Beside him, his brother stirred and moaned in his sleep, growing restless, until at last he woke and sat up, listening, gazing in one direction and frowning.

The rain battered loudly on ground and metal, it splashed on the soft earth and the leaves of trees. The sky flashed with light, but there was no thunder. Fury coursed through the clouds, lightning after lightning, never striking the earth.

Nillith stood and walked to where the roof reached outward into the night. His eyes shone a moment with ruby light, then faded to dark. "The woodlands, how far are they?" He spoke quietly against the roaring rain.

Tawori rose and went to stand beside him. Nillith had meant the deep woodlands that are the Alassian domain, for Tawori had told him that they were growing near.

"We are close," said Tawori, his own voice silvery over the storm. "The rain carries the scent of our trees. I think perhaps a day walk."

"I think ... no, I'm sure of it. I sensed fear. I don't know how far. And strife. Maybe ten miles, maybe eight. Maybe more ... That way!" He pointed north into the rain that fell tirelessly filling the ground with rivers. "Someone is out there. I can't sense that far now, but I heard them in my sleep. I heard them calling me."

THEIR PAWS STRUCK the ground with muffled thuds, raising wet leaves and spouts of soil. They galloped into the night, charging southward at great speed. Around them the jungle was dense. Above them, the dark stormy sky hid behind a black canopy. Only the rain seeped through the leafy roof in heavy drops, in streams, and torrents.

The riders held themselves astride with difficulty, barely seeing the path ahead, shifting their weight instinctively left or right to accommodate for a sudden dodge as time after time a tree appeared out of the night to stand in their way. They cried out, if a kaara collided against a fellow runner, or bumped against a tree, but never did they slow their pace.

When they reached the forest's edge and the kaaras paws sank ankle-deep into boggy ground, still the riders pushed them to run faster. A hunting darkness was at their heels. The bristlewolves' howls drew nearer, and the beasts gushed from the jungle into open land, hefty creatures with the spiked fur of the porcupine and the wide-toothed mouths of sharks. Behind them, trampling the earth, rode a swarm of archers on horses swirl-eyed from the chase. The rain beat and howled.

Lightning split the sky and the thunder boomed. The radiance lingered an instant; then darkness closed around the hunted and the hunters.

"Tarkins!" Aruhin rode ahead of the pack on her white kaara, Izzisho, and she had seen three winged creatures flying fast above the jungle, dark against the lightened sky. She looked at the falyn beside her, riding the red furred Onnara, his sword drawn and his body hunching into the wind. "Theidrin!" she called. "We will not reach the shelter before they come! We must make our stand, here!"

The falyn looked at her, his eyes black with anguish.

"We'll have no hope here!" he shouted.

"We cannot outrun them on this marsh!" cried Aruhin. "We have to fight! You must give the order!"

Lightning lit the night, carving the silhouette of a draconic beast plunging head-first in falcon dive, wings flat against the elongated body. At the last instant it spread its wings and zoomed with the gale, spouting fire from its jaws over the kaaras and their riders. Screams and roars filled the bog. Kaaras tripped, slipped, and crashed into one another, their riders tumbling from their backs.

And the bristlewolves were upon them.

In unison, the hunted turned and fought. With swords, with fangs, and claws. Blood grimed the soil and lightning turned the earth crimson red. Rain beat down over the battlefield. The draconic creatures whirled and screeched, breathing fire over enemies and allies alike. Arrows rained unseen.

"Archers!" Theidrin yelled, pointing back toward the forest. "Give cover!" At his command, the warriors rallied in pairs, a sword for a bow, and let loose their arrows. In the distance the horse riders broke their line and dispersed.

Roars and howls were swallowed up by the almighty thunder; then the three draconic terrors filled the sky with their screeches. They swooped down spitting fire, lifting their prey into the air and releasing them to their deaths.

Amidst the chaos of battle, the bristlewolves' howls died out, and the beasts paused all at once. The kaaras pounced at their throats without hesitation, tearing flesh from bone. Fire lit the sky as one of the tarkins fell like a shrieking comet. It struck the earth, raising a billow of mud, and skidded for thirty yards with its wings flung out, trampling everything in its way. Then it lay wailing and breathing smoke into the ground.

A ruby glimmer breached the stormy dark, and the fugitives looked to the south. There, atop a small grassy mound, they saw the guardian erect against the night, arms reaching toward the battle, eyes glowing with red crystal radiance.

Silence drowned the field.

"The tarkin! Slay the tarkin!" cried Theidrin, his voice like an eagle's call in the emptiness of the sky.

The tarkin's throat was gashed, and the beast screeched its last cry. Loud wails echoed it from above. Another of the terrors plunged headlong, ejecting a whirlwind of flames that turned rain into vapor. It did not break the dive, but whacked the ground head first and lay bone-broken and dead.

Vast wings beat the air and slapped the rain in great gusts as the last tarkin landed on the carcass of its kin, perching like a hungry vulture and shrieking dreadfully. It planted its taloned wings in the mud, crouched forward, and breathed a wall of fire. A shadow leaped from its back, white hair flapping behind it like drapes in a windstorm. It raised a hand in command and pointed to the red-eyed figure atop the mound.

The guardian fluttered. He was pitched backward with arms and feet aloft and for a moment was suspended as though floating on water. Lightning opened the sky. A sludge of darkness towered above him, deep black in the blinding flash. It dived down upon him and crushed him on the ground. The guardian screamed with a voice young and wounded. Then the sky closed, and the thunder crashed.

The night howled and snarled with bristlewolves freed of the restraint and maddened with rage. The tarkin screeched and spit fire. Standing before the beast was Lenthieh, a twisted smile on his face. A blade reached for him, alight with current, and Lenthieh sprang back, his hair grazing the blade. His footing faltered, and he stumbled. Above him the tarkin smacked down a taloned wing at the sword wielder, who dodged it narrowly. The wing dug a hole in the grassy sludge and was stuck.

Tawori plunged forth, quick as a spark, this time driving Wanninh, the bringer of lightning, deep into Lenthieh's chest. The surge of power lit up the night, jolting from raindrop to raindrop. Lenthieh bawled, and the tarkin spewed fire. Tawori dived through the wave of heat and beyond it, cutting the fire in half with his sword. He slipped over the mud, caught himself, and bounced forth again. The tarkin's tail smacked him from behind, tossing him into the air and away. The beast spread its wings and took flight with a gust of wind. A barrage of arrows chipped at its scales as it rose higher and higher, and it veered northward and fled.

Tawori didn't watch Lenthieh flee. He got to his feet, winded and coughing, and began to run through the battle raging around him. He scrambled up the mound to where his brother lay, glowing eyes fixed on the sky above, rain beating his face, the scarred hands grasping his drenched woolen jumper, grabbing, pulling, tugging desperately at the unlife inside him, fighting to catch his breath.

"Nillith! NILLITH!"

He heard Tawori's voice and saw his life force shining strong and steady above him.

"Nillith, I can help!" cried Tawori. "Lend me your power! Hear me! Hear me, brother! You have to share the guardian's power. I can help you! I will help you! But I need your power, Nillith. Share it with me. You must do it now. Nillith, now!"

The unlife crushed his chest. His mind was aflame with a cold so intense that it split his skull. His eyes burned like coals in their sockets, and his throat felt as though it had been slit open. He heaved a breath in, and forced out a word: "—can't!"

"You can do it! You have done it before, remember? I told you. I told you, I remember. Nillith, please. PLEASE, BROTHER! Give me the power to save you! I beg you! FIGHT!"

Tawori's feelings raged louder than the storming rain; his fear and anguish broke through the iciness of his own darkness-drenched heart, and washed through him like a flood, rousing him. He reached out with all his will, giving himself wholly to his brother's feelings, embracing them, becoming them. He saw Tawori's eyes fill with a ruby glow, and saw him straighten up. A warm touch lay on his chest and his torment stilled.

He drew breath.

Then Tawori began to lift his hand, and the unlife thrashed inside him, clawing at him like a beast dragged from its den. His chest rose with the pull and he grabbed Tawori's wrist, but was pushed back down. An anguished bawl escaped him. He kept his eyes on Tawori, kept his focus on him, for should their bond break now, the unlife would devour them both.

"Bring a living beast!" yelled a voice. "Hurry!"

His vision went black and he felt his consciousness fade. His hand hit the mud with a flop. Cold and emptiness filled him. He held on to Tawori's presence in the dark. At last he heard him speak. "It is done. It is done, brother."

Then everything went silent.

THUMPING RAIN DROWNED the sound of battle. The enemy was bested—it fled, hunted, into the jungle. Those who did not follow in pursuit, gathered at the grassy mound where the guardian—who was only a boy not yet grown into his third decade of life—lay unmoving, so that to some it seemed he had perished. But Tawori held him as one holds a sick child, and when he looked up, his eyes were fierce and his words urgent. "We must get him out of this rain," he said, "quickly!"

Theidrin kneeled down beside him, looking first, in disbelief, at the guardian, then at Tawori with grievance. Stiffly he said, "We have a shelter a few miles south of here. You may take him there." The falyns looked at each other a moment, then both turned to Aruhin when she spoke between them. She said, "Make haste, Tawori."

Theidrin stood and began giving out orders, to search the fallen for survivors, to make prisoners of Lenthieh's followers, to kill the servants of the unlife.

A kaara came trotting up the slope, and the Alassians made way for her. Her black fur speckled with orange and ash was thoroughly soaked, and stuck to her body as she moved. With her yellow eyes she sought Tawori's gaze, and when he saw her, he spoke in surprise. "Yinna?"

She blinked her greetings. She lowered her face and sniffed the guardian. Even so washed by the rain and dirtied with mud, his scent was the scent of Akihalla. Yinna bumped her head against him, grunting softly, and licked his scarred cheek. The cold chill of darkness was in him. Yinna lay by the sons of her late mistress and roared her wish.

Tawori lifted the guardian, and with aid sat him astride the kaara's back.

"He will live this time yet," said the falyn helping him. Squeezing Tawori's shoulder, he added, "It's good to see you, my friend."

"It is good to see you too, Beriun. I knew not if you lived." Tawori's eyes moved from Beriun to Aruhin. He sat behind his brother and passed an arm around him. Yinna stood, and set off galloping into the night.

The rain fell sideways in the gale. In the distance, lightning struck. Thunders boomed and clashed. Tawori unfastened his jacket and let it flap wildly behind him. He hugged Nillith tightly against his chest, taking one of his icy hands in his own, infusing the touch with his life force. He had taken much strength from his brother in ridding him from the unlife. He feared dreadfully for his life. He thought he could feel his presence slipping away, at every stride of the kaara getting weaker and further from life.

IN TAWORI'S ARMS, the guardian dreamed of a cold, deep nothingness pressing all around him. In it he sank as though in waters where the up and down often switch places, never knowing where lay the surface and where the abyss. For a time that seemed unending, he dreamed this dream of nothing and knew he was in a place between life and death, and that if he fell too far from the surface, he would lose his way forever. The notion did not frighten him, for there was no fear in this dream, only the turbulent waters pulling him this way and that. In the iciness of this dream he found a haze of warmth and stretched a hand to grasp it, holding on to it with the feeble strength he had left. After a long time the warmth grew, and a path opened that would lead him back to life. He ran along it with urgency, but with dread found himself drowning in a pool of sludge, so that as he ran he swam and he stayed in one place going nowhere but under. Until at last all stilled. He was no longer submerged and no longer running, but floating on thin grass. Red tulips and clusters of white whispers surrounded him. There was a pond nearby and trees bathed in daylight. His father sat smiling by his side, his face dimpled and kind. He said, "Now lie in the sun for a while. You will soon feel warm."

YINNA SHOOK THE WATER from her coat and settled near the guardian child. They had laid him on a thin rubber mat in the middle of the shelter's widest room, where a fire burned hot and bright under a high, dark ceiling. She began cleaning herself and the boy—though because they had covered him with pelts, she could tend only to his short hair and scarred face. When, pleased, she deemed her task complete, she nestled close to him and purred for long until his breathing eased, becoming deeper and softer. Then she, too, slept.

. . .

Tawori watched Aruhin soothe the flow of his brother's sickened energies, as she had done months before. At long last Aruhin rested her hands in her lap and looked at Tawori from across the fire.

"He will be all right," she said. "His dreams are as clear as spring water."

Tawori was relieved to hear her words and ashamed to be listening for her voice.

"He is not the broken thing he was a year ago," Aruhin said. "Perhaps you did what was best to heal his hurt, and you brought us our guardian, in the end. Perhaps. Perhaps you did what was best. I only wish I had known." She looked down again. After a long silence, she returned his gaze.

He was relieved to look into her eyes, and ashamed to be doing so.

"I am happy that you have your family back," she said, and she tried to smile.

That was hard to watch, but he did watch her try.

Her voice was shaking when she asked, "For how long have you known?"

It took Tawori a moment to understand that he should answer. "He was five," he said.

"Of course. That day. That was . . . over ten years ago." Her whispered words were nearly lost in the crackling of the fire. She did not try to hide her pain.

"He was not the only broken thing, Aruhin." Tawori's throat hurt. "When I learned of him . . . Even after I learned . . ."

Nillith lay breathing softly. He did not usually sleep serenely for long and he might soon stir and moan.

Without thinking Tawori caressed the scars on his face with the back of his fingers. The need to feel those scars sometimes arose when he found him sleeping soundly. He longed to feel the hurt that had been done to his little brother, the hurt he had failed to prevent. "Look what they did!" he blurted out. "How could they? Why would they? Who would have the heart to do this?" He glanced at Aruhin and only then heard his own words. "He's . . . he's so young!" he said, "So sweet! You should hear him laugh, Aruhin . . ."

She dried her tears with the tips of her fingers. "I am glad your brother lives, Tawori," she said.

He did not reply. They both looked away.

THE WARRIORS returned from battle, and the room filled with Alassians and kaaras, wet, tired, and wounded. The injured were tended; then those who were able gathered elsewhere. By the fire, the guardian slept soundly, dreaming of life and light, of his home, his father, his childhood. He watched the days of the life he had forgotten rise with the sun from the east, when his father and Tashira had been his whole world, and set on the west, when that world was taken from him. He relived his life, remembering himself. He explored the woodlands with his father, fought the unlife in the river, found humans near the great, thundering waterfalls. In mind and heart, he sat at the council. He stretched his essence to every Alassian in Irieth, and through them fought the might of the humans' weapon. He learned his own strength anew, the firmness of his will, the clarity of his focus, and the depth of his love for all living things. When he awoke he was whole, one with the flow of the world, born in the power of the guardian and tempered by the cold touch of darkness.

To the watcher it appeared that the young guardian, having sat up waking from his sleep, was now staring into nothing as though in a trance or in shock, his eyes shining red with power.

"Guardian?"

The call was repeated a second time, but there came no answer.

Meyvath set aside the waterskin and the plate of food he'd been instructed to offer. He made as if to stand but paused halfway, hesitating, debating whether he should call for help. He knew the others were discussing issues of great importance, and unless imperative, he did not wish to disturb them. He mulled over the matter, neither standing nor sitting, and while he did, the shine of the guardian's eyes faded. The youth turned his dull gaze to the kaara lain asleep at his side and caressed her face.

"Guardian?"

He did not answer, but looked around the room.

What he saw was a wide, empty hall with a lively fire in the middle, white walls, and a green floor with yellow and blue lines painted over it. A great many kaaras slept on the floor, sitting with their legs tucked under them, or curled up and wrapped in their tails. There were a few Alassians, also sleeping, except for one nearby, a willowy falyn with wavy hair grazing his shoulders. He was sitting onto one foot, frowning, and uncertain. On the ground beside him were a plate with food and a waterskin, plump and full.

The thought of water made him swallow. His throat felt parched and his tongue was dry as paper. He pointed to the waterskin. "May I?"

Brows drawn together, the willowy falyn nodded.

He took the skin and drank avidly. As sweet water washed down his throat, he opened his senses to the surroundings.

He learned that this room was built underground, that a number of Alassians were gathered on the floor above, that Tawori was with them and that he was angry and resentful.

"My name is Meyvath," said the falyn.

He replaced the cap and put the skin back where he'd found it. He stood up, and a draft made him shiver. He was naked. Clothes were hanging on cords that stretched across the room. He found his underpants, his socks, his once white trousers now dark with stains, his shirt, and his woolen jumper. His boots were too soaked to wear, and he left those to dry. The shivers continued, so he took a pelt from those he'd been sleeping under and wrapped it around himself. Then he strode out.

"Uh, wait?" called out Meyvath. "Where are you going?"

Up a set of stairs, through a long corridor brightened by daylight, left, past three empty rooms with closed doors.

The fourth door was where he wished to go. He pushed down the handle and entered.

IN THE AMPLE ROOM, desks and chairs had been piled up against one of the walls. A storm battered the broad windows, buffeting and wailing. Two dozen Alassians sat in a circle of chairs with wooden seats and shiny metal frames. Some wore human clothes, others Alassian garments, all were covered in mud and bruises, their clothing long-traveled and battle-worn.

They had been gathered here since dawn, arguing at first, then exchanging news, then again arguing. Two of them were on their feet. Theidrin, having accused Tawori of betrayal, stood within the circle of chairs, his angry gaze to the windowed wall where Tawori paced back and forth with his arms crossed.

"And now you come to take leadership," had said Theidrin. "No one will acknowledge you as our leader. Not after you've kept us ignorant of your quest for five years, Tawori! You have no right to lead us now."

"And why would I want to lead you? It is not I who is guardian!"

"He is your brother! And he is but a child. He cannot lead. You expect us to follow you, just as *he* follows you."

"You know not of what you speak!" Tawori had cried, checking his pace and facing the other. "I lead no one but myself. For all these years I have followed my heart; and it is I who followed my brother here, not the other way around. He chose to leave the safety of Ydalon. He chose to come here. He found you and brought us to you. I have not led anyone, and I certainly would not lead him. This quest is his own. As much as I would have kept him hidden, kept him safe and miles away from Lenthieh. Even so, here I am. Because his will demanded it. He is guardian, not I. He chooses the path and I follow it. As you all should follow it. As you all will. When you see him for who he is, when you see the will of the guardian in him, you will follow him. Not me, Theidrin, him. Him you *must* follow!"

When the door opened, everyone turned to look and

the conversation ceased.

Tawori strode across the room, his face turning from an angry scowl to a gloomy frown. "Are you well?" he asked. "It has been only hours."

"I'm fine," he replied. He glanced at the people sitting in a circle, and at the one standing; then in a low utterance meant only for his brother to hear, he said, "My name is Redien."

Tawori beamed at him. "That it is!" he said jubilantly. He gave him a fugitive hug ruffling his hair. "It is good you have remembered!"

He smiled at his brother's sudden joy. Then frowning, he asked, "Lenthieh?"

"He has fled. Alas, he has fled. Wounded and defeated, but we suspect not for long. Come sit with us. There is much you should hear."

Silence reigned as he crossed the room, but he heard what others wouldn't. Scrutiny, curiosity, judgment, and deep in everyone's heart a profound sense of relief.

A burly falyn brought an extra chair, and he took his seat at Tawori's side. His brother made the introductions.

The falyn who'd been arguing until a moment earlier was called Theidrin. His hair, a mellow ash-white color, wound over his left shoulder in two thick braids that dropped down to his lap. He had a handsome face with a strong jaw and a determined gaze, but his heart was filled with worry and doubt and with a subtle sour taste, which Redien thought might be envy or something deeper still he couldn't quite place. Theidrin had been a fighter for the Alliance of Ydalon, and Redien remembered glimpsing him through the shadows of his nightmares.

At Theidrin's side sat Aruhin, whom Redien already

knew by name. Now he saw her simple beauty and heard the gentleness of her careful heart. When her eyes met his, she wished to speak, but instead she smiled and bowed her head, and her long ivory hair brushed the floor, like drapes.

Many others in the room, Redien had never met but knew by their hearts and minds, for they had often hunted the unlife with his father. The oldest among them was a falyn named Nuren, whose chalky hair was plaited thinly and tied in a thick braid that on the floor circled his feet. Last to be introduced was the burly falyn with an unkempt mane of alabaster dreadlocks, sitting beside Redien. When he heard the name Beriun, Redien's vision dimmed with the echo of darkness, and he recalled the words "*Leave him, Tawori. He will not survive the night.*"

He shook the memory and focused his attention on his brother.

"Beriun, too, fought for the Alliance. So that makes six of us including myself. Six survive of the eleven who first opposed Lenthieh. Yet more have stood up to him. Every Alassian in this room is a warrior of the light and Irieth's champion, trained in wielding the power of both keeper and guardian. Except Meyvath because he was made a warrior only a decade ago and his training is incomplete." The willowy falyn who had remained by the door looked anxiously toward them. "We have fought many battles together—"

"Yet not enough to earn each other's trust," Theidrin interrupted.

"Whilst more than enough for reprisal," Tawori retorted.

"Too many have died, Tawori," Theidrin said, "and I do not speak for our kind only, but the humans also. It was a slaughter we found at Oxwish, a grave loss that might have been averted."

"Their deaths weigh on my conscience," said Tawori. "I will carry the guilt always."

"What good will that do?" Theidrin shifted his gaze from Tawori to Redien. "When Lenthieh attacked Oxwish, we were not there to protect it. We were tracking the two of you, following a trail that from a cave near Tidfyl led north and east. When news of the attack reached us, we hurried back, but by the time we arrived, Oxwish was in ruin. There were no survivors and no sign of the keeper or his army."

"Why do you call him keeper?" A tense silence filled the room. All eyes settled on Redien. "One doesn't become keeper by killing his father and stealing his power. I don't know what one becomes then, but not keeper. So don't call him that. The title is not his."

The wind blew rain against the windows. It was the only sound.

Old Nuren grunted. "The title belongs to the one who holds the power," he said. "Perhaps you will shed light on what misfortune befell Miriethal the night of the human's attack. Tawori told us a little of your tale. We would hear an account of it from you now."

"No." A palpable tension rippled through the circle of warriors.

"No, young guardian?"

"Just not now."

Nuren's gaze impaled him right through, but it was another's eyes Redien peered into. He was having trouble keeping the memories in the past. He closed his eyes against the fever that flushed his cheeks and made his bones ache. His mind felt awfully sluggish.

"We will hear the tale when he is ready to tell it," said Gwendier. Redien met the falyn's unfriendly gaze, which did nothing to hide the reprimand in his heart. "The touch of the unlife is plain on his face. He's had scarcely any rest, when he needs plenty." Like Nuren, Gwendier's face showed the signs of old age, but while Nuren had withered through the centuries, Gwendier still had a powerful, solid figure. He wore the uniform of the Alliance, and his hair was gathered in a thick bun at the back of his head.

Nuren's heart grumbled on, but he said nothing more.

"After Oxwish was destroyed, we had two options." Beriun shifted his imposing size on the little chair beside Redien. His voice was deep and rich. "We might go east to Terica and there seek a new alliance with the humans, or we might return to Sa'dar and bring the fight back to Lenthieh. We did the latter." The burly falyn looked at Theidrin, who resumed his tale.

"We salvaged a transport from the remnants of the Alliance base and spent some time studying it. At last we felt ready to make the journey, greatly thanks to Nishath, who is no longer among us.

"Once here, we made our way into the jungle and sent scouts to spy on Lenthieh. We found kaaras hiding in the west. We had thought them all dead, but they still lived, although small in numbers. Among them were several of our warriors, lucky fugitives, some of whom you see here"—he addressed the circle with a nod and a glance—"though only last night there were more . . ."

The falyn's heart was bitter with resentment. His eyes skipped twice from Redien to Tawori and back, before he said, "We believed we had the numbers to strike at Lenthieh. We were wrong. He has grown stronger. Stronger than our scouts had anticipated. He has bolstered his ranks with greater numbers and has many terrible creatures at his command. The bristlewolves and the tarkins are only the fastest among them, but there are more. Stronger and deadlier things. It is as if"

"He has made ready for me."

"he knew we would strike," concluded Theidrin.

There was silence. It hummed with skepticism.

After a moment, Aruhin spoke softly. "I do not believe that last night he foresaw your coming."

Redien shook his head. "Nor did I think that I would see *him*. I failed to sense his presence. I cost us the advantage." He clenched the seat of his chair so tightly that his fingertips hurt. "There were many of you, and many that hunted you, all crying out to me and, yes, the darkness of his flying beast shrouded him but that justifies nothing. I should have sensed him, I should have been ready and I wasn't! I messed up. I was slow and I was weak."

His words silenced the humming of their minds. A long moment went by as they watched him mutely.

"Yes," Beriun said, "now I do believe he's your brother."

Tawori's laughter burst out silvery.

"Beriun," said Aruhin, "I do not think your timing is appropriate."

But his brother's amusement made Redien smile.

"Oh, all right," the selyn said, "you do have a sweet smile."

Had his cheeks not been ablaze with fever, he would have blushed. He averted his gaze and watched Tawori shake with laughter.

"And about your ranting," Beriun said, "the two of you have saved us. Which is more than we could have asked for."

"But it isn't enough," said Redien. "It hasn't been enough before, and it wasn't enough this time."

"You are alive," Tawori said, the laughter swiftly forgotten. "It is all that matters."

"But how many have died?" he asked the pavement beneath his stockinged feet. "And how many more will die?"

"You cannot save everyone."

"But I should. I should save everyone."

"You did all you could. You will do better next time."

"Next time I will end it!"

He flinched at the sudden fury in Tawori's mind. He looked up and saw that fury on his face. "Next time, I will not leave your side, brother."

They gazed at each other; then Tawori patted his shoulder and his features relaxed into a tired smile.

"Still, the guardian speaks true," Gwendier said. "Lenthieh was vulnerable. Such an opportunity will not come again. Worst yet, now he knows the guardian is near, unless he trusts that he has killed him."

"He doesn't."

Gwendier's unfriendly eyes sought Redien's. "How could you know?"

"Because he wasn't trying to kill me."

The old falyn's mind asked the question a second time.

"Four years in a cold cage of stone. Looking at

nothing but darkness, listening to nothing but silence. I lived, because he wasn't trying to kill me."

"You say he wants you alive?" Theidrin asked.

"I don't know what he wants." He turned to Tawori. "Will he have made for Irieth?"

"We believe so, yes. He not only was gravely injured but lost his army of wolves, two of his tarkins, and most of his archers. We think he has retreated to Irieth and it will be some time before he can strike again."

"His beasts fly fast."

"Yes," Theidrin said, "but not over long distances, and an attack here would require more than tarkins. He would need to bring an army. An army would take at least thirty days to travel here, and that only if they ran as though their lives depended on it."

The tawny floor of this room was polished to a shiny mirror. Redien could see his shade reflected in it, in the faint light of this stormy day. On a sunny day, he might be able to see his features clearly, perhaps his scars, too. He had not looked into a mirror since his last day in Ydalon so many months ago. He wondered whether he looked any different, now, than he had then.

"What do you intend to do?"

He dragged his gaze to the falyn and blinked a few times before he saw him clearly.

"Sleep."

Theidrin waited. "And after that?"

"Rest. Until I am well. Then I will make for Irieth."

"That isn't wise. He is stronger there than he would be here."

Redien nodded, he knew that was true. "But there's strength for me there also."

Mistrust drenched Theidrin's voice, "And what strength is that?"

He coaxed his tired gaze about the circle of warriors. Their eyes scrutinized him. He had spent his childhood hiding from these eyes; now here they stared at him, though so few they were. "Alassians," he replied.

Theidrin's doubt rang louder than the words the falyn spoke so fiercely, "Do you expect to be welcomed there like a prince of old come home? You might be guardian, but nobody knows you. Nobody owes you allegiance. Just because you were praised, here, for tilting the scale of battle in our favor, do not expect the same to follow in Irieth."

"You might be wrong, Theidrin," said Ehanna, a youthful selyn with a fruity voice and silver hair that fell in waves over her breasts. "Many of our warriors back home will side with the guardian if he presents himself to them. They wish to be rid of Lenthieh. They will seize the opportunity at once."

"And what if they don't?" said the falyn Omoin. "What then? We will have walked into Lenthieh's clutches, and this time knowingly."

"When they witness the guardian's power, they will know there's a choice to be made," Beriun said.

Theidrin stood up waving a hand hastily. He said, "And which choice will they make? Who would side with this child guardian? This weedy little boy?"

"Has he not proven that he can fight?" said a falyn with short braids adorned with bronze rings and brown feathers, whose name Redien had forgotten.

"He has proven that he possesses the guardian's power," Theidrin said, "nothing more."

"I beg to differ."

"The child who stood outside the keeper's home," Aruhin said softly, "in plain daylight and with no reason to be there." Theidrin turned to look at her, his hostility in check. "Miriethal's secret child. How many of us guessed at first glance last night that he was that child? How many in Irieth will have the same reckoning when they see the shine of his eyes and hear the youth in his voice? Will that not sway their hearts?"

"It will," agreed Ehanna.

"Doubtfully," argued Nuren.

Theidrin remained silent.

Redien had shut his eyes against the faint daylight. The world was spinning. It wasn't an unpleasant spin, on the contrary he found it inviting as well as dizzying. He was hugging himself tightly in the heavy pelt which seemed to give off no heat and did nothing to quell his shivers. A bitter cold enveloped him and he might as well be standing naked in the snow-blowing winds of the Caerphil. His heart throbbed in his head, and nausea had taken up residence in the hollowness of his throat. He wanted very badly to lay down.

He stood and made for the door.

"Wait," Theidrin called.

He didn't wait.

"Nillith!"

"That's not my name to you," he snapped. He turned and faced the falyn, regretting his own tone and knowing that the falyn resented it.

Tawori had followed him and stood beside him quietly.

"My name is Redien."

There was a pause in Theidrin's mind before he nodded, and almost apologetically said, "Redien, we must discuss what is to be done."

"I'm going to sleep." He turned and the way out disappeared into blackness. He felt arms around him, heard a scuffling of chairs. After a moment he saw again and straightened himself up.

"You are cold as ice," Tawori told him.

"I'm naked in the snow," he murmured, fighting a shiver.

"That is an odd thing to say." His brother passed an arm around his shoulders, and with a final glance at the room, helped him out and down the empty corridor. "Don't think about snow. Think about the sun. Think about the Red Reef on the open seas."

"Oh, no, no," Redien groaned. "I have seasickness."

He leaned into Tawori and listened to him chuckle.

"I do not think you can call it seasickness if you are not at sea, brother," Tawori said, "but let us do something about it."

10
THE CIRCLE

THE SOUND OF RAINFALL came in through narrow windows high on the walls. Tawori rekindled the fire, which soon burned hot and bright in the dark. He removed his boots and wet socks and a layer of muddied clothes, then sat warming his limbs in the heat of the fire.

Redien was eating cold food: lentils, greens, and a small piece of cured meat. The meal was tasteless, as far as he could tell, but it helped ease the sickness in his gut. He felt better already in the comfort of the under-room, near the fire and surrounded by the restful sleep of many. The beautiful kaara he had awoken next to, an hour or so earlier, yawned a sharp-toothed yawn and shook her downy head like a lion shakes his mane; her black coat flecked with orange and gray shimmered in the firelight. She opened her big yellow eyes and rubbed her face gently against him, groaning with pride, though a note of melancholy wavered deep in her heart.

"Who is she?"

"Her name is Yinna," Tawori said. "She was our mother's kaara companion. I had not seen her since Mother died."

The kaara hummed. She rose and arched up her back in a slinky stretch, then came closer and settled down curling her body around Redien. She seemed to doze off again. He felt compelled to stroke her cheeks, and when he did, she purred softly. Her heart ached with loss and now so did his, although hers knew what it had lost while his did not. He looked at his brother. Tawori's white, still gaze glanced back at him.

"How did our parents die?"

"So you ask." But then Tawori was silent; his eyes went to the fire and he blinked slowly. His hand slipped under his soiled shirt to feel a hot bruise that made breathing painful. "There was a battle against the creatures of darkness," he began. "They came in great numbers when we did not expect it. They struck at the city's heart. It was sudden. We were unprepared. Our mother was expecting you, you were to be born soon. Her power was weakened and she was unfit to fight. Our father died protecting her. His name was Llangdath. He was a great warrior, greater than I will ever be. He fought alone and against too many. He could not keep her safe. When I found them, she alone still lived, and she was gravely wounded. I brought her to Miriethal. Something was poisoning her, he said. He did not say what, he did not say 'unlife,' he said not what did it, only that she was poisoned. He took her to his home. If the keeper's power would not save her, nothing could. And nothing did. When I saw him next, Miriethal told me that you had died with her."

Tawori's tone was defenseless, naked. Tiredness weighed him down, not only physical tiredness but of the mind, a long endured loneliness awakened tenfold.

"Why would he lie about me? You would have wanted to know."

"I would have wanted to know..." Tawori looked past the firelight at memories far away. "I think... I think the truth of that night blighted Miriethal. It haunted him just as the ignorance of it haunted me."

"Lenthieh...?"

"I do not know. I thought, perhaps. But if he was there that night, I do not know of it."

They sat in silence. What little appetite Redien had had before, was all but gone. He put aside the rest of his meal and took a few sips from the waterskin.

"And so it is Redien." Tawori looked at him and smiled. "Yes. Yes, indeed. Redien, you should sleep now before someone comes to question you." His brows rose and he tilted his head to the entrance; the warriors who had been gathered upstairs were coming in, some looking toward them with questions in their minds.

Redien lay on the thin mat and curled up in the nook between Yinna's legs, snuggling close to her soothing, warm presence, freely given and most welcome. He rested his head on her front legs, his back against her belly, and fell asleep.

He slept peacefully, waking once to relieve himself (and then the sky outside was black with night). At his next awakening he found his body rested and ever so hungry. The wide room was nearly empty. The kaaras had left, Yinna had left, and so had his brother. Only three Alassians slept in the dark corners. Meyvath was once again with him, waiting for him to awake. The willowy falyn offered him water and food, which he accepted saying his thanks to Meyvath's relief and satisfaction.

"I must go tell the others that you woke."

He left hurriedly.

Redien guzzled the water and ate to his fill, then made his way out into daylight. He breathed fresh air and stretched his gaze into the distance. The day was young and the sky was filled with puffy clouds pierced sharply and brightly by the rays of a sun high and warm.

He had exited a hulking edifice three floors in height and one in depth, gray walls and wide windows. Now he stood enveloped in a yellow beam of sunlight at the center of a small courtyard; hard black pavement heated the bottoms of his feet. He noticed a few kaaras and Alassians ambling the passages between half-destroyed buildings reclaimed by nature, bramble bushes and patches of moss growing wild all throughout.

He turned to meet Aruhin's gaze; she was walking toward him and stopped by his side.

"Greetings, Redien," she said. "Tawori went hunting."

"With Beriun." Two miles to the northeast; they had caught prey and were in high spirits. "They're heading back," he said.

A screeching caught his ear, and he raised his gaze to see a falcon swoop down, then land neatly on Nuren's forearm. It beat its wings to gain balance, before folding them gracefully. The old falyn stood a few steps from the entrance of the shelter. He was dressed in Alassian clothes, worn and stained with use and battle: a loose chest-robe with strings wound around the forearms, a long skirt, and a wide cotton belt. The robe and skirt looked as though they had been blue, sometime ago; the strings and belt were white or so they had been, a time long before that. Against the squalor of this desolate village, the falyn looked even more scrawny and aged.

The bird chittered a moment, but fell silent when Nuren spoke the words of the ancient tongue. It listened. It spread its wings and flew. A second falcon took its place. This one wailed and snapped its beak at Nuren, but when the falyn spoke, it listened eagerly. Then it took flight, and away it went.

"We did not know when you would waken," said Aruhin; "you have slept a full turn of the Haven and a while longer. We will gather for council when all have returned."

That should be soon, he thought, no one was very far. He did not need to ask what they expected of him at this council; he was ready for it, as ready as he would ever be.

"Thank you for leading me out of the nightmares," he said.

She was puzzled.

"Tawori told me what you did for me in the place of the Alliance. You ended the nightmares. You brought me back to the light."

Aruhin bowed her head, and with that gesture she was beautiful and full of kindness. "It was Theidrin who found the way. I followed his guess. Theidrin is our hunt leader. Our lives and the lives that were lost weigh heavily on him. He did not mean to insult you with his harsh words. He wishes only to protect us."

"It's all right. Although, it was unpleasant to be called a little boy. But Theidrin assumed wrong, and I couldn't explain myself. Well, I *felt* weedy, but I am better now." He smiled and she smiled too.

"In your words I hear a likeness to your brother."

Redien shrugged. "I had forgotten the sound of words, but he made me remember. He speaks a lot."

There was a pang of sadness in her heart, quickly brushed aside.

"That he does," she laughed.

They stood conversing in the sun until a breeze blew softly from the east.

Aruhin led the way through the broken buildings. She walked with the slender grace of willow branches in the wind, her straight ivory hair flitting behind her, down to her knees. Her thin jumper, the color of prunes, trembled lightly in the breeze, and her knitted skirt, a wan unripe mulberry-pink, swept back and forth over her dark leather boots. He walked beside her, stepping lightly over hot little stones that probed the soles of his feet. The road suddenly sloped, then wheeled left and disappeared giving way to rows of half-fallen red brick houses with white balconies. Low, green hills rose up behind them, then sank, and past those was only white sky.

As they neared the left turn of the road, they heard a mellow roar from between the buildings. Yinna trotted out with her fur shining handsomely with reflected sunlight, a black sapphire with tufts of gray and smudges of fiery orange. She stopped in front of Redien, looking into his eyes and blinking slowly. He scratched her hot cheeks. She was smooth like satin. She hummed and nudged him with her nose. He knew what that meant: *ride with me!*

He leaped onto her back—a much easier task than he remembered—and with a rush of sudden triumph the boy within him awoke. His heart raced, and he cheered her on as she sprinted through files of empty red buildings, the wind whistling wildly in their ears.

When she slowed to a trot, he saw they had come around in a circle and were returning to Aruhin.

He leaned back smiling, one foot buried in the kaara's hot fur and the other hanging from her side, her flanks shifting slickly under his palms with each step of her proud walk.

Aruhin cupped her hands around her mouth and yelped a call at the sky. Soon a snowy kaara came running. His eyes were a pale aqua-blue. She hopped on his back, light as a feather, and rode with both her legs hanging to one side, graceful as a princess of old.

The kaaras took them beyond the village to where a hill rose softly, toppled with long grass and tall chestnut trees. They climbed the hillside and dismounted at the top. A few warriors were already gathered there and more were traveling up the same way to join them.

Redien stood gazing northward where the land dived softly toward a sea of trees: the woodland domain of Irieth. He spotted Tawori and Beriun walking uphill on an old cobbled path, growing slowly bigger and nearer. They carried between them a plump boar hanging from a pole by the feet. When they reached the top, they laid down their burden.

"We brought something to look forward to," Tawori said. He took the quiver and folded bow from his back, then grinned, tilting his head at Beriun. "Though someone will struggle to keep his mind off evening supper."

"I certainly will," Beriun said candidly, "and I won't be alone in that."

"Now that we are all here," Nuren called them, "let us sit."

Sixty-two Alassian warriors—dressed in all sorts of attires, armed with bows, quivers, swords, and daggers, their long white hair flying in the wind—sat in a circle on the grass at the top of this hill overlooking to the south a human village and to the north the woodland domain of the Alassians. A few kaaras settled nearby and they would listen at first, though soon they'd doze off.

A somber silence descended over the hill.

"I woke up in the middle of the night," Redien began. "I remember this unsettling feeling as though I'd been having nightmares; only, I knew I hadn't. I thought about the humans, and sure enough, there was that feeling. Dread, and panic. They knew something terrible was about to happen, they knew they were going to die."

He recounted the night in detail, from his awakening, to the sighting of the object in the sky, and to how his father had commanded him to share the guardian's power. At first he had not known how to do this; he had not known it could be done. He'd watched his father weave threads of the keeper's light over Irieth, and in his example, he had stretched the guardian's essence to its limit.

"I believed Miriethal to be my father, until Tawori told me otherwise," he explained to the warriors' confusion at his use of the word "father."

"We fought the blast of the explosion, a power nearly overwhelming. Time seemed to come to a standstill, and I could see it all. I knew who needed help. I came to their aid and acted through them when they couldn't. I was . . . determined." He met the gazes of the warriors. A murmur had grown in their minds.

"Continue," Nuren said.

"Do you not believe me?"

"On the contrary, brother." Tawori spoke quietly by his side. "I think they believe your every word."

"Then what's the problem?"

"What happened next?" Nuren insisted.

"Next it was over," he said. "I felt drained. I was baffled stupid, like I'd lost my wits." He'd healed his wounds, and sometime later he'd watched a tarkin land over the debris. On its back was Lenthieh and a second person who might have been a falyn or a selyn or neither.

"And what of Miriethal?" Nuren asked.

"He had been tending to his wounds. He saw Lenthieh and called him by name."

"Was he gravely injured?"

"Nothing he would die from, although I am sure he felt the exhaustion as much as I did."

"How long after the explosion was this?" asked Theidrin.

He shook his head. "As I said I was exhausted . . . and maybe I'd healed my wounds too quickly. After that I couldn't get my mind straight. Everything around me seemed strangely still and silent. I don't know how much time passed." He told them what little he'd seen of the fight between Lenthieh and his father, how useless he had been; they wished to know more than he could tell them. "My father ordered me to run away with Tashira, so I ran."

He saw the jungle burn around him and heard the

crackling and swooshing of fire. The scream pierced his mind, and his fingers dug into the soft earth. His father's voice rose louder and louder over the quickening of his own breath.

"Redien."

He found Tawori's gaze. "What?"

"You were . . . distracted."

"Yeah. Did you ask me something?"

"Theidrin did."

He beat the dirt from his fingers and looked at the falyn who gazed back at him but said nothing. Nuren spoke in his stead, hardness in his heart. "Did you witness Miriethal's death?"

"No. When it happened Tashira was taking me away from the battle."

"Yesterday you claimed that Lenthieh killed Miriethal," the old falyn said, "yet now you say you did not witness this. Your words are void, nothing but a child's fantasy."

Buried beneath the hostility in the falyn's heart, grief burned as deep as Redien's own. It weighed on Redien's voice as he replied, "I heard him cry out in my mind; I felt his pain as my own. I felt his life force fade. I listened to him die. I listened as hard as I could until there was nothing left to hear." But he could hear it still: his father's screams, the stifling pain, Tashira's flanks between his thighs, his fingers buried in her fur. Stop. Turn back. Turn back!

Weak child.

"I told you my father was weakened by the humans' attack, but his life was in no danger. Lenthieh attacked him, and this I saw. I was not with him when he died, but

I know how his life was taken from him and by whom. I know because what Lenthieh did to him, he later did to me. I knew what awaited me when he found me."

He told Nuren of how in the forest he had been captured, shot down, and bound. He told of Lenthieh's chanting, the words in that harsh language that had shaken the world. He told of the creature that had overwhelmed him and had drunk his life force, how it had mangled his essence forcing it out of him until consciousness had left him. "When I came to my senses Lenthieh was in my mind, and he was furious. I don't know what he did, or intended to do. I couldn't stop him. I thought he would kill me, but he didn't." He could taste the blood in his mouth and feel the choke in his lungs. "He was furious," he said again.

"He failed to take your life," Theidrin said.

"No. I was alone, and there were seven of them. I was at his mercy. If he wanted me dead, I would be dead. The guardian's power is what he wanted. He'd taken the Light from my father, and from me he would have the power of the guardian."

Theidrin held his gaze for a long moment. "Lenthieh told us that Miriethal had passed down the Light to him."

"He lied to you."

"Perhaps he left Miriethal no choice."

"He wrested the Light from him along with his life."

Theidrin shook his head. "To force one's essence from one's body, we do not know of a way if not through the guardian's power, which you hold. So how could Lenthieh have taken the Light by force?"

"He has just told us how," intervened Gwendier, speaking as bluntly and as harshly as the day before.

"Through a language we know naught of? A tongue unknown in history?"

"Unknown or perhaps forgotten," Aruhin said.

"We have long wondered how Lenthieh controls the unlife," said Ehanna in her mellow tone. "Now we know."

"And I suppose we trust the boy's word without question," Nuren argued. "Only by witnessing his memories we will know the truth."

"You are not serious!" cried Aruhin. "He is our guardian!"

Theidrin laid a hand on Aruhin's shoulder and looked at Nuren. "That will not be done," he said.

The old falyn shook his head, but said nothing more. Beside him, Gwendier set his cold gaze on Redien.

"It is not without question that I believe his word," Gwendier said. "On the contrary, I asked myself many questions, most of all, why does the guardian live? Why having him in his grasp, did Lenthieh not end his life and let the power be lost? Why if not because he did not wish it lost? Miriethal is dead and Lenthieh holds the Light. These facts are irrefutable, yet Lenthieh's claim is not. His succession wasn't witnessed. The power he possesses over the unlife is beyond our comprehension, and beyond our comprehension may be other powers he is yet to reveal.

"If Lenthieh wishes to gain the guardian's power, if he has the means, but has thus far failed to acquire it, it would explain why he would not kill him, why he would rather risk the chance of the guardian slipping away from within his grasp. If he believed that, were he to try again, he may succeed one day where he has failed."

For a time the wind whispered words in the tall grass.

It spoke of the sky and the earth, of the coming of rain and the smell of flowers.

Redien met Theidrin's gaze. "And did Lenthieh try again? In four years, surely he had plenty of time to attempt the deed again, if that were his goal."

All eyes turned to Redien. He said, "I don't think he did."

"You don't *think* he did?"

They waited for him to say more.

The sky had grown heavy with clouds. Daylight seemed to darken.

"In the place where I . . . where I . . ." He rubbed his scarred wrists and swallowed dry. The pull of their expectations drew the words from him, "I woke up in the dark and I thought maybe a day or two had passed, because I was so hungry. I was bound as they had bound me in the forest. I was gagged and couldn't speak. I couldn't work my focus, I couldn't see. I was in a small empty room and it was cold. There was a door, always shut. No lights. No sounds. Only silence. I couldn't sense anyone or anything. I was alone. I'd never really been alone before . . . never truly alone. It was like I was . . . missing something."

Beside him Tawori stirred, his heart screaming against the pull that impelled Redien to speak.

"The air was *filled* with darkness. The unlife . . . was in the walls, the stone, waiting, watching, thirsting. It made it hard to think, to stay awake, to . . . remember. The days, and the hours . . . they were endless. Always silence and darkness. Then they . . . always . . . they came to . . . a-and I . . . I couldn't see them. I couldn't sense them, as if they weren't there. Only what they did made them real. I-in the dark . . . They . . ." The pull eased, and he swallowed back nausea.

They were looking at him and what they saw filled them with pity. He removed his shaking hand from his mouth and took a deep breath. He would tell them what they must understand.

"They never spoke to me, or to each other. But the nightmares did. The nightmares were loud. Always the nightmares. After some time, I became confused. I confused real memories and the dreams. And I began to forget, so that room, I'd always been there. In the darkness. I forgot there was anything else. I forgot how it is to see, to not feel pain and hunger and thirst all the time. The nightmares became real. They *felt* real. So I could never awake. Sometimes I could tell the difference between the nightmares and the silent dark, sometimes I couldn't. In the nightmares I saw many things that pretended to be real. I saw Lenthieh try to take my power, but I don't think he was ever even in that place. I don't think he ever tried again. If he had, I would know, I think I would know. Because real pain always cut through the nightmares."

Tawori's presence had grown deafening. His heart wailed with guilt and regret, and his mind stormed with anger. He was glowering down at his hands clenched in his lap and didn't notice when Redien looked at him. Tawori blamed himself for those years of suffering. Redien had come to know the terrible regret in his heart; and it pained him. Tawori had freed him from endless torment, yet he struggled with dark feelings, as if he'd been the very cause of it. But his brother had given him back the joy of life, he had sustained Redien gently and patiently, giving freely and unconditionally. Redien loved him completely.

It was with that love that he willed the essence of his being to join him with his brother. This time there was no hint of the dreadful wrongness of many years ago, no fear, no pain. This felt right, and easy as breathing. Then his brother could hear him, hear his heartfelt gratitude.

Tawori looked up to meet his gaze and wiped away tears before they could spill. "You'll make a fool of me, Nillith," he fussed, smiling, his heart warm, and his mind quieter.

"These are no coincidences," said Beriun, giving his friend a long, hard stare. "Eighteen years ago your parents' deaths. Your brother hidden by Miriethal. Then the humans at our doorsteps. Miriethal's death and Lenthieh's return. The keeper's power changing hands. The unlife doing Lenthieh's bidding. War. These are all one and the same."

"There is no knowing it," Tawori said.

"I tell you, this is not the will of the world at play. But it is someone's will, all right."

"Why deny the possibility, Tawori?"

"Deny?! I do not *deny*, Theidrin! Always putting words in my mouth. Be quiet! you said. Let the others speak! Well, I have been quiet! I sat here listening to you pass judgment on my brother, question him, demand that he speak of things he should not be asked to speak of. I waited for you to satisfy your curiosity. Because my opinion was asked, I said, There is no knowing it. And if you cannot fathom it yourself, the meaning of my words is: we do not know the truth of this, and if anyone knew, it would be Miriethal."

"Yet he would not speak of it with us," said Theidrin. "Although he told *you*."

"Miriethal told me nothing!"

"So you keep saying. You would have us believe that while our keeper had your brother hidden away, you for once bit your tongue and let that be, without knowing why he was doing this. But we all know that you are incapable of forbearance, Tawori."

"Theidrin, that is quite enough."

"No, Aruhin, it isn't enough! He's hidden the truth from us far too long. I want him to tell it now. Tell us all he knows! Enough lies!"

Tawori sprang to his feet with clenched fists, ready to burst. He stood frozen like stone for a moment, then spun around and walked off.

Redien rose and watched him descend the hillside, stopping where their words would not reach him. If he had looked through the guardian sight, he would have seen a thread of ruby light stretching between them, but with his gaze to the world of things, all he saw was his brother's back bent under the weight of Theidrin's enmity. Tawori could feel now what the falyn felt, and the depth of it harrowed him.

Tawori kicked a rock with the tip of his boot. The rock rolled down the slope, hitting another rock, and then another. He shook his head, put his hands in his pockets, and gazed into the distance to where the light of the sun broke through the clouds, painting yellow lines on the dense jungle canopy.

Redien sat down and looked at Theidrin. "Can you believe my words?" he asked.

"I can. I believe you have told us the truth as you

know it."

Redien bit his lip. "Tawori didn't even know my name until I told him. That was yesterday. Some of you heard what I said when I walked in. I had forgotten my name, as I'd forgotten other things. A year ago I asked him if he knew it, but he couldn't tell me. He didn't know.

"It has taken me a long time to remember life before my imprisonment. Something happened in the battle the other night that helped me remember, as if a mirror shattered and I can finally see what's on the other side.

"But I began remembering many months ago. One of the first things that came to me, was how I met Tawori. I was five years old. You know the day, when you saw me. I heard arguing and went to see. Tawori was in our garden, wielding a sword in anger, threatening my father, who would have fought him rather than tell him about me. But I didn't want Father to get hurt. I intervened. I forced Tawori to drop his sword. That's how he learned that I am the guardian. He learned that I am his brother, but nothing else. He left vowing to my father that he would tell no one what he'd discovered. Then he never returned, and he never spoke with my father about me again. I know this without a doubt because Tawori told me so—and if you think I would not hear a lie, you are mistaken."

Theidrin's remark died on his lips.

"My father used silence to hide the truth from me. In those days he expected something terrible to happen, but he never spoke about it. I was afraid and didn't know why. I was only five. I didn't know it was my father's fear I felt. It taught me obedience. 'The outside isn't safe for a child,' my father would say, and that was my truth. Not until I was a few years older I understood what he was not telling me, that he was hiding me from whatever it was he feared. By then I knew of the unlife, I knew of the Light, and I knew that I was different from my father and every other Alassian out in the city. I was the guardian: only *I* could see the world for what it truly was, only *I* could hear the minds and hearts of others as if they were my own. That was why I knew about the people outside, but they didn't know about me. I understood that my forced isolation had to do with my being the guardian, and a child at that. So I accepted it as a burden that comes with the power. And I did the only thing I could. I decided that I would become stronger, that I would train my body and mind so that one day my father would not have to fear for me anymore . . . But then, when it was time to fight, I wasn't strong enough."

"You were just a kid," Beriun said from across the space left by Tawori's absence, "and strong enough to save thousands from the humans' weapon."

"But not from war. And I was not a kid, I was the guardian. And I failed. I ran."

The clouds had turned gray above the hill. The air, which had been warm and humid, was now windy and cold. In the north, the jungle loomed for leagues, dark and forbidding, hiding only beneath the line of the horizon, as a sea stretching to the ends of the world.

"Redien, how did you come to be guardian?" Gwendier asked. The falyn sat erect between the slighter, shorter figures of Nuren and Ehanna, whose gazes both were fixed on Redien, one full of disapproval, the other wonder. "Were you told why the power was given to you?"

"I was told that I was chosen," he said. "But that isn't true."

"No, that cannot be true," Gwendier agreed. He folded his hands in his lap. "And have you always had the power?"

"Since I can remember."

"Were you taught how to use it?"

"Taught?"

"By Miriethal. Did Miriethal train you in its use?"

"No, not that I remember. He taught me how to fight when I was eight, and he taught me how to read and write when I was five. I was often tasked with the study of one book or another; and sometimes Father guided me through meditation. I remember those teachings. The guardian's power has always been a part of me. I don't think it needed teaching."

"And healing?"

"I'd watched my father do it. One day I hurt myself and he wasn't there." He shrugged.

"There has never been a child guardian in our history," Gwendier said. "Did you know this?"

He did not.

"And do you know how the guardian's power is passed to another when this other is chosen?"

Again Redien remained silent.

"The guardian will pour his or her essence into the chosen one," said Gwendier, "until all is given and none is left. Thus ending one's own life. For the power to live on, the guardian must make the final sacrifice before time. And the chosen one is pledged to honor that same obligation. This is not a burden that would be laid on an unconsenting child. So why was it?"

He watched Gwendier shift his cold gaze from warrior to warrior, as if challenging them each to answer his question. Redien had no answer to give. His heart had suddenly grown painful at the thought of his mother in her last moments, and his first.

"Perhaps it was by necessity," Gwendier continued, "might the power have been otherwise lost. Or perhaps it was to save a life, I wonder. And once it is given, the power cannot be taken back. So now Miriethal has an infant child with the means to bend reality to his will. He believes he must hide him; a child is a white canvas, weak is not all that he is. Furthermore the boy is skilled, there has not been a guardian in living memory with the skill to act through another's will. So, we must concede that Miriethal had reasons beyond our ability to guess, for acting as he did."

"He would not speak to me," said Nuren. The falyn's old heart was as clouded as the sky above, toward which he glanced. "Miriethal was not himself after the deaths of Akihalla and Llangdath. He believed he'd failed in his duty as keeper. He considered himself responsible for their deaths and, I thought, for the death of their scion. I did not imagine. He had always been the quiet sort, even before he was made keeper, even as a boy. But he cherished the company of others. He was a caring leader, always seeking to understand and to help, until that dark day. He became distant and sullen. He locked himself in his house, hidden and alone, or so I thought. I believed he was hiding from his grief. I never suspected it was his grief he was hiding from us."

The old falyn looked at Redien.

"When we saw you as a small boy in Irieth, I

confronted Miriethal. 'What is this about a child? What have you not told me?' I asked him; and he replied, 'I am not quite sure myself. I was not here to see.' But I'd had enough of his evasiveness, so I pointed a finger at him. 'Do not play me for a fool, son!' I told him, and asked, 'Who is this boy? Is he your offspring? Do I have a second grandson?' At that, Miriethal was saddened, and he said to me, 'I wish it were so, Father, but you know that Ewin is dead.' Ewin was Lenthieh's mother," the falyn explained to Redien's wide-eyed stare.

"'Do not play tricks with my heart, son!' I told him, and then, 'I know very well that Ewin is dead. Now, will you let me come in, or have you things to hide?' But he did not invite me in that day, or any day thereafter. He became cold and evasive, and then he stopped speaking to me altogether. He did not trust me with the secret . . . But you, you he let in."

Tawori was taking his seat by Redien's side, glancing between him and the old falyn, and holding back a smile.

"You he trusted with the secret," Nuren said bitterly.

"H'm. Or, he trusted I'd make such fuss if he refused to see me, that everyone would hear what I'd come to ask, and his secret would be secret no longer."

"You would have done that," Beriun said.

"I would have done that," Tawori agreed.

"Enough of this." Gwendier lifted his stern gaze from Tawori and Beriun and addressed the circle. "We cannot decide, now, Miriethal's reasons for hiding the guardian. The wrong guess may do more harm than no guess at all. We waste time wondering the why and the who. It is of no further benefit to discuss this matter. We must move our attention to practical things. What is to be done next? Will we strike Irieth? Do we have the strength?"

"I wish to know the guardian's thoughts on the matter," said Theidrin.

Redien forced himself to look away from Nuren, whom only now he had really seen, and turned to Theidrin. He said, "I won't ask for permission to do what I must."

"You mistake my words," the falyn answered. "You are our guardian, and I am hunt leader. I will hear what you would have us do."

Redien hesitated. Then he said, "I would add your strength to mine. I would have you fight by my side when I face Lenthieh."

"Then tell us what you need from us."

All eyes were on Redien.

"I need to know about Irieth, or what is left of it. You had scouts survey it?"

"We did. Omoin and Suni." Theidrin nodded at a falyn and a selyn who sat together, their honeyed-white hair tied in buns atop their heads. They were unlike one another in age and character: he was older and sharp, she was younger and blunt; he wore dark Alassian clothes, she bright human garments. Yet there was a resemblance in the way they sat erect, composed. "With them were Nishath and Tziha, but they have perished in battle. They scouted the borders of Irieth and sent birds at its heart to follow Lenthieh—"

"What use is this now?" Omoin spoke brusquely. "Already there was much we missed, darkness we could not see, hordes of creatures that seemed to spawn from nowhere. Our ineptitude has cost us lives. Too well has Lenthieh concealed his strength. We cannot know what defenses protect him."

"The Alassians in Irieth, are they his prisoners?" The falyn stared at Redien with reprimand. "How many are there? Are they confined or free to come and go?"

"The war has claimed many lives, little guardian, little wolf," Suni said. Her voice was young and crisp, with none of Omoin's hardness. "Our numbers are greatly thinned. Less than a thousand walk the streets of our city. No one leaves unless Lenthieh commands it, and then his most trusted go with them, his followers and foul creatures. There are many more who fight in the human lands across the water. They, too, are unwilling servants of Lenthieh."

"What binds them to him? If they go as far as the human lands and Lenthieh is not with them, why not desert him?"

"Because of the others," Meyvath said, and his mind said that he had spoken without thinking. He glanced about nervously.

"The others?"

The falyn's mouth hung open and dumb before he replied, "The ones in Irieth;" then he pursed his lips and it was clear that no other word would come from him.

"Do you know nothing, Guardian?" Omoin's spite was sharp as a blade. "You want to know what became of Irieth. Then listen well. It is a swamp, black with death and rot, rebuilt on its own grave, roads and houses twisted and filled with a foul smell. The creatures of darkness roam it day and night, preying on rodents and birds, snakes and jaguars alike. No creature can share a home with them. It is no place for the living. It is a prison where Lenthieh keeps his bargain. Should any who fight beyond the water betray him, their loved ones, a family member, a close friend, a lover, will meet a cruel end. Their lives are his to do with as he pleases."

"They are hostages . . ." Redien mused. "Then given the power, they will take the chance."

"You plan to incite a revolt!" cried Theidrin. "That's what you meant with there being power for you. Not a power that would assist you, but one that would fight your battle for you."

"And I theirs for them," Redien said.

"But can you?" the falyn pressed, "Can you share the guardian's essence, and with so many?" He glanced at Tawori as if checking with him, before adding, "We were told that that ability has eluded you, if not until the other night."

Redien met his brother's gaze. "I was only in need of a small reminder," he said.

On the chiming notes of Tawori's laughter, he stretched his essence to each of the warriors, swiftly and effortlessly. Then their hearts and minds were joined, and each of them felt what the others felt.

Surprise was quickly replaced by the thrill of excitement and triumph, the relishing in a power which had been long missing. Meyvath was taken by fear and looked about in alarm, but Aruhin turned to him and said, "It's all right, young one. It is the guardian's power that you feel, our hearts and minds that you hear." And her heart brimmed with joy and warmth, and longing and hurt, and she smiled and laughed while a tear ran down her cheek.

The warriors sat in silence listening to one another and to their guardian, who was new in their circle and unfamiliar to them. They studied him, peering into his mind and heart. He let them prod as they pleased, glad for the moment to be rid of their questions, and content in the newfound silence. His gaze wandered about the hill, beneath the branches of the wide chestnut trees and atop the tall whispering grass.

Plenty of food was cooked that evening, and gaiety and lively chatter swept over the fire-lit hill under the clouded sky. Instruments were brought from the village and music filled the night. Meyvath played two small drums, striking one with the flat of his left hand's fingers while beating the other with the heel, palm, thumb, and fingertips of his right. His strikes were slow and relaxed, at times light as summer rain, at others heavy as falling stones.

A selyn named Seriwa played a lute with a short neck and countless strings, pegs, and ridges, its sound sharp and rich as a harp's. Gwendier sat beside her with a second, much bigger lute in his lap, a tall instrument with a small rounded body from which four plain strings tensed to the pegged head, a foot above the falyn's shoulder. At Gwendier's plucking of the strings, they produced a lingering, mournful sound, above which Seriwa's clear strokes rang bright and full.

After dinner the drumbeat and clear sound of the small lute turned silent, and only Gwendier's lament lingered on. Tawori took a seat beside the old falyn and began to sing in the ancient tongue, the speech from before the time of dawn, from the time of stars and of the other world. His voice soared, soft and full of sorrow, lingering on each syllable so that the words and the sound of the lute seemed to wait for one another, none willing to engage the next note before the other had.

No one was speaking now.

"A lament for the dead," Beriun murmured to Redien.

The chanting continued, the same verses repeated over and over, filling the night completely, until, abruptly, silence.

The fire rustled.

Seriwa plucked the strings of her lute and a lilting melody rang dulcet and pure. Tawori began singing a happier tune.

"This is a song of healing," Aruhin said as she came to sit at Redien's side. She asked if he liked the music and the singing, and was pleased to see the answer in his smile.

Other voices joined Tawori's as the night went on, falyns and selyns singing together. The drumbeat struck merrily, and a flute began to trill.

It was late and Redien was curled up on the grass drifting into sleep, when he heard Tawori's voice crooning softly on the shy notes of the lute. Half in dream he listened to the quavering in his brother's voice and the sweet ache in his heart. Till a deep slumber took him.

He was woken by Tawori's gentle touch. "It is about to rain," his brother said. "Come to the shelter."

The music had stopped, the campfire was red with embers, and the smell of rain rode the cold wind from the east. Beriun waited for them on the path, holding the longer lute over one shoulder as one would hold a log of wood. Farther ahead, Gwendier and Seriwa were descending the hillside like shadows in the night. There was no one else in sight.

He followed Tawori, minding only not to stumble or slip, barely noticing the heavy drops beginning to fall. Once in the under-room he found an empty mat, lay down, and slept.

Yet, soon he would have woken in a chilling draft, had his brother not fetched for him a warm pelt and tucked him in; but that his brother did for him, for that is what older brothers do, Tawori thought, yes, that is what they do. He sat with Redien and watched him sleep, warm and untroubled the little wolf, the unwavering light.

It had been a good night after such a painful day for his sweet brother. "In the end, all I could do was watch," Tawori murmured. "You did well, little brother; you did what I could not . . ."

11
THE HEART OF ALL

HEAVY RAIN FELL without respite all the following day. Redien stayed in one of the upper rooms of the shelter, helping those tasked with the crafting of arrows, straightening shaft after shaft and chipping pale flint stones into arrowheads.

"You could choose one of our spare bows for yourself," Ehanna told him. She was feathering the arrows, binding split quills to the shafts using long, thin twine which she wound between the feather's barbs. She was skilled at the task and varied her method according to the materials at hand.

Redien shook his head. "I'm not proficient with the bow," he admitted, "I'm still learning."

"Guardian, a word?"

Nuren stood by the door, stern and forbidding. They stepped together into the corridor. The old falyn carried a slim sword, gently curved like Wanninh, though an inch or two shorter, the scabbard made of ivory, and the hilt wrapped in snowy leather strips. Nuren lifted it flat in front of him, his hands clutching the two ends of the sheath. A single pearl, silvery-white as the moon, was set midway the scabbard's length, circled by six drops of gold, like stars.

Redien stared at it dumb. His quivering hand rose to touch the moon and the stars.

"I never knew to ask its name."

"It is Mirenh," Nuren said.

"Mirenh," he repeated. "What does it mean?"

"Moonlight," said the old falyn. "I have decided that you should have it, if you'll accept it."

He nodded silently, overwhelmed by a pang of emotions.

"Then have it," Nuren said.

He took the sword and squeezed it tightly as if afraid it might truly turn into moonlight and vanish. The full moon on the scabbard was pale and lustrous; he imagined he could see himself reflected in it and in each of the six tiny stars, if only they had been a little bigger.

He found himself looking out the open doors of the shelter and realized he had walked there in daydream. Outside, the downpour fell sideways on sudden gusts of wind. The rain called out to him . . . or was he the one calling?

He unsheathed his father's sword and leaned the scabbard against the wall. He stepped outside.

In the center of the barren courtyard he stopped and closed his eyes to listen. The rain sang in his ears, battering on the hard pavement, splattering on leafy brambles and tree leaves, drowning in the soaked soft fabric of his clothes, flapping and skidding on his face tilted upward to the sky. He was drenched in the sap of the world. When he opened his eyes, he knew they shone with ruby light.

The rain paused. Suspended. Silent. Obedient.

Redien cut the air with Moonlight, and water drops followed the blade's path. He shifted his balance, swirling the blade, moving swiftly. The water danced around him, whirling, spiraling, running along his fingers and on the surface of his blade. Water rippled on the hard ground in expanding waves that climbed upward in a whirlpool, ascending skyward against the pull of the earth.

To the guardian sight the rain was like the falling of a million stars, and the ground shimmered and glinted like a sea made of diamonds. Leaves and brambles fluttered in the wind, brushed by its white push and filled with the world's beating life force.

A crowd gathered inside the shelter to watch the guardian perform the eroh, the ancient combat forms of water and earth, and to watch the rain dance to the rhythm of his footsteps splashing on the puddled ground. They watched enthralled, their eyes fixed upon a mystery they had never seen before. This power, reborn in the young guardian, was unlike what they had known it to be. They looked in awe at the power, and not at the guardian; no one noticed that he was crying as he danced, his tears mixing with the rain.

When he stopped, he held the water still and offered Moonlight flat on his hands to his father's memory. He bowed, and imagined he could glimpse Miriethal bowing in return, smiling kindly.

He let his vision still, and the water roared, crashing onto the pavement with ferocious strength.

When after some time he hadn't moved, Nuren came to get him out of the rain.

"You take care of that, now," the old falyn said once inside, handing him the ivory scabbard. "Dry it, oil it. You do know how to care for a sword?"

He nodded.

"Good, good," the falyn said, "we wouldn't want it rusting away. Take good care of it."

"I knew he had died," Redien said. "I knew it without doubt."

Nuren's mouth flopped open.

"But I saw him in my nightmares so many times . . . I doubted what I knew."

The old falyn's hand holding the scabbard sank. His eyes looked into Redien's, who caught and held them with nothing but the need of his heart.

"Then I forgot who he was," Redien said. "I knew he was someone important, but I couldn't remember who. I couldn't remember. He was someone important, but I couldn't remember him. Time moved on and I . . . I became convinced that he was a prisoner, like me. He was the only other prisoner in that place. I hoped I would meet him one day, then on that day, we would both be free.

"But when I was rescued, he was not. I left him behind. Again. Just as before." He took a quivering breath. "Until now." He brought Moonlight's hilt to his chest and bowed to his father's father. "I met him, at last," he said. "He is with me now, and we look upon daylight together. Thank you."

His silent tears became shivering sobs when Nuren hugged him. The old falyn was scarcely taller than him, his arms frail and thin around Redien, but warm and comforting. Nuren held him until the sobs ceased.

Together they descended into the under-room, where they sat talking about Miriethal, his life before Redien's birth, and the life he had led with Redien as father and son.

It was later in the evening and the room had filled with a flurry of activities, when Aruhin came to speak with Redien. She had him look through a pile of clothes she'd scavenged in the village and stacked up near the brightly burning fire.

"Did you and your brother play a game of slash and stitch?" she asked, raising her brows at his densely repaired clothes. "By the looks of it, I'd guess you won?"

"I lost at every round," he admitted, and smiled.

From the pile of clothes, he chose a gray long-sleeved top and a pair of dark teal loose-fitting trousers tight at the ankles. He coiled a cloth sash three times around his waist, fastening it with a flat knot at the back, and slid Moonlight's scabbard in it above his right hip. Then he slipped back into the tattered jumper he'd been wearing, a size too big for him.

"I like the color," he said, shrugging at Aruhin.

She smirked. "What color was it? I can't tell."

"And I have forgotten," remarked Tawori, grinning at them from a little away.

Others came to choose from the pile of clothes, including a young tabby kaara who snatched a fine yellow scarf from under Aruhin's nose and swept the floor with it left and right before bouncing away, chased by a determined admirer of the finery.

. . .

THE FOLLOWING DAY Redien woke late and found the others nearly ready to depart. He was grateful they had let him sleep for long, as this had been their last comfortable night for some time. The rain still fell, and the sky showed no sign of clearing. Half an hour later they rode into the storm with the wind hissing in their ears. The kaaras' paws squelched at each stride, sinking in the grassy mud. Six dozen mighty kaaras ran in loose formation, each bearing a rider or a bundle of food, pelts, or weapons. Yinna bounded at their heart, powerful and surefooted like a queen of the wild, the slight figure of the guardian on her back, bent against the wind and the rain. He looked small and slender against those around him, his cloak of dark pelts flapping madly behind him.

For half the morning they ran without pause and came to the forest's edge where they stopped. The kaaras drank rainwater from puddles in the mud and rested under the cover of the trees. Soon they set off again, the Alassians going on foot and the kaaras walking among them. The jungle swept over them, dense and gloomy. Above them, the sky was green with life, green with the smell of countless plants, green with the rain that crawled leaf by leaf, in dribbles and drops, trickling down the bark of trees, patiently and stubbornly, all the way to the earth that drank from it and still lay hard and thirsty, filling the air with the scent of moist soil.

Walking in the damp woodland was more comfortable than riding in the open against the wind and rain. The march warmed their bodies and dried their clothes, and by the time they sat to eat a brief meal, the ground felt wet and cold against their bottoms. They mounted and rode in single file, then walked, then rode again. At night they lay in wet discomfort, Alassians and kaaras snuggling close together like a mob of mongooses, always with the guardian at their center. He made no complaint, for the nights were cold and miserable. Still, his slumber was easy and deep, and he slept gladly in the jungle's embrace, full of life and the screams of birds and monkeys and rodents—he was used to the cold, used to a floor of stone while the woodland's ground was gentle, used to dreary solitude while others, living and breathing, surrounded him now.

They kept guard four by four and would not let him take up watch. "You should rest and save your strength for when it is needed," had said Theidrin, and the others had agreed. But when it was Tawori's turn to keep watch, Redien sat by his side for a while, listening to the night, to the dreaming minds of his traveling companions, and to his brother's heart. That night was also hers to watch; she stood many steps from them, immobile as a stone statue looking into the night. His brother did not look at her, but knew she was there and often thought of her, his heart swelling and mourning.

Redien couldn't bear it any longer. "Is it because of me?"

Tawori stirred, sighed, and was still. At last he hugged a knee to his chest, and said, "It is not because of you."

"But it is, in part," he insisted.

Tawori continued to gaze into the darkness of the trees. "I hurt her. I cannot return to her."

"But you want to."

"I want many things," said his brother. "I want our

mother and father to be alive. I want this war to be unmade. I want the scars on your face to have never come to be . . . I cannot have these things."

"But those are things of the past. I don't understand."

They remained silent for a while.

"How did you hurt her?" Redien asked.

"I broke a promise I never should have broken."

Tawori's mind was a shambles of contradiction: guilt, love, anger, loss, desire. Memories raced through him as feelings, images, echoes of tastes, words, touches—too fast, too many to grasp. His face was coarse against it all. It hurt to watch.

"For seven hundred years I walked by her side. Then, no more. I chose to walk alone. She let me go."

"When?"

"When I lost everything. There was one thing I did not lose, so I cast her aside."

"Why would you do that?"

"Because I was weak," Tawori said. "I needed to suffer. But she did not deserve it, and I did not think of her. I cared only for myself. She suffered because of my weakness."

"You are cruel."

"I was."

"No, you *are*. You are cruel to yourself."

Tawori shook his head. "I am only fair."

"I don't understand you."

"Of course not. You are fourteen."

"Eighteen."

"Fourteen." Tawori smirked.

"You are wrong," Redien said, a little louder than he had intended. He lowered his voice. "You are wrong. I understand that you are ashamed of returning to her, but why you say it's fair, that I don't understand. You want to be with her. And Aruhin—"

"We are going into battle, brother."

Tawori had interrupted him before he could tell him what he must; but then he saw it, how he was eighteen, or fourteen, and had not understood. "You are afraid," he said.

"I am."

"That she might die?"

Tawori made no reply.

"That you might . . ."

They gazed into each other's eyes. A dark dread filled Redien's senses. He was struck dumb with it. When he understood what he felt, he forced himself to look away.

He would not allow fear to take him. Whenever he thought about what awaited at the end of this road, he thought of what he must do and how he must prevail, never of what he might lose along the way. To allow such vision of failure would crumble his resolve. He must have no weaknesses. He must look to the light. In his nightmares he saw loss, failure, despair; yet when he woke and looked upon the world and upon his brother, his heart saw hope again; he would cast darkness out of his mind and reach for what must come to be, willing it into existence. Every morning he turned his back on the nightmares. There was light where he was headed: it shone brightly upon his face and cast dark shadows behind him, always behind him. If he kept heading forward, kept chasing the light, then darkness would forever fall behind him.

He must not falter, he must never turn from the light.

Redien looked at his brother, now, and saw the burden that weighed on his heart, the weight of those he might lose, and of those he might depart from in victory or defeat. Tawori chose to suffer now, in the prospect of a darker tomorrow. Redien had not known this about his brother. How was it that after all this time he had not known? How had he been so blind?

When he looked at the path ahead, Redien saw no one. He walked the bright way toward the light and others followed him. Tawori had been by his side when Redien had needed him; in Ydalon, when he had been lost and broken, his brother had walked beside him. But even then, although sick and exhausted he had followed Tawori on sea and on land, in the city of man, into a cave, and to the cold mountains, even then, his brother had walked beside him, never ahead of him. Tawori had taken him only where Redien himself had wished to go—although at times Redien had not known he wished to be somewhere, until only after getting there. He had never seen Tawori walk ahead of him, in the light, and so he had never seen the shadow he cast. Then one day Redien had taken the lead, no longer beside his brother. He had not stopped to ponder when this change occurred, or whether it was right or wrong.

Only now he saw the place Tawori had chosen for himself. His brother walked behind, last of the line, in the shadow of many. Because to watch over them, he must be the last to come. And so the light was hidden from him by those before him. Tawori walked the same bright path, but he walked it in darkness. And if he were last, and alone, where would he find strength when he needed it? Tawori could not bear that burden alone, no one could.

"You must speak to her," Redien said, and shivered. The wet, cold night had seeped into his bones.

"Go to sleep," Tawori said softly.

"You can't care for everyone and have no one to care for you."

"It seems I have you to care for me."

"But I can't," Redien said, "I don't know how. I'm fourteen."

Tawori chuckled and smiled, although his eyes were sad. He nodded at the sleeping kaaras and warriors, and said, "Go get some sleep, Nillith, before Theidrin wakes and finds you sitting here shivering like a weed. I'd never hear the end of it."

Redien fought a yawn. A great tiredness had come over him. They had traveled many miles that day, and the day before, and the one before that. He could hardly keep his eyes open.

Yinna was asleep, curled up in her tail. Redien huddled in her warmth and fell asleep.

The night passed, and there came many nights and days alike. Then one morning, the rain ceased its relentless downpour. They were entering the deeper heart of the jungle where the trees grew taller and closer together, larger and older. Eight days later they came to a place where the ample tree trunks merged in clusters, their roots spreading like giant hands with countless fingers slithering in and out of the earth. Here, Redien bade them stop.

Yinna halted at once, the others a moment later. Theidrin rode back swiftly.

"How much farther?" Redien asked him. The ancient

trees in this part of the jungle were familiar to him, but the place itself was not. He was peering ahead through the guardian sight.

"Another full day at this pace."

It was early afternoon, and daylight broke timidly through the dense canopy.

"We shouldn't go any farther today," Redien said.

"I thought we could leave behind us as much as ten more miles before nightfall."

"The path ahead is full of darkness." He gave Theidrin the sight so the falyn could see the blackness of the trees, the absence of light, the absence of life. Like mist hiding the world of things, darkness hid the flow of life. "I think if we go any farther, he will know."

"Send scouts ahead!" Omoin said. He dismounted and walked to them. "Lend us the sight, and perhaps we will find a way that is clear of the unlife."

Redien joined his essence with Omoin's, but as he did, he said, "I sense only emptiness ahead. I don't think you will find a better way."

"Be careful, Omoin," said Theidrin; "stay far from the unlife. We must not alert Lenthieh to our presence before we are ready."

With a nod, Omoin took his leave. "Suni! Tsaela! With me!" Their eyes shone red and bright. They talked briefly, then set off running in different directions.

Redien slid from Yinna's back, and the kaara bunted her head against his chest. He thanked her scratching her cheeks, then she went to sit on the grass and began cleaning her fur.

Redien sat with his back against the whitened bark of a lupuna tree whose top crowned the canopy high above.

He hunkered down between its tall, wide roots with his arms on his knees, and gazed through the eyes of the scouts. He saw the jungle darken step after step as Suni and Tsaela advanced, one going northeast, the other northwest. Omoin was moving northward, slowly and more cautiously, sometimes deviating east or west. The unlife ahead of the falyn was denser. Soon he could no longer advance safely. He turned back, and began retracing his steps. By then the others were entering darker woods, their pace slow and cautious. It wasn't long before they, too, headed back. Then Redien let the focus fade from his sight.

Tawori had sat cross-legged beside him with a wide concave stone on his lap. He was using a big rounded rock to grind a red substance into fine powder, stirring and crushing it. He unscrewed the black cap from his metal bottle and poured a little water over it. Then he mixed water and powder to form a paste.

"It is customary for the keeper to paint the guardian's four markings, beginning the ritual at its heart where it will also end. But today we have no keeper. So it was decided that I should draw your markings, because of the bond you and I share.

"The four lines represent the strength of your focus, the life force within you, and the essence of your being. They are a symbol of the power that resides in you, and that will bind us together in the battle to come. You will then draw the single stripe over the eyes of our hunt leader who will do the same for another, and they will do the same, and so on to the youngest of our warriors, Meyvath. Lastly, if things were as they should be, Meyvath would draw a dot on the keeper's forehead and a line on his lips, closing the circle. You might have seen those markings on Miriethal's face. The red dot is a symbol of centrality, for the keeper is where our purpose begins and where our battles against the unlife end. Alas, we are without light. Today Meyvath will draw the single line over my eyes instead. The circle will be closed yet.

"The paint is a symbol of our union in the struggle to come. It is how we make ready to meet the unlife on the battlefield. May we remain strong together, and prevail. Here. Hold the stone while I draw your markings."

They sat facing each other. Redien held the heavy stone in his lap and Tawori dipped the tip of his middle finger into the paint, crimson red on his pale skin. "A line on your forehead," he said, touching the bridge of Redien's nose and moving his finger upward. "May your focus be unwavering. Beneath your eyes, two lines." With his little fingers, he drew beneath Redien's eyes and outward. "May your sight never falter. A line on your mouth." He pressed his wet thumb over Redien's closed lips, then slid it downward to his chin and neck. "May life remain strong in you and untainted, brother."

Tawori bowed his head, and Redien did the same. His brother moved to the side and Theidrin, who had been watching them, took his place.

"Give the mortar to Theidrin. You must draw a line with your two fingers from side to side: here, to here."

He wet his index and middle fingers in the red paint and did as he was instructed.

"May life shine strong in you, Theidrin," said Tawori.

Theidrin's gaze was hard. He said, "Redien, I was filled with prejudice when I first met you. I believed you to be too young to be worthy, too young to be trusted. I thought you weak and yielding. I have watched you and heard your heart's desire. I see your resolve. And I see your strength. I judged you before I knew you. I was wrong to do so." The falyn turned to Tawori. "We have lost many lives in this war, Alassian lives, our friends and families, and human lives. The Alliance is no more: *you* were its downfall. I will fight by your side because I must, but I do not stand with you. I don't know who you are, Tawori, except a liar and a deceiver."

Tawori's guilt slithered inside him like a snarl of snakes.

"I can't forgive you," Theidrin said.

"I do not ask to be forgiven."

Theidrin scowled and bowed stiffly; then he stood, taking the stone and paint with him.

Tawori lowered his gaze and was silent. After some time, he said, "The ritual demands that we speak the truth of our hearts. Others may come to speak with you, or with me." And indeed others came, the red marks bright across their eyes.

"I have thought of your quest," Gwendier said, seating himself on one of the great lupuna roots, as if he were sitting on a throne. He spoke to Tawori and looked solely at him. "We cannot know what today would be, had you not sought the guardian on your own and kept the secret to yourself. I do not condemn you." He was silent; then he nodded. "That is all I have come to say."

He left as solemnly as he had come.

Beriun came and kneeled on the ground, making himself small. He bowed low, then straightened back up. "You might not remember," he said, "I was with Tawori when he freed you from Seligor."

"I remember."

"Forgive me! I spoke wrongly that day. I'd seen great evil at work and I spoke out of wickedness. Never again will I say ill of the suffering, and I will not proclaim a life lost, if there is any hope to save it."

"I remember the sound of your voices," Redien said, "it was like daybreak after an endless night of silence. I didn't understand your words and their meaning was unimportant. Their sound reached me from beyond the nightmares. It was the sound of hope."

"I kept this," Beriun said. From his gray and brown jacket identical to Tawori's, he produced a small folded paper. "To remind myself of my weakness." He unfolded the paper and handed it to Redien. It was a single page, torn and ragged along one of the edges. Thin words in black ink were written in a frail and uncertain hand. The sickness and frailty that had inhabited Redien in the first days of his freedom, he had almost forgotten. "You wrote these words?" Beriun asked. "I thought so. Had I been the one to find you, I might have ended your life. There would have been no thanks. And now there would be no hope. I will not forget." Beriun took back the note, folded it, and put it in his pocket.

"You had seen . . . great evil, you say?"

"I heard you speak to Nuren," Beriun said. "You weren't the only prisoner in Seligor. There were others."

"Others?"

"Mutilated and ill-treated. Long dead, most of them."

"That's enough, Beriun," said Tawori.

"No!" Redien glowered at his brother, then at Beriun, then at his brother again. "What of them?" He heard the anguish in his own voice. "The ones who lived, what of them? Did you free them? Did you leave them . . ."

"No, we would never leave them there." Tawori squeezed his shoulder, staring into his eyes with a tortured frown. He spoke softly. "We found one falyn and two selyns alive. We took them with us." A headshake. "One of them died before we reached Oxwish, the others a few days later. You were the only survivor."

The jungle air was thin. It had seemed fresh and clear moments earlier, but now he was struggling to breathe. He stood and walked away.

He leaned against the thick bark of a tall tree and let the memories take him.

Tawori watched his brother sink down against a tree.

"I should learn to keep silent," Beriun said.

"He never asked . . ." Tawori looked at his friend and shook his head. "He never asked, and I didn't have the heart to speak of that place. When he asks again, I will tell him all there is to tell. But I hope it won't be tonight . . . tonight he needs strength."

After Beriun left, Tawori watched his brother sit with his face turned to the darkening forest. He looked like a little wolf again, alone and fragile, needing protection, needing a brother to watch over him, but not for long. Soon his determination would shine once more, strong and unyielding, drawing others to him and weakening the grasp of darkness on the world. How he had changed since their battle with Lenthieh, since gaining his rightful place among his people. He would not need his older brother to watch over him for long. Redien was strong, stronger than Tawori. Tawori had known this ever since he'd learned of his brother's existence thirteen years ago.

On that day, Tawori had met his better, and had vowed that his brother would succeed where he had failed.

He heard steps and looked up.

"Aruhin?"

"I did not mean to steal your thoughts," she said.

Whatever thoughts had been in his mind were gone. He watched her take a seat by his side, as one might watch a bird coming to peck at a crumb of bread: holding very still and silent.

"I wish to speak with you," she said. "Will you listen?"

It did not occur to him that he should reply.

Aruhin spoke the words she had come to say, but she saw that Tawori did not hear her. He had that aching look in his eyes, that look he'd been watching her with day after day. He brushed her lips with his thumb, and his hand stroked the back of her neck. He tasted as he always had, like hot summer rain.

"This isn't right," he whispered. His breath wafted sweet warmth in her mouth. Then he was silent, his lips kissing hers. He drank from her like a thirsty animal after the long arid season, his arms pulling her in.

He caught a shaking breath. "This isn't right," he panted, "I'm sorry."

Suddenly the jungle was around them and they were not alone. He *should* be sorry for ending the kiss, Aruhin thought.

He drew back averting his gaze, and murmuring, "I shouldn't have . . ." but meaning something else.

"You didn't listen," she scolded him.

His eyes darted to hers, his expression alight with docile surprise.

"No, I didn't listen," he said. Then the light was gone, and he was frowning.

She looked at him soberly. He had sat back, folding his hands in his lap, squeezing them hard.

"All right. The next time we speak, then, will you listen?"

"I will try."

"And we'd better be somewhere private," she said, "maybe *I* will not listen." She glimpsed him smirk with that crooked smile she so longed to see, before the mournful frown returned. She could see the weight of his fears and knew it was not her place to ease them. He was strongest when he set himself apart, strongest when he stood alone, and in that, they were not alike. She had come seeking his heart because she could not face tomorrow without it. He had given it to her. She would ask nothing more. She stood and left without another word.

SILENCE DESCENDED on the jungle like a blanket of mist. After nightfall, few words were spoken. The leaves hung still on the trees, and no animal sang or cried in the dark.

In the night a chill spread through Redien's body. Darkness closed around him and weighed on him, pressing him against the hard ground. Cold rain fell, battering hard on his skin, pricking his eyes and blinding him, beating him and drowning him. It fell ruby red, muffling all sounds. It was the blood of his companions, of his brother, of every creature of the forest; it was the sap of the trees, bleeding out red and thick. The world had died. Everyone in it had died. Their blood spurted hot from his mouth, so strongly that his howling cries made no sound. There was death. Death was in everything around him, and death was inside him. The guardian's power scorched him. Threads of red light pierced his flesh, pulling him into the air and tearing him apart, and his blood trickled down along them. In that absolute silence, he sobbed. His voice was all that was left in the world. Everything else was darkness and emptiness. He was alone.

When he woke, he did not hear the words he said but knew that he had spoken. He stared at the canopy of leaves overhead, blue and pale yellow in the dim light of the cloudless night. No wind shook them. He listened for the sounds of the wild, but all he heard was the sleeping of his companions, their breathing and dreaming. The jungle smelled wrong; there was no aroma of moss and damp earth, and he did not smell wood or flowers.

He filled his lungs with the scentless air, then let his quivering breath escape his lips.

Close by him, Tawori said hushed, "You will defeat him. You will thrive. I will be by your side when you do. Now sleep, Redien. Sleep a while longer."

He turned to his side and gazed into his brother's eyes, black with night sight and painted red. He pulled the pelt tighter on his shoulders and soon welcomed the stillness of a dreamless slumber.

At first light, he stood watching the jungle with dull white eyes. He listened to the silence and inhaled the odorless air. He could see cracks in the ridged bark of the trees. Here and there the naked wood was exposed where sections of the bark had broken off and fallen onto the ground, withered and white like molted snakeskins. The foliage was rich, but many of the branches were dense with dry leaves. One of the biggest trees, which had majestically fanned out roots twice as tall as the tallest

Alassian, had its trunk cracked at the midpoint, and from there, it was sickly contorted deadwood. When he shone his gaze on the canopy, he saw that its life force was parched and black. He could see no birds, and only a few insects sparkled in the branches, in the air, and even in the soil. The unlife had taken over this part of the jungle.

As he watched the upsetting sight, he opened his senses to the warriors behind him who were making ready to depart. It brought him comfort to know them by the feeling of their hearts and minds, and a great strength filled him whenever he let their presence in.

Above them all and louder of them all was his brother, whose presence crackled and sparked even when he slept or meditated, ready to burst with the strength of a hurricane. His friend Beriun, by contrast, was placid yet not soft; he was like a brook that digs deep between rocks, flowing steadily with the will and patience to shape mountains. Aruhin was gentle, light and inconspicuous, yet sure. She was the silent falling snow, beautiful, playful, and unforeseeably changeable. Theidrin was like the blue sky when the wind blows and the foliage on the trees rustles; and Gwendier was like a boulder in the shallow waters of a cold and clear stream, immobile and impassible.

He knew them now as though they were a part of his own being, because only with them, and in the flow of the world, he was whole at last.

He reached within himself for the essence of his being, the center of his power, that splinter of the world's fabric that had been given to him, which was not born of him but made him who he was. He let it out as easily as he let out breath, for that, he knew now, was its true nature. It was its purpose to flow and unite him with all things. He had only to keep the tap open, keep his heart and mind open, let himself be filled, be still, and welcome in the world.

He looked for the red threads of power that should pierce the whiteness of his life force, but this time there were no threads, only a misty fog, a faint red glow in the air around him which went as far as he willed it to go.

He turned to face his companion's astonishment, their red shining eyes gazing back at him. There was no need for words. They could hear his certainty, as he heard their surprise: this was new to them, yet it was as it should be.

When he had first shared the guardian's power at his father's request, he had done it all wrong. He'd watched Father stretch his essence and reach out, and so he had done the same. He'd taken control and forced his power to obey him. The effort had been straining, and he had come out of it weakened and stupid. Worse even, he had risked emptying himself of himself. He understood now the mistake, and the risks. He must not force his presence upon those who spoke to his heart, but rather, he should let himself be filled with them, let them drink of his power and draw strength from his will. This required great certainty, for he must keep sight of himself in the midst of them all, or be lost in the crowd of their voices. He must steady his focus.

He walked to Yinna and hopped on her back. Tawori took his place at his right side, Beriun at his left, Omoin and Suni were behind them, Nuren and Gwendier ahead, Theidrin and Aruhin led the way. They rode out.

The trees closed around them, trunk after trunk of tall, silent stillness. The brightness of their sap waned as they rode deeper, until only darkness filled them root to leaf. They were shadows of a once living world, for here, life was no more.

The kaaras' paws thumped on the ground, resounding like the beating of drums. Their gallop lifted fine soil, like long-awaited gasps of relief.

As bright stars in the night, the riders shone with white life force; and red gemstones gleamed in their eyes. They looked out at the trees, up at the sky, and down at the earth, watching the unlife that pressed all around them weakening the ground beneath them, which shook and threatened to give way. The unlife would crush them, and the earth would open wide and swallow them. But their wills combined held it whole. Together, they forged deeper into darkness, at each step closer to its heart.

12
BLACK SKIES

IRIETH LAY FALLEN at the bottom of a swamp reeking of rotting bodies and sulfur. Her once glorious houses made of wood and living trees, flowers, and gleaming jasper, were only a memory. In their place were waste and debris, decomposing matter turned soggy and foul. No grass grew for miles, and the trees produced no leaves, flowers, or fruit. Life had no place here. All that remained of the jungle's ancient heart were the naked gray husks of centuries-old trees, too stubborn to die and too sick to live.

Darkness had prospered in the flora's blight, thriving on death and disaster. It swam in the black water of the swamp, seeping underground and drenching the roots of the old trees, feeding poison to any life that still lingered.

The Alassians endured the misery of the swamp from boardwalks of blackened wood built above the deadly waters, and from inside small houses with crooked roofs, twisted and wrong, cold, and damp.

Beasts from the Realm Beyond lurked in the blackness of the water and the trees. Winged terrors flew in the ever hazy skies, circling the air like vultures and wailing as though with grief. At times they dipped to land on the misshaped roofs, their hooked talons digging into the wood and their wails turning to anguished whimpers. The stench of burnt flesh hung heavy about them. Day and night they cried their lament, beating the air with their wings and scorching it with fire, always watchful, always waiting.

On this day, which had begun as any other day, with sunrise brightening faintly the perpetual grayness of the sky, Lenthieh was seen walking the boardwalks with hurried steps. The hem of his dark robe dragged over the floor and his long hair waved behind him.

In the last year of his reign, his face had grown stained with the unlife. His eyes were veined black, and purple rings hung beneath them. An irked scowl twisted his parched lips.

Young Alassians in leather and silvery armor accompanied him, bearing swords and bows, and radiant with the Light. At their passing, the city folk got out of the way, pausing to look, whispering, and wondering.

Lenthieh came to a narrow wooden walkway that stretched over the swampy water to a circular platform at the city's heart, its floor smeared with dry blood, water sloshing beneath it. It was a place feared by the city folk, where this lord of the unlife worked his wicked magic. Lenthieh raised his arms in welcome and spoke in the dark speech. His taut voice echoed in the silence, carrying past the borders of this world into what lies beyond.

And the Beyond answered. Black smoke rose from the

swamp, concealing the water, the wood, the sky, and daylight. The people of Irieth cried out in fear.

Then a stiff silence fell, and the black smoke sparkled with ruby fireflies.

Lenthieh's voice thundered with defiance, "FACE ME IF YOU DARE!"

Silence answered his challenge—silence, and red-glowing fireflies.

An anguished cry chilled the air. Another followed. The lights flickered and died like candles blown by the wind. And the city screamed.

REDIEN HOWLED AT THE madness of a thousand minds assaulting his consciousness and wrenching his sight. He crouched over the warm body moving beneath him, instinctively tightening his thighs around it and digging his fingers in the thick fur. He begged for a breath to fill his lungs, but none came.

A roar cut through the havoc of his mind, and he heard voices. *Danger! The world is shrinking!* "Guardian!" *It will swallow us! It will swallow us!* "Redien!" A steely grip caught his arm, and he drew a staggered breath.

He forced his mind to snap open with a painful, almost audible crack. The sharp pang tore a groan from deep within him. He sensed fear and reached out toward it. It eased. His sight began to clear, and he saw white hair fling before him like spiderwebs in the wind. The jungle was dark and ominous about him. His head throbbed as if he'd smacked it against a wall. He put his hand over Tawori's on his arm, and looked at him. "He has them!" he told his brother, "All of them! He called to the darkness, and it came at his command. The unlife has them."

"Then the battle is lost before it begins!" cried Omoin from behind them.

"There is no turning back!" shouted Beriun, his voice booming over the thumping of the kaara's paws. "We will find no allies ahead! We must make way through our brothers and sisters."

"What have you seen?" Tawori's eyes pierced the gloom of the jungle, like red gleaming stars.

"The city is clouded in black smoke. The people choke in it, they are driven mad by it. There's a platform deep in the city, the only place not taken by the unlife. Lenthieh is there, but something about that place ... I think there's power there. *His* power."

Tawori's hand gave one last squeeze, then let go. His brother patted the gray tabby kaara he rode. "Take me to Theidrin," he told her.

Redien blinked after them, watching Tawori's hair slither like sea spume. He wiped the tears from his cheeks with his sleeve. The pain had dulled. He brought forth his focus, and returned his gaze to the world of energies and to the unlife.

WHEN THEY NEARED the city, Redien did not see its wooden houses and walkways. He saw darkness; and within the darkness, the lives of countless Alassians flickered in and out of existence. Their screams and incoherent words filled his ears, and the sharp edges of their minds stabbed and tore at his sanity. He shut his eyes and breathed through clenched teeth, narrowing his focus, isolating the ones he needed to protect, the ones he must share his power with. He shut out everything else in the effort to keep himself from tumbling into madness. It was like pressing his hands on his ears against the roar of a thousand voices, much of the noise still came through. It made the hair on the nape of his neck stand up.

He heard the howls of bristlewolves and the wails of winged terrors, as the kaaras' paws began to beat on hollow wood. He braced himself and looked. A wide ring of black smoke pressed all around, moving with their advance. Solid houses emerged out of nonexistence, only to vanish again into darkness. Alassians, his own people, washed out of the smoke, breaking like waves onto the warriors' blades, their pulsating life force tainted with the unlife.

Redien had not yet drawn Moonlight. He dived his hands in Yinna's fur and shut his eyes again, seeking not to see or hear, but to feel. He turned his mind away from his companions, away from Theidrin's gaze searching the path ahead, from the wound burning in Nuren's thigh, from his brother's rage infusing Wanninh with lightning. He breathed deeply once, then twice; then he pushed. His perception rippled, broader, farther, spreading like water over marble, till he knew all living things in the city—living and *un*living. And he found it, a place where nothing was to be found. He pressed his heels into Yinna's flanks and she adjusted her course. The others followed them.

Water gurgled from beneath like an earthquake, and Redien opened his eyes. He was on a narrow boardwalk, no more than two feet wide, which hovered a foot above the swamp. The gurgling became a loud gushing as thick black tendrils spurted into the air. For an instant they towered above him, waving and shaking; then they dived. Redien clawed the air bringing his arms down, tugging at the unlife and casting it back into the water, pushing and crushing it against the bottom of the swamp. Yinna broke off her sprint and roared. Her left flank sank. They fell.

The cold water nearly drowned him. He swallowed a mouthful of the bitter fluid and the taste throttled him.

Gasping and coughing, he found his footing. The freezing water was only waist deep. Yinna tussled with it, pounding at it with the full force of her front legs, thrashing and wrenching, biting and snarling. He tried to grasp the tendrils of darkness between her legs with his mind, but he couldn't see them while the water splashed brightly with her efforts. So he plunged his hands in it, closing his fingers around slippery flesh. Tendrils coiled around his bent knees and pulled him down. He lost his balance . . . caught himself . . . then his legs were pulled from beneath him. His face slapped the water and he skidded. His nose hurt with pressure. The back of his head smacked something overhead, and he went under. Water churned around him. He was walloped by wooden piles and tried to grasp them, but the pull was too strong. His breath escaped him.

Then suddenly the tendrils let go. He pulled his head up gulping. His right hand found support as he retched and heaved, spitting the foul taste from his mouth.

The darkness had drawn back, and the tendrils that had caught and dragged him had vanished. He was where darkness wanted him to be. Alone.

But Tawori was riding toward him, his kaara bouncing through the waist-deep water like a dolphin, drops and splashes skittering brightly out of their way. Tawori leaped from the kaara's back and somersaulted past him, thumping down onto the circular wooden platform, the blood smeared platform, the *support* Redien was holding on to.

Tawori did not look at Redien, but stared at the intense, white light.

"You have come here to die! Uninvited, as always, Tawori," Lenthieh yelled.

Beneath the keeper's light, Lenthieh's face was full of anger. His eyes were darkened by a shadow, a dullness of the light, and his voice was raspy, changed.

"Come out of the water, brother," Tawori uttered, his gaze steady on the enemy. "Draw your sword."

Redien pushed himself onto the platform. His clothes were drenched and heavy. He drew Moonlight and turned his back on Lenthieh. Stepping behind his brother so that their backs nearly touched, he peered at the unlife around them, above them, and beneath them; and he watched Lenthieh through his brother's eyes. Lenthieh stood immobile, his sword held loosely with the tip pointing to the ground. On his left stood a falyn in silvery armor, on his right a tall selyn wearing leather, and behind them were two other falyns. They shone with the keeper's light, which threaded from Lenthieh to them and to other Alassians who stood on the boardwalks surrounding the platform—two of them engaged in combat with Tawori's kaara.

"Ickh benn'ahk!" Lenthieh commanded, his voice full of power.

Many things occurred at once. A tarkin screeched and a gust of fire lit the air; the warriors of the light emerged from the wall of black smoke and saw Tawori and their guardian facing Lenthieh and four of his followers, but as they saw this, the water around the platform gurgled and the unlife jolted into the air spinning like a whirlwind, engulfing the stage and hiding everything from sight.

Redien dodged away from the howling darkness, carelessly jostling his brother who glanced his way, and for a lethal instant their eyes met.

Shock and pain shoved Redien forward. He felt a cold gust ruffle his hair as he looked down at the blade protruding from his chest. Thin, hard steel.

The blade withdrew, and Redien's body lurched back with it. He collapsed on hands and knees, his mouth open, no air coming in or out of it.

Tawori sprang forward swinging Wanninh. The blade sang with lightning. The three falyns closed on him, covering Lenthieh's retreat. Tawori pressed them back, fending and delivering blows with staggering ferocity, his blades sparking and crackling at each blow. Redien knew this although he did not see it. He knew it because Tawori knew it. In the same way, he knew that their companions were battling Lenthieh's followers beyond the swirling darkness.

Lenthieh's sword had stabbed him beneath the heart, cutting through his breastbone and severing an artery. Blood streamed copiously from the wound. His breath was caught in the sharp searing pain. He concentrated, feeling the pain with every bit of his awareness, and his life force gathered of its own volition. His flesh tickled and heated, and he took in a breath of cool air.

Gripping Moonlight's hilt, he stood. He wrapped his senses around him like a blanket; he could feel the unlife spinning at arm's reach. And he turned to face Lenthieh.

It wasn't what he saw but what he heard that struck him with fear.

Lenthieh was at the center of the platform holding up his bloodied sword. He was chanting quietly in that harsh speech that gave him power over the unlife. Redien could hear his voice clearly in the sudden dulling of everything else. He remembered the sound of the words and their rhythm . . . It was the same chant he'd heard five years before.

He drew his hands together and seized Lenthieh's life force, striving to silence the invocation. Lenthieh stuttered and his lips sealed shut; but his light intensified, glaring blindingly; and then he cried out a word, barking like a maddened beast.

Darkness's chill closed in behind Redien, reaching through the field of his heightened senses. He dashed forward.

The selyn at Lenthieh's side moved to intercept, and their swords clashed. Redien's arm recoiled with the impact. Their swords grated as the selyn drove his blade downward, then swept hers in an upward swing. He half-turned out of the way feeling sharp air brush his cheek. His defense was wide open but she was slow and he had the forward momentum. He pushed off his right foot and kicked her in the gut with the sole of his boot, sending her crashing against Lenthieh.

Lenthieh held strong. He clasped the selyn's arm and helped her to her knees. He was again speaking quietly, his eyes alert. His sword, still above him, drew a half circle downward and came hollowing through the selyn's neck.

In the instant the keeper's light left her, her shock invaded Redien's mind. He felt the blade split the dense tissues in his neck and knew he was about to die.

"Ackh ekka u ishjish'ehk!" Lenthieh's voice commanded.

The sword drew back, searing her flesh.

Redien's eyes were latched onto the selyn's face. Her mouth opened in a soundless O which widened on, and on; and as it widened her eyes broadened, wholly white, her brows lifted, higher, and higher. Her legs unhinged, and she crumpled to her knees like a hump of flesh. She shook convulsing, and screamed. Her spine bent with a backward lash, and her arms spread wide. The unlife clawed her chest from within and crawled out.

It was a horrific thing with no face except for an empty hole that was perhaps its mouth. Its flesh was liquid black in the guardian sight, dense and vitreous, obsidian-like. It had tentacles for limbs, slithering and twining about its body like snakes. It emerged, leaving behind a bloody, empty cocoon.

It charged with surprising speed.

Redien pushed against it with his mind and the wave of one hand, but his focus moved through it as if it were smoke. Standing behind it, Lenthieh lurched backward, hit by the force of his push.

Redien brought up his guard too late. His sword tumbled from his grasp as the thing slammed into him, and he fell, the horror's weight crushing him and caging him against the floor.

Through Tawori's eyes, Redien saw Wanninh sink its length into the horror's body, and from the hollow blackness of its mouth the horror cried a deep, pain-stricken bellow. To which a high-pitched screech answered. A shadow swooped from above and sank its sharp talons into Tawori's shoulder. Tawori was lifted into the air and tossed like a dirty rag. He rolled and skidded over the wooden floor as the tarkin stormed on top of him in a flurry of motion, biting and clawing and beating its wings like a hawk.

Then Redien couldn't see through his brother's eyes anymore; he heard him yelp, and yelp, till his voice became silent.

On top of Redien, the horrific creature shook and squirmed, snorting and huffing. The opening that was its mouth drooled a bitter fluid onto his face: it reeked of bile and burned his skin. Redien stared into the hole, glimpsing four thin fangs, each the length of a finger.

He was searching blindly for the hilt of Moonlight. He couldn't find it. His right forearm held some of the horror's weight lifted above him, its slimy secretions scorching him inch by inch. He felt its many limbs search his thighs, his hips, his chest, rummaging around roughly and doggedly. They tugged at his clothes and rubbed his skin, scorching and scratching him. He abandoned the search for his sword and slammed his fist at the formless face. It tried to bite him, the fanged hole closing and opening soundlessly like the mouth of a fish. With his free hand, Redien grabbed the formless face and stabbed his focus into it.

Nothing happened, except his palm and fingers burned.

The obstinate, malicious touch slipped under his shirt and began quivering with gruesome excitement. For a long, dreadful moment Redien felt it brush his navel with the tenderness of a lover. Then with sudden, implacable urge it delved.

An unrestrained scream broke from Redien's lips. He jerked with spasms as bit by bit the horror burrowed deeper inside him, sucking and tugging. It fed fire to his blood, drinking his strength and setting his mind aflame with agony.

Redien's sight dimmed. He saw the creature of darkness turn from liquid black to solid gray flesh, smeared with blood. Redien's screams died down to feeble whimpers and his hands fell limply.

It was happening again as it had happened before. He had no strength. He couldn't stop it. He tried to hold on to his life force, hold it in and stop it from leaking, but he couldn't. It was leaving him. He was dying. His eyes filled with tears, his heart crammed his chest painfully, grieving angrily . . . He was *angry*. Grieving with a terrible anger, striving to break free from hands that held him still. A gag was in his mouth and power surrounded him like a shell containing the spark of his rage. He was struggling but couldn't break free; and his little brother was dying! His little brother was dying!

"I said, ENOUGH!" Lenthieh bawled. "Ackh ieh annen!"

Lenthieh's voice came to Redien muffled as if from behind a curtain of silence.

Above him, the horror wailed. Without warning it yanked its limb upward and Redien's body arched after it, unwilling to let it go. With a grunt the creature broke free, and moved away. Redien's body fell back, flat and still. His head dropped to one side and for a moment he saw a bright red glow: an orb and its trail, or was it the sun beyond thick mist? He didn't know. He thought it was a light, a red, living light.

"Control your thirst!" Lenthieh yelled. The falyn clamped his hand over Redien's mouth and forced him to look up. "And you, stop whining!" he barked. "This is what you came for, is it not? Your punishment?"

Redien did not try to reply, he tried to breathe. He managed, somehow, to inhale through his clogged nose, and that half-choked him. He coughed into Lenthieh's hand and breathed, and that was all he could do, breathe, and look into the falyn's leering eyes.

"Listen to me," Lenthieh said, pressing a finger onto his own mouth, "Listen! You know you deserve this. I would not hurt you if you did not deserve it. I tried to be merciful, to spare you the suffering. Yes, I planned it that way, but you spoiled it. What right did you have to interfere? You were nothing. Nothing. A lump of flesh, that is all. You should have not insisted on being born. All this pain, all this strife, it was all your fault. I would never hurt a child, not unless I had no other choice. I did not want to do it, believe me. But you resisted me. What was I to do?" He waited for an answer. When none came, he said, "But I am trying to fix it. I *will* fix it. Your pain will end, it will *all* end when you give in, I promise you. I promise. Oh, it would have been easier, yes. If you'd let me have your mother, it would have been easier. But I forgave you that impudence."

A searing rage screamed within Redien's body, and his heart throbbed with it. One beat, then another, and another. He moved his hand—or was it Tawori's hand? And was it he or Tawori who moved it? It was his hand that Lenthieh caught and pushed against the platform's floor. The falyn spit as he yelled, "You ruined everything! You stubborn parasite! You fed off her like a leech. A vermin! That's what you are. You wanted her power for yourself, but it was my power, mine! You took it from *me*. I nearly *had it*. Can't you hold him still?!" Lenthieh snapped his gaze up. "Just hold him still! You can do nothing, Tawori, don't you see? You are pathetic. Always so eager to challenge me, and with what? What have you to challenge me? Weakness? You disgust me! I will end your pathetic existence, I shall have to. Yet another evil act staining my hands because of *this* one." He looked down, his mouth wet with spittle. "You leave me no choice, child. Though it pains me. It pains me to do harm. He was my friend, did you know? We were friends, once."

Lenthieh bent closer. His small pupils darted left and right, undecided on which eye to stare into. "But I will do it for you. I will kill him for you, for your sake. Because this time you will learn, won't you? Answer me! Nod, like this. This is what I tried to teach you all along, that you have nothing in this world, nothing at all. When you will have accepted that, I will make you my servant. You will serve me as your mother would have served me. Though she would have been a glorious queen. You will be my pet. Oh, if only he had not hid you from me. I could have done with you so easily and kept you forever as my child. But you turned my father against me. Yes, you did, you heartless *brat!* You stole from me! So now, I will take from you. Watch me."

Lenthieh forced him to look to the side, pressing his face against the floor so he could see Tawori kneeling at the edge of the platform, arms hidden behind him and his mouth gagged. His face was red with burns, his clothes torn and bloody. His eyes stared back at Redien full of tears and anger. A figure in silvery armor bent behind him, one loomed over him, and yet another lay dead. The green-scaled tarkin shook and whimpered nearby in a pool of black blood.

"Watch me kill my dear friend for you," Lenthieh said, "my young prentice... my clever spark." He kicked aside a sword as he walked. "I do this for you." He seized Tawori's scalp, forcing his head back, and brought a blade to his neck. It was a fine, tempered Alassian blade, the hilt wrapped in honeyed yellow leather. The cold, thin edge slashed into the flesh with little effort.

Tawori's blood gushed like water from a spring, pouring down his chest, drenching his clothes and dripping onto the wood. The heat was somewhat a relief, because Redien had been dreadfully cold on the platform's floor, where his body, he saw now, lay sprawled with the clothing in disarray, his bare abdomen smeared red, and his eyes unfocused. Yet his knees hurt from the hard floor beneath him. Clearly, he had been kneeling like this for a while with tiny rocks digging into his knees—into his brother's knees. He could not stand up, his brother, his brother could not stand up because their hands—his brother's hands—were held in a steely grip twisted behind their back. There were hands on their shoulders—on his brother's shoulders—strong hands that pressed them down on their sore knees, with the tiny rocks jabbing at them. A wall of energy encircled them, a barrier made of the keeper's light. They were trapped inside it. And they couldn't breathe. They needed to breathe but their throat was gashed open and they couldn't.

He had only to think of the wound, and keenly, the flow of Tawori's life force surged at their neck where it held waiting, impatient, frenetic, untamed like the molten blood of a waking volcano, a wrathful, raw strength that with submissive eagerness bent to Redien's will as he fed it to the pain and the mortal wound. Their flesh heated, sealing itself. And they drew breath.

They breathed, and filled their body with the flow of all things. The swampy waters beneath them, the earth down below, the wood on which they knelt, the air that filled the sky and the sun's heat hidden above the cloud of darkness. They drew breath from the living, from the Alassians, the kaaras, and all creatures of life. They pulled it all in, and their body shook with power.

They shone their ruby gaze upon Lenthieh's face and saw it twist in sudden fear.

Raw and terrific, they let the lightning spark.

The blast flared brighter than the keeper's light and for an instant swallowed everything.

Then suddenly, it vanished.

Lenthieh collapsed, and so did the two falyns. The tarkin's head hit the wooden floor limply, and the horror of darkness crumpled up and was still.

Free of the falyns' hold, their body pitched forward, lightning still coursing through them. They caught themselves with both hands on the floor, breathing hard. They saw the hilt of Wanninh and moved to grasp it—to stand up—their wills collided, and they tumbled headlong onto the wooden floor.

Redien relinquished control.

Tawori pushed them onto their hands and knees and freed them from the rope tangled about their wrists, then he pulled off the leather strap crammed into their mouth. He got them on their feet and took a step forward. Kneeling beside Lenthieh who lay shuddering, he turned him around and pressed their right hand over his abdomen. At once, Redien understood.

Tawori lifted their hand steadily, and together as one they tugged at Lenthieh's life force and at the essence of the keeper's power. A globe of light took form in their grasp, shining white like the moon, warm as the heat of the sun, and heavier than stone. They bent their fingers around it like hooks. It weighted their hand down, pulling itself toward Lenthieh like a magnet, striving desperately to re-enter him.

Lenthieh raised his hands, clasping theirs, clinging to them and to the power, and all but lifting himself up. " . . . My . . . light . . ."

"It was never yours," they said, and yanked it away.

Lenthieh convulsed, taking a heaving breath that arched up his belly stiffly. Then he fell back and was forever still.

Weightless, the Light hovered small and fragile in their palm. Tawori brought it close and their eyes watched it shine, white and pure. They felt its warmth upon their face. Tawori hesitated. Yet watching from within, Redien did not share his brother's doubt. He leaned their body forward, and parting their lips took a shallow breath, a taste of the heat and power. It made them shiver.

Then Tawori opened their mouth wider and breathed in deeply with profound relief. Hot dampness filled their lungs, and a blazing heat flooded their gut.

They sat there baffled, looking up at the black sky. A deafening silence surrounded them, and gusts of intoxicating sensations filled them, making their body quiver. For a time they felt each other's presence and the Light, and nothing else.

Darkness pressed around them, snatching at them with icy fingers that turned to smoke in the blinding heat of their life force.

"We must cast it out."

"Cross the borders . . ." Tawori said.

"Close the doors."

" . . . I need your help, brother."

"You have it. But we must do it now."

Tawori got them to stand with great effort. Gathering their arms to their chest, they took a deep breath. With a fierce violent push and their arms opening wide, they cast the Light through the city and into the forest, and beyond it. They reached up in the blackened sky, toward the light of day and the sun, and beyond. Down, into the swampy water, into the earth and the hard crust of the world, and beyond. They washed away all darkness in a wave that shook reality. Then, with a sound like thunder, they closed the doors shut.

Tawori fell to his knees.

He was surrounded by silence and felt utterly alone. The keeper's light within him fluttered weakly like the flame of a dying candle. He could no longer feel Redien's presence. The sky above him was clear blue, but Tawori's sight was blurred and shadowed. All he could see clearly was a puddle of blood, and his brother's body in it.

He began crawling toward him. It was long, arduous labor. Again and again, Tawori had to beg his battered body to move, to keep going, a little closer, a little closer, nearly there, just a little closer. Twice he saw the world vanish, and a land of darkness unfolded before him. Cold, stale air made his teeth chatter. Then he found himself stranded on this wooden platform, forgetful of his whereabouts, but seeing Redien lying in a puddle of blood, he began crawling toward him.

At last, his hands felt a slight heat as he pressed them over his brother's wounded abdomen. Redien's eyes focused on him and blinked once, and then twice. Tawori didn't speak. He watched his brother blink, and he watched him take one breath, and another, and another.

IT WAS LIKE THIS that Beriun found them, and when he spoke to Tawori, his friend did not seem to hear him.

"I have nothing to give," Tawori muttered, "I have nothing left."

Then Beriun understood.

THEIDRIN OPENED HIS eyes to the light of day, and gazing about him, saw the bodies of his kindred lying unconscious on the wooden boardwalks and in the foul swamp. He looked up at the clear blue sky and knew the battle was won.

He hurried to his feet. "Wake the others!" he told Gwendier, shaking him into wakefulness. "Omoin, gather the hunters! Seize Lenthieh's followers. Be swift, they awaken!" He crouched beside Meyvath. "Are you hurt? Can you stand? I need you to see to our kindred. Tell them of the guardian. Tell them that the reign of darkness has ended."

On the wooden platform, Theidrin kneeled, clasping Tawori's shoulders. Shaking him gently, he tried to wake him from his haze. "You must let me tend to your brother!"

Tawori did not seem to hear his words or to be aware of him in any way. He was covered in blood and burns, and quivering, his jaw and lips trembling with a terrible cold. He was pressing his hands on his brother's abdomen and would not remove them.

Beside him, Beriun had set a hand on the guardian's forehead and with the other gripped his thin right hand, infusing the touch with his own life force, keeping him among the living.

It was only when Aruhin kneeled beside Tawori and spoke to him softly, that he began noticing the world around him. He turned to look at her, and it seemed then to Aruhin that his eyes watched her from somewhere far away. "I can't, Aruhin," he murmured, "I could never learn."

"I know," she said, "I know. But your friends are here. Let Theidrin heal your brother."

It was clear that Tawori had not known Theidrin was there, for when he saw him now, he promptly took his bloodied hands away. Then he watched with a hopeful light in his eyes until his brother's chest rose with deep, easy breaths and a tranquil sleep came upon him.

"He rests now," Aruhin said. "You should rest too. Come, Tawori. Come here." She wrapped her arms around him, and as she pulled him in, he surrendered, at once, to unconsciousness.

EPILOGUE

It was a warm, sunny day. The jungle was filled with the scent of flowers in bloom, the soft dampness of the earth, and the hard, clear fragrance of wood. The air chittered with birdsongs, with *witt-witts*, chirrups, and purrs. There was in the distance the clamor of water falling from high stone steps and diving into deep pools. A little farther up the slopes, where the thicket-covered ground opened to the sky, giving way to soft short grass, the pale, ageless people of the jungle sat beneath the afternoon sun, talking with fine youthful voices to the humans among them.

«There is no use in discussing blame.» The speaker was a tall, stout male of their species whom the others called Keeper. «Nothing of the past can be changed. We are not here today because war happened: war did not bring us together. We are here because our two people have learned and are willing to listen, and to see one another, truly see one another. This is why we are here.»

His name was Tawori, he'd said earlier, greeting the humans in perfect Taelic and with the accent of one born in the capital city of Methyr, although clearly he was not born in any human city, for he was Alassian. He looked young and personable despite his species's pallid skin, the long white hair, and the otherworldly gaze of his tiny pupils like lonely hunting panthers in an endless snow-field. He was well-mannered and his sense of humor was light on the mind. Yet for all his friendly words there was a demeanor in him, a sureness in his gaze and gestures, that set him aside; and it was almost as if a light from somewhere unseen shed its radiance solely on him, so that his presence could never quite be overlooked.

Some among the humans believed he must be a prince, or perhaps a military leader—for he had said that he was among those of his kind who'd fought with the Alliance of Ydalon. Others simply found him charismatic and gave no thought to the matter of his lineage or what the title of keeper entailed. They listened to his words with wholehearted attention, scribbling on papers, flashing cameras, filming, and recording history.

«Five years ago my people lived secluded in this jungle,» the keeper said. «We called this our domain, but was it ever so? Or was it merely a place of concealment from an outside world that had grown so changed we no longer knew it? Five years ago your people, despite your science and technology, were unaware of our existence, ours and that of many other things, some peaceful things and some much less so, things we have kept you safe from for millennia.

«Today all this has changed. The world cannot go back to the way it was. My people cannot return to hiding in this jungle and pretend that this is the extent of our realm; just as you cannot simply forget that we exist.

«So I see only one way forward, one path that we must walk together, different as our two people may be. For I understand your perplexity. We are not what you are. We are not human. We do not call this world by the name you have given it, and we do not believe in any god you worship—although we do believe in the world's will that governs all, and *that* you may call a religion, or a philosophy, if you prefer. So, you see, we are not so different you and I. Strange as we may seem to your eyes, alien, or demon-like, we are as much creatures of this world as you are, and we wish to live in harmony with all who inhabit it.»

A long silence followed his words.

At the keeper's side sat one who seemed very young among these ageless people. His hair, unlike the others', was short, and his face and body were terribly scarred. It was difficult to look at him and see not only the scars but a kind, quiet gaze and the supple body of a healthy youth full of life. He had been introduced earlier as someone of importance. His people called him "Guardian." He had been sitting beside the keeper without uttering a word, watching, staring, and sometimes smiling.

In this silence full of musing and contemplation, the keeper spoke to him in their native tongue, which sounded like the burbling of a mountain river. The guardian smiled, replying with few words. To the Alassians and the few humans among them who understood their speech, the exchange was enigmatic, for what the keeper said was, "How fares the awkwardness?" to which the guardian replied, "Like a kaara skidding on ice."

Now the keeper began laughing, his voice light over the sunlit grass. He shook his head and looked at his guests. «Well, then, how about some food?» he said. «I hear nothing brings people together like food. Would you care to join us for supper?»

Thank you for reading Alassian Born!

I had the best time of my life writing this book. It would mean the world for me to know that you have enjoyed reading it. If you have, please, help me spread the word. Let your friends and loved know. Take a moment to add a review or a rating online. An author's voice gets lost in the crowd, but you, the reader, your voice will be heard. Help me by helping others find my book.

Great places for reviews are Goodreads.com, Amazon, and any online platform or shop where you purchased or received your copy of this book.

Thank you for supporting me and my work.

Lynn Oakwood

Sign up for Lynn's newsletter to receive updates on new releases, behind the scene, special offers, and more.

Sign up using the contact form on Lynn's website: **www.lynnoakwood.com**.

THOUGHTS FROM THE AUTHOR

Writing Alassian Born changed me. I found myself again—the self which, during the course of my life, I had learned to hide so well that I had forgotten it existed.

Alassian Born took me on a journey of re-discovery, a journey of healing. Like Redien, I had to remember who I used to be, before life happened. I had to understand and accept my wrongs, my limitations and flaws. But most of all, I had to accept the truth of myself.

If like me, you are someone who doesn't quite fit in the box, I hope that reading Alassian Born made you feel a connection.

You are not alone.

L.O.

Acknowledgments

Not many people were involved in the creation of this book. As a self-published author (and incurable perfectionist), I did most of the work myself. However, a great number of people should be thanked for being of support and inspiration to this book. Here are some of them.

The original inhabitants of Meviland. This might sound silly, but trust me, it isn't. You know who you are! Without you, I might have never found the courage to write again, and certainly, the time for Alassian Born would have passed without it being written.

A message from the past to Davide Bonni, because you were the first to believe. I cherish the memories of the days we spent plotting and exchanging what we didn't know were *first drafts*. Your stories were the best, and I lack your limitless imagination . . . although your writing was a total train wreck.

A huge thanks to Daniel, for all your help and support.

To Bernard, for generously volunteering your time.

Lastly, my thanks to Hazel and family, for providing a safe home at the beginning of my journey in discovering the English language. I was a little, lost sheep, and you opened the doors to a new world.

LYNN OAKWOOD is an Italian-born speculative fiction author. Currently located in the Netherlands, Lynn spent ten years in the United Kingdom, where she worked in the video game industry. Lynn's academic background focused on sciences and Chemistry. Her literary preferences revolve around fantasy and speculative fiction, with Ursula K. Le Guin and J.R.R. Tolkien among her favorites. Her creativity is further inspired by her fondness for anime and video games.

In addition to her writing pursuits, Lynn engages with a wider audience on Twitch, under the name Mevidia, where she shares her passion for gaming and storytelling.

Website: **www.lynnoakwood.com**
Twitch: Mevidia

Also on:
Twitter: @LynnWritesBooks
Instagram: @lynnoakwood
Goodreads: Lynn Oakwood

www.ingramcontent.com/pod-product-compliance
Lightning Source LLC
LaVergne TN
LVHW030318070526
838199LV00069B/6496